In Little Place

"O pardon! As a crooked figure may
Attest in little place a million. . . ."
Henry V

Novels by Grace Irwin

LEAST OF ALL SAINTS
ANDREW CONNINGTON

GRACE IRWIN

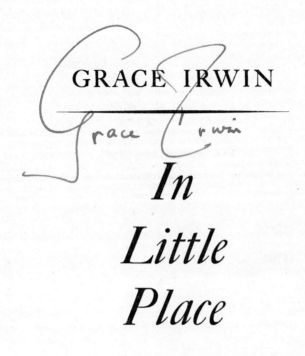

Grace Irwin (signature)

In
Little
Place

A Novel

WM. B. EERDMANS PUBLISHING COMPANY
GRAND RAPIDS, MICHIGAN

First printing, April 1959

Library of Congress catalog card no. 59-8748

Printed in the United States of America

TO MY FAMILY

Preface

I CANNOT STATE that any resemblance of persons and events in this book to those in real life is purely coincidental. No Toronto schoolteacher can write a book about present-day Toronto schoolteaching in a vacuum. As far as I know I have avoided personalities. Those who find themselves the more admirable characters of this book are to be congratulated; those who look for themselves in the less admirable do so at their own risk. I apologize for Aran. I've done my best for the woman but she is unmanageable. The worst about letting a middle-aged school teacher into a book is that she tries to take over. The faults and insufferable qualities of her personality are fully recognized and deplored by

Yours truly
THE AUTHOR

One

THE PRESIDENT'S GUESTS had gradually but inevitably gravitated towards the point of interest. A few couples still strayed along the main hall of the Museum or in one of the Chinese galleries at the far end. Dr. Ransom and his family chatted cordially with half a dozen intimates at the top of the shallow steps where they had formed the receiving line. Not far away some others, late-diners or constitutionally ascetic, displayed no interest in food. But it was ten-thirty, the smell of strong coffee lifted the air and from the first ring of groups, decently separated like the inmost ripple from a stone thrown in water, almost a hundred people shifted or held positions irregularly concentric around the long refreshment table beneath the square lofty skylight.

Deliberately detached and trying not to draw attention by her detachment, Aran Waring stood watching them. She looked as though she had come up the steps and slightly away from the throng in order to search for some particular person, or persons, who would likewise be searching for her; as though meantime she was happily observing a pleasurable and interesting spectacle. She knew that she gave such an impression, and in it lay her security. No one, glancing up or across at her unselfconscious pose catching her alert half-smiling glance, would dream that she was debating whether to force herself to stay another conventional ten minutes and take an apologetic farewell or to dispense with formalities and make an unobserved departure. Dr. Ransom, in spite of his uncanny memory and his unpurchasable faculty of greeting people whose names he did not know as though they had been the recent object of his fondest thoughts, would not miss her. It was all very well to tell herself that she should stay; social contacts were valuable; spending five days of the week and often a sixth with adolescents she should welcome these opportunities for conversation with interesting and important people. Surely at the age of forty-five she had the right to let down her tired eyebrows, remove her frozen expression of animation, and go home to bed!

The struggle, always sharpened by her Methodist conscience, between what she wanted and what was, she felt, expected of her engendered a faint belligerence. Important and interesting people forsooth! By whose standards? She recalled a trip through Hollywood years before, when she and her mother had lunched at a restaurant "frequented," according to the bus tour brochure, "by the élite of the film world." They had gone in with carefully concealed expectancy, scanning the near-by tables for a glimpse of Gable, or Colman, Shearer or — who could tell? — Garbo? And they had scarcely been seated when a fellow employee of the Board of Education flung around her the affectionate arms of one exiled Torontonian meeting another. "Of all places to see you," she had exclaimed. "Did you feel us all crane our necks when you came in? With that hat and air we were sure you were one of the film stars." Similarly how many of the strangely assorted group drawn by the President's courteously diplomatic net had come to meet interesting and important people — or at least to be counted of the number?

That was hardly fair, really. These were important people; only a bitter mind attributed all success in attaining promotion to mediocrity and social manipulation, and she had no reason to be bitter. Interesting too, doubtless. But how could anyone make or hear an interesting remark in such a babble? Was it possible that she was becoming allergic to noise that the increasing loudness of conversation affected her with acute physical discomfort? These voices were fairly well modulated. The flat, raucous, all-Canadian, juvenile cacophony which greeted her in Rivercrest cafeteria at noon hour was mercifully lacking; the concentrated essential soprano which made refreshment time at the Christmas party of the University Women's Club a shrill war on the aural nerves was here relieved by masculine bass and diluted into echoes from the high ceiling. Yet the effect was the same. Trivia, brief questions and scarcely longer answers, an occasional joke by a determined raconteur, of which the nub was lost as someone else came up, or as one of "those assisting" chose unerringly that very moment to bombard the listeners with petit fours: this was all that could be expected of the most intelligent, and to what purpose this waste, especially when not a soul in that outwardly vivacious gathering would notice her departure — she would see to that! — or care that she had been present at all.

That was the rub, she admitted ruefully, her smile brightening spontaneously as she lifted her head to acknowledge recognition of Professor Husband, who stood with his wife and an unknown couple, three or four cup-balancing groups away. She toyed with the possibility of following up his greeting, threading her way through the mob, asking about the next Classics Club meeting, being introduced to the strangers, shouting vivaciously to Mrs. Husband about the noise, the crowd, the composition of the sandwiches, the need and difficulty of going on a diet — and abandoned it. She liked Professor Husband and his wife: they talked well and she was always at ease with them . . . but not here. And pleased as they would be to welcome her, try as they would to include her, it could not be done, although she, and not they, would realize the fact and the reason.

She had no man with her. Except in the receiving line as guest of honor, or as one of the attractive young girls who pushed plates at the guests and chatted to acquaintances with varying degrees of conscientiousness, there was no place for a manless woman in such a gathering. Never had she felt so sharply her unanchored condition. Or perhaps, once before, on the same trip to the West Coast, when her constant sense of responsibility in making decisions and bookings, looking after luggage, tips, and entertainment for herself and her mother had so exacerbated her that for a brief ashamed period she had wished to be married: not particularly, gloriously, ideally married as she always did, but just married, so that what was vaguely thought of as "the man's part" could be lifted from her tired feminine shoulders. Now, against her better judgment, she experienced the same feeling. For this reason, she knew, many women married what they did — *as* they did would be kinder but less truthful. And for this reason many of those who didn't, clung possessively and catered thoughtfully to widowed father or bachelor brother. At a bridal shower not long before, Aran had met the elderly widow of a once prominent Toronto clergyman who, in one of those quick confidences evoked by assurance of sympathy, had talked about her difficulty in making herself go into society since her husband's death. "You don't know," she said, looking into Aran's compassionate eyes, "how hard it is to do everything alone when you have had someone else to plan for you and take care of you for forty years."

Aran had assured her that she could imagine. Characteristically she had not asked the older woman to consider what it would be like to have no other experience. Now with the recollection came a story which perversely amused her more than at first hearing, so that she laughed involuntarily and lifted her empty cup quickly to her lips to conceal it. Goodness! this would never do! A spinster who stood serenely alone at the edge of a convivial group was one thing. A lone spinster who burst into an uncontrollable whoop at nothing at all was a case for the psychiatrist. But it seemed suddenly desperately apropos, Miriam Singer's story. Miriam was her own age, an intellectual, a missionary's daughter, who from early training, circumstance, and preference had few social contacts among the ultrasophisticated. Recently, however, she had found herself at a cocktail party among Bohemians in New York and had described with relish her encounter with one woman to whom the marriage ceremony was such an oft-told tale that it was used only to punctuate her liaisons. Her incredulity when after a pointed inquisition Miriam confessed her own deplorable celibacy had sounded particularly funny imitated in Miriam's clipped English accent: "But my dear! you don't mean that you've never *been* married?"

That, shameful to admit and dark with abnormal portent since Freud made Kinsey possible, was her own state. It was a state so gaily accepted by herself and so unquestionably accepted as her own choice and responsibility by her family, friends and — praise be! — successive generations of pupils that its social disadvantages seldom now brushed her consciousness, much less caused her embarrassment. Therefore, doubtless, this unwonted feeling of outrage at her sense of exclusion, of unimportance as a person in her own right. She liked dressing up; conscious that her figure was better than it had ever been, she resented as wasteful the increasing paucity of occasions on which it could look its best, as now, in long moulding folds of black crepe — a pre-war dress perennially modish. Since the war women going out together felt conspicuous in evening dress, especially driving their own cars and walking increasing distances from parking lots. Only at formal, all-female gatherings was there any likelihood of the majority's "dressing" and what a waste of sweetness on desert air that was, Aran thought rebelliously.

Quickly ashamed of such childishness she tried to alter the course of her thoughts. Usually, on finding them unduly self-centered, she looked around for someone to help, someone lonely or self-conscious. Tonight she had been unable to find anybody. The only other unattached women, Dr. Edda Porter of the Oriental Language Department and Myrna McTavish of the Museum staff, had come together and established themselves as authoritative consultants and dispensers of information regarding several debatable exhibits in the west gallery. Devotedly academic, they conveyed, even in evening dress, an impression of dedicated erudition which gave meaning to their presence and which she herself never achieved even in the classroom. They had been affable and had obviously not required her.

In the cloak-room where she checked her fur jacket on arrival Aran had been glad to meet Dr. Lockyer, whose husband had recently retired from the Rivercrest staff. She had gone down the receiving line in their pleasant, reticent company and genuinely enjoyed exchanging comments with them on Ming porcelain, dynastic robes, carved jade. Acquaintance after acquaintance she had greeted, secure in a temporary sense of belonging derived from her common interest with Mr. Lockyer and reciprocal hospitality with his wife. But on their desultory return journey her friends were greeted by a family group. The young doctor present had been best man to the Lockyers' son the year before. Reminiscences; questions concerning common acquaintance, information regarding unknown people and events inexorably forced the outsider to the fringe of the little group. To look bored or forlorn was to impose upon hospitality; to look brightly interested and try to take part in the conversation was an impertinence. The worst — or the best — of it all was that her former companions were completely unaware of her sudden isolation. No one ever seemed to think that Aran Waring could feel self-conscious, ill-at-ease, undignified, unwanted, alone.

No one had, though she felt all five increasingly as she drifted towards the distinguished mass of humanity coagulating around the entrance hall. Casually, making a comment here, stopping brightly to reply to a greeting there, she had found herself, still unblessed by impediment or interruption, being served with coffee and looking, if any stranger turned and met her eye, as though she were just leaving one set of friends to exchange some vital information with another. Professor Jones of the Math Department and his wife, whose son had been a favorite pupil of hers and a star in the Rivercrest Collegiate Drama Club, acted as a temporary haven for a few cheerfully shouted remarks. Then a stout, white-aproned woman bearing reinforcements for the coffee-urn cut her off from them, and turning, she found that the same movement had catapulted them into a larger group, evidently of Bridge Club associates. It was at this point that she had come up the steps to evaluate the outward and inward struggle.

At this point in any novel she would have found herself in mirth-provoking and productive collision with someone else likewise meditating escape: a visiting bachelor diplomat from Britain, an eminent surgeon from Montreal or Vancouver, recently widowed, or, in the modern style, with a wife conveniently but problematically in an institution for incurable mental cases. Apology and laughing riposte would lead inevitably to camaraderie, to discovery of tastes in common, to an offer of escort and an arrangement for dinner next evening. Aran, her strongly marked dark brows relaxing whimsically, was thankful that she had left long behind her the habit of expecting such encounters. It had passed with her twenties — particularly with her late twenties, that period when a girl, for whatever reason unmarried, feels that now surely the great and awaited event will take place. For a time she had greeted every invitation like this as an opportunity, examined every new acquaintance, not — perish the thought! — considering whether he would like her, but whether she could like him, whether he could possibly measure up to the requirements which she must have in a husband or continue — as she was. It had passed, she remembered, suddenly on her return from her last summer trip to Europe just before the war. As though it were yesterday instead of seventeen years ago, she remembered glancing up at her mother from a letter in her hand and saying the words which had marked her unconscious achievement of freedom from fear. "You know, I think if

I could live with Eric here" — she gesticulated towards the letter from a young Scandinavian whom she had met in Rome — "for three months of the year, and with Cliff" — a middle-aged Englishman who had been their constant companion on the Mediterranean cruise — "for another three, and with Jack Spence" — a young actor for whom she felt a more than motherly regard — "for three more, and with someone else who has something none of them has, for the last three, I'd marry. But if I met the someone else I shouldn't want the first three at all. So unless God produces him for me, I'd sooner not."

Bold words — but she had meant them, and they had marked her release and accounted for the fact that she was usually completely unselfconscious with men, or at least as unselfconscious as she was with women. Only occasionally did she become exasperated, when an explanation was expected of her that she could not give for fear of sounding egotistical, or when someone — never someone who knew her — sought to dampen the enthusiasm of a young admirer by suggesting that she could not be "normal." Normal, indeed! Aran controlled an unrefined snort. From what she knew — and she knew a good deal — of the feelings and attitudes of most married women of her acquaintance, she could show them heels in a canter as far as normal emotional reaction was concerned. Why could people not realize that an incurable tendency to be guided by the head did not indicate lack of heart; that an instinctive prescience concerning the passing and dissipation of unguided emotion by no means quelled the violence of the emotion itself? She had been a very young teacher — in her mid-twenties — when a handsome, mature-looking boy in third form, dropping in one Sunday afternoon to discuss his school and home problems, inquired bluntly if she had a steady boy friend and, with the same air of seeking factual information, why not? At a loss to explain an attitude incomprehensible to him, and only glad that it did not occur to him to regard her as helpless in the matter, she had referred vaguely to the recent accidental death of a dear friend, feeling uncomfortably dishonest although telling the literal truth, in that she was donning the role of a heartbroken fiancee. Her tact and ingenuity had been more seriously taxed when the boy made earnest tentative proposals to fill the vacant place himself. How long ago it seemed! one of the schoolboy crushes with which she always tried to deal tenderly. Some years later the question had come up again, when an ex-pupil, not this time a sentimental admirer, had urged upon her the desirability of marriage, with masculine certainty that a life without a man was a life wasted, and in language flatteringly reminiscent of Viola's:

> Lady you are the cruelest she alive,
> If you will lead these graces to the grave,
> And leave the world no copy.

His plane had been shot down over Africa — she paused for the momentary salute of mental silence which she seldom failed to accord at the recollection of any of the sixty-two boys on Rivercrest's honor roll who had passed through her classes. Later still — she must have been thirty-three — there had been the delicate approach of one of her brothers, in whom concern for his young sister's future had overridden the silence in which all matters of sentiment were usually passed over in the family. His carefully worded suggestion had been to the effect that she weigh a lonely future against the consideration of "making the best of" some possible young man — it had warmed and also amused her that, in spite of the complete dearth of desperate suitors on her then horizon, he had taken for granted that her volition alone was necessary. Amused and rather surprised because — Oh, why try to explain even to herself? She would have to write a book!

And why not write a book — an autobiography? She checked the impulse to laugh this time and, determined to see the thing through dutifully, began to thread her way across to the President's party. Who on earth would read her autobiography when she had two books already written concerning which no publisher had shared her enthusiasm? But the urge to write was strong upon her, an urge only felt at times of deep feeling and conviction. There must be other women who, like her, felt the indignity of her present situation. She had a name ready too, *The Sex Life of the Canadian Female Too Fastidious to Have One.* Rather long, perhaps, but sure-fire for sales. And no more misleading than the average title either.

Her smile was quite unforced as she waited to speak to Dr. Ransom. The stupendously large gentleman, whose dress shirt-front escaped his waistcoat in a celluloid bulge just above his trousers, continued, ignoring her presence, to bombard the smiling President with details of the chemical composition of the best manure he had found for his farm in Essex County. Aran, on the edge of groups all evening, and on the edge of this one as a slave to duty, felt a surge of imperious self-assertion,

"Pardon me," she said clearly, the voice which she sometimes used to quell obstreperous classes, rising above the agriculturist's insistence that the President visit him for the express purpose of analyzing the fertilizer for himself, "I'm later than I intended to be already, Dr. Ransom, but I do want to thank you for including me in your party. Good night."

"Delighted," the President's voice boomed after her, getting rid, she trusted for his own sake, of the offal enthusiast with the same non-committal heartiness. She did not look back to find out. Walking well, but unhurriedly, she skirted the groups till she reached the turnstile, was the first to collect her wrap in the empty cloak-room, and escaped into the comforting asylum of her car in the parking lot.

Muriel's light was out when she arrived home, but Boojum, her spaniel, plop-plopped sleepily down the stairs to make her feel, as Muriel always put it, "cherished," and performed her solitary trick of lying on her back, floppy-pawed with an expression of adoring abandon. When her stomach was duly stroked she righted herself and disappeared up the stairway to be waiting head on paws, Aran knew, on the landing. Slipping out of her jacket, Aran looked at herself in the long hall mirror with rueful self-approval before she switched off the light and followed Boojum upstairs. There she went straight to the bathroom mirror, the kindest and best-lighted in the house, and stared quizzically and encouragingly at the face which never would have been missed from the night's celebrations.

"Never mind; you never looked better," she told it soothingly, and the curved mouth grinned swiftly back in response. "And if it's any comfort to you, though you're no Helen of Troy or Lily Langtry, I doubt if either of those femmes would have got much further under the same circumstances tonight."

With sudden reaction from the evening's strain she was frantically tired. She opened the Bible for her nightly reading and, after glancing through five verses without grasping their sense, decided that such adherence to dutiful ritual was dishonest, turned off the bed light and flung herself down, separating the pillows and lying flat on the mattress to relieve the tension at the back of her neck; then thrusting her arms up under them as she sometimes did to induce sleep. Yet after some moments while her brain raced in her tired head, she got up and, moving quietly, found her pen and the remnant of a writing pad which she brought back to bed. The idea of a book had not left her since its first sardonic incursion into her mind in the Museum. Now she realized why it was important to her alone — no one else would see it — to begin it immediately. She glanced at her watch. It was only eleven-forty. Twenty minutes of the day still remained. For five minutes more she sat propped against the maltreated pillows; then, with a sigh, remembering Kipling's saving advice to all writers, she scrawled in large, unusually legible characters:

17

Praise Famous Men.

And underneath:

I must be mad to begin an autobiography. What ground have I for thinking that there can be any interest in the life-story of a middle-aged woman, unknown outside her own city and not well known there, a woman who has accomplished nothing of outstanding significance in any field, in an era of outstanding feminine achievement? Only the fact that, though I still look young enough to be whistled at occasionally on the street — at a distance, I'll admit — it is exactly one hundred years today since the large-eyed, calm-browed woman whose black-framed, white-capped picture was all I knew of Grandma on my father's side, gave birth to her eldest son, my father, in a well-built homestead on the hills of Western Ireland. Only that — and the terrific sense of destiny which has possessed me since childhood and possesses me still as positively, in spite of increasing unlikeliness that I am destined to any earthly distinction. Oh, yes — and the paradoxes of my life.

Well, there it was! A rotten start but it had to be made, if there was anything of interest in the exact date. At any rate, she had obeyed Kipling's mandate to write, at all costs to write, even if paragraphs, pages, chapters were to be scrapped later. Even if there never would be another paragraph, Mr. Kipling?

She slept.

Two

"HAVE YOU EVER THOUGHT of connecting the mood of a verb in English or Latin or French — any language for that matter — with our common use of the word 'mood': He was in a resentful mood that morn ——"

Dr-r-r-a-n-g! A shout of laughter coincided with Aran's despairing shrug. Before the second of the three fire-drill signals the class, which she had just settled into receptivity in order to begin her lesson on the Subjunctive in a way fondly designed to give a reasonable motive for the memorization of grammatical forms, struggled from their thirty-two folding seats with conventionally noisy pleasure and streamed out by the rear door. The aim of fire drill being to empty the school as quickly as possible, they felt happily justified in standing not on the order of their going. Half of them at least would have preferred to get on with the lesson; but no one would have admitted it. Not to welcome any interruption, even one involving only a trip down and up two flights of stairs and a few shivering chattering moments in the February wind, would brand one as a brain.

Aran sighed philosophically, sauntered down the aisle, remembered to close the open door before going to take up the position at the head of the west stairs as charted for her on the fire-drill memo. There was no provision on the chart for leaving her post in the case of actual fire. She would, she presumed, stay there, copying the admirable but not too intelligent example of the Roman sentries during the destruction of Pompeii. Leaning over the stair well, she waved at Hilda Wright and Reg Purvis at their posts below and, tilting her head back, saw Dorothy Simpson threatening her with a book from above.

"Aran, of all the rotten times for fire drill." She swung around with a reproving eye at the young colleague who came up behind her.

"And what, Miss Maxfield, are you doing away from your appointed post? Northeast stairs at the landing if I'm not mistaken."

"Oh, blast the northeast stairs and the landing!" Terry Maxfield's annoyance was too genuine and nervous for banter. In the years of Aran's friendship with her as pupil, confidante, student-teacher, and now colleague, she could seldom remember seeing her fair, rather Alice-in-Wonderlandish face so flushed with anger. "I ask you is there any earthly use in trying to plan a period ahead?"

"Not much. Don't let it raise your blood pressure." Aran spoke with a calm she did not always feel. "After all, according to regulations there has to be one fire drill a month. We haven't had one yet and the month is nearly over."

"That's all very well. But I've had my name entered all week as giving Nine-E a test this period. You know what brats they are?" Aran nodded. She did by reputation and was thankful that her Grade Nine — since she had to teach one at all — was the more intelligent and tractable Nine-F. "The only time they will work is when they know there's a test coming. I couldn't have it yesterday because of the Hockey Hall. Tuesday was a half-holiday. Monday they had two other tests, they informed me — I found out afterwards that one was to write a vocabulary and the other was to hand in their notebooks for Health Education — so I set it for this morning. It is a full-period test; I'm giving the same one to Nine-C and G the next two periods. And they just had time to get started when the bell went and so did they — "

"So did mine," interrupted Aran, in a vain attempt to soothe.

"I know. But yours will settle down again. These — Aran, I hate to see them come into a room. And they were buzzing like bees down the stairs and out into the yard asking one another the answers. And it's not fair to the other classes when they've seen the questions and had a chance to talk about them. I'm sorry — but I felt so rotten I had to come and tell you. There's the bell now."

"I am sorry, dear. It's a shame it had to happen just then. There's nothing to do but carry on with the test in spite of it. Listen to those laughing adolescent voices! Don't be humorous, Walwyn, you don't need a drink. Haven't we wasted enough time?" She turned to finish her cheering mission. "Forget your illusions about the way my classes settle down. My lovely reasonable 'from the known to the unknown' introduction is shot — either it must go or I won't reach the end of the lesson."

"Well, I must run. I always have to cry on your shoulder, don't I?"

"There is another shoulder applying for the privilege of being cried on, I understand."

Terry stopped and wheeled around, her blue eyes bright again.

"Oh, I have something to tell you about him. See you in your spare."

She dashed down the hall at what was technically a walk — running in halls being forbidden — and disappeared into the new wing. Aran shut the back door behind the last of her sauntering pupils rather emphatically for warning and walked with self-renewing vigor to the other which she closed in similar fashion. Inside she waited, leaning in apparent nonchalance against it until the noise subsided. Fortunately she seldom had to decide what to do if it didn't subside, but she wished it would happen as quickly as it once did. These days there were always some — well-meaning usually — who were impervious to a hint.

"If I may interrupt, Nasmith," she began at last. "I think it's my turn. Elsa, could you leave the social contacts till later? I doubt if you remember that I was saying, just before the school didn't burn down —— "

At the end of period six Aran Waring reached her post in the corridor too late to do more than nominal "hall duty" to the rotating classes. Fortunately her defection was less noticeable because of the fact that her room formed a dead end in the old wing of a school erected in the nineties, apparently on the sole principle of surprise. This isolation — at least compared with her former situation, where there had been other classes at either end and across the hall — would have gone far to reconcile her to the deplorably inefficient planning of its Victorian Romanesque architecture, had she felt inclined to deplore it. She seldom did, finding in herself a tendency, which she frankly attributed to increasing senility, to defend some of its extravagances against the vaunted superiority of functional planning. Granted that the system of rotating classes, of which she thoroughly approved, made the old open cloakroom and desk shelf inadequate, was the installation of endless rows of lockers, so built that, after the first week of any new term, twenty percent could be made to open or shut only by a violent kick, a faultless substitute? To say nothing of the locker lists, the forgotten combinations, the broken locks, the forgotten books, the between-period trips to lockers "by special permission," the irregularly given admonition to keep lockers bolted and combinations secret — inevitable for progress undoubtedly — but was it in all points preferable to her own collegiate days, when the freedom of the school's unlocked classrooms had only on two or three occasions — spoken of in hushed tones — tempted any to petty pilfering? And though she knew her heterodoxy, she found something refreshing in buildings containing space with no particular practical design, an odd little room or alcove or balcony, without special purpose in the scholastic system but able to serve a dozen purposes of interview or confidence or need to be alone. After all, it was often the leisure moment, the uncalculated idea, the decorative extra, the apparently useless encounter which proved fruitful and memorable in life; in a building, spaces not strictly utilitarian could have the same effect on the soul. She still felt a twinge of regret at the demolition, four years before, of the oldest part of her wing of the school, a demolition which had taken with it a fascinating, unused wooden staircase leading to an unexpected empty sunroom, just where the corridor turned off to the old art room on the third floor. The new wing contained an art room with fluorescent lighting, a household science section of gleaming utility and a fitted typewriting room, all three the object of inspection for visiting celebrities and the subject of annual gratulation in commencement speeches ever since. Presently her room and the rooms above and below it with their comparative seclusion, their sturdy wooden cupboards, their old-fashioned push-up windows and their non-working air-conditioning would be torn down to add a bally-hooed seven mills to the next year's tax bill by the erection of metal-fitted, indirectly lighted classroom units, with green — instead of black — boards and transom windows. Well, the lighting would be an improvement; the present lights could hardly be worse.

The last class had entered Mr. Paton's room, next down the corridor. Where was hers? Then she remembered and smiled with the added pleasure of a forgotten treat. She had been so busy just before the bell, altering Monday's assignment, because her class had reminded her that ten of them would be away that period at special orchestra practice for the Kiwanis festival; so busy explaining, to the slow satisfaction of the painstaking Stanislaus Sienkiewicz, Virgil's use of *hi* and *hos* for vividness instead of the expected *hi* and *illos* — Stanislaus always brought his open book and grave puzzled face up to the desk when the class was dismissed and Aran invariably placed an individual need before nominal mass supervision in the hall outside; so, she had forgotten her spare period.

"Whoops!" she said, entering her open door. (Pupils at Rivercrest entered by the front and left by the rear doors, a sensible arrangement which resulted in an incorrigible ambition on the part of at least one seeker after truth in every class to enter by the rear, and a sense of crowing achievement if his entry escaped the teacher's vigilant eye.) "Likewise, Yippee! Or in other words, Callooh, Callay!"

She sat down at her desk, stretched her tense figure and wriggled her toes in a moment's lovely idleness. The luxury of four spares a week on her present timetable still caused her to feel grateful. The previous year she had taught thirty-nine of the forty periods and been shocked at the resultant strain. Back in her early thirties she had taught without intermission — for years giving extra classes in Greek or conducting rehearsals after hours without more than temporary healthy exhaustion. The difference was in her age, she supposed. Or was it? There seemed such an unending amount of work to do in her spares which she knew she had not taken home in earlier years. She looked at her desk, a desk which she usually advised her Ontario College of Education student teachers to take as a horrible example of what to avoid for efficient teaching. One set of Grade Nine tests, two of Grade Eleven vocabulary reviews! The pile of scrawled paragraphs under her Daily Calendar — ? Goodness, they were her Grade Twelve's attempts at independent translations of Virgil — the day she became thoroughly disgusted with their lack of initiative and their pen-posed waiting to copy down blindly and erroneously whatever the victim presently translating should piece out with her assistance. That other pile was Grade Thirteen Latin prose — thirty-six of them to be minutely corrected with textbook references. But when used she to do such things? Some of them, at least, in regular periods while the classes went on with the next day's assignment. When she began to teach, the classes had marked their own period tests with fair accuracy. Now with the most well-meaning there was so much trouble in explaining and re-explaining the marking scheme, in quieting disputes over errors, in acting as arbiter on special cases — after which, if she collected the papers for checking, she usually found a dozen wrongly marked — that it was more time-saving to do it all herself. She recalled Ancient History periods where a third of the time was given over to reading. There had been Latin classes where rapid workers had been allowed to look at issues of *Punch* for a reward. These days even the best of her classes required steady oral prodding to cover shorter and shorter assignments; and the anecdotes, the games, the addenda, with which she had always sought to enliven their study and give background for their enlarging experience and thought, had to be discarded or introduced most sparingly. Well, she would attack that pile of translation immediately; otherwise the salutary effect of her experiment would be lost; there were few things more demoralizing than for pupils to be confirmed in their sneaking suspicion that some of their work was thrown in the basket unmarked.

She drew the papers to her, setting aside to make room a neat typewritten half-page requesting "as soon as possible" — that meant Tuesday — a summary of the month's attendance. She would *not* spend this precious period marking her register with a Morse code of dashes and dots, adding days — and now half-days — present, days and half-days absent, entering *G* for religious and other granted holidays, working out the average attendance, the perfect aggregate, the actual aggregate, the percentage of actual to perfect to two places of decimals. That could be done before nine or one o'clock whether or not half a dozen messages or questions interrupted.

"Huge grief the young man's bones burned," she read from Bill Sherman's effort, "neither tears failed his cheeks."

There was a knock and Terry Maxfield glanced in through the single unfrosted pane of glass and opened the door almost simultaneously.

"I hope I'm not disturbing anything important. I should be working myself but I did want to see you before the week-end and I've got a class detention with Nine-E."

"Poor Terry." Aran shoved her papers away, pulled a loose chair forward and motioned her to it. Anyone facing a Friday afternoon detention with a class of Nine-E's man-eating caliber should be given all the encouragement at her disposal. "I'm fond enough of you to waive the joy of reading Sherman's up-to-date translation of the Boat Race. Listen to this! 'In memory (that's *immemor*) of his decoration and his friend's salutation he disturbed Menoetes' — I'll say he did! Well, thank goodness he has disturbed him from the lofty stern and not from the deep pup which I should not have put past him. Oh, Terry, when I read things like that I don't feel I'm earning my salary."

"That's when you are earning it," said Terry stoutly. "If they can't do better with your teaching, it's entirely their own fault."

"You always were prejudiced," Aran said, feeling warmed, however.

"Rot! You taught me three of my four years Latin and one of Ancient History. And I observed you last year. So my opinion is quite up to date. It's my own teaching that reduces me to despair."

"Terry, you were far and away the best student I had last year. I told Dr. Moorhouse so when your application came in."

"*You* were probably prejudiced that time. And they were your classes, remember, with you sitting at the back to keep order."

"I didn't have any occasion. They worked very well for you. And it wasn't just in Latin. Miss McManus said the same about your English lessons, and she isn't easy to please. Terry, you handle the youngsters well, you are keen on what you have to teach — besides knowing something about it, which is a help — and you were the only student I had who showed decided ingenuity in presenting your topic and in dealing with their questions."

"You always make me feel better, Aran." Terry's long blue eyes were grateful and her beautiful sensitive mouth with the strongly marked Cupid's-bow upper lip looked a little less as though she might burst into tears. "But in a way that's the worst of it. I do care about teaching. I've wanted to be a teacher ever since Grade Ten. I like the kids. I never had trouble with C.G.I.T. groups at church, or youngsters at camp in the summer. But what's the use if you can't get them quiet long enough to hear what you have to say?"

"Don't exaggerate. Eleven-B was telling me the other day about a lesson you taught them on *The Ice Floes*. They said it was the first time they'd ever really enjoyed poetry."

Brightness rippled across Terry's face and was gone again. "Eleven-B are dears — most of them. I got to know them last year from the time I spent with you and Miss McManus In fact, if it weren't for Eleven-B I'd have resigned in October, I think. But Eleven-G and Ten-D — though they wouldn't be bad if Carol Liscombe and Sandra Luck and Hartley and Obalanski didn't egg them on. And then Nine-C, Nine-F — and Nine-E! I lie awake nights dreading my next period with them."

"Terry, it's your first year. They know it's your first year. Everybody expects difficulty then. I remember a class — Two-C in those days — when I came to Rivercrest. I had a double period with them before lunch on Tuesday — see how the scars linger — and I used to go home regularly and lie down most of the noon hour while Mother made sympathetic sounds at me."

"I wish I could believe it was just first-yearish-ness. But what if I have Nine-E next year in Ten? They won't all be wearing little haloes! At least my Tens don't. You never seem to have any trouble with discipline."

"My soul!" Aran was less genuinely astonished than if she had not often heard the same comment, but it always struck her with an inner amazement. "I've *never* been satisfied with my discipline. No, I have nothing to worry about. Naturally by this time I can handle anything that comes up — otherwise I'd have quit years ago. But it's a matter of keeping a jump ahead of the youngsters. That isn't my ideal of order. I have a dream of a day when my classes file quietly into my room, whether I'm there or not, open their books and wait expectantly for me to begin."

"After saying: 'Good morning, Teacher.' "

They both laughed.

"You must have heard Mother. She had an amazing little song which her pupils sang to her back in the nineties in Phoebe Street School.

Good morning, good morning, kind Teacher so dear!
How gladly we greet you to all doth appear.
Our schoolmates we welcome, each one with delight.
Our hearts are so happy because we do right."

Terry giggled. "I can imagine Nine-E singing that!"

"It would be a jolly good thing for them. Listen to the sound psychology of the second verse:

Good morning, good morning, our dear little school —
pride in group possession —
How happy we are while obeying each rule —
that's auto-suggestion for you! —
For love is our motto in work as in play — "

"To judge by some of Nine-E who are going steady, that line would pass," interposed Terry.

"*So hurrah! hurrah! for each happy day!"* concluded Aran firmly. "Rather a weak ending but more conducive to outgoing co-operation than the 'What's good about it?' wisecrack which often greets my 'good morning.' "

"I thought all the youngsters were supposed to be cowed and browbeaten in those days. School was a place of horror."

"Not according to Mother's stories. She used to make taffy on the stove on winter Friday afternoons and each youngster had a big piece to suck as he went home. I imagine the situation varied considerably with the teacher — as it does now. I know when Mother married after teaching the newsboys' class — a class with special hours so that the boys could sell their papers without missing school — three of them came to see her and declared that their education was over since she wasn't to teach them any longer."

"There, you see," said Terry despairingly, "they seemed to care, to want to be treated reasonably. They were willing to be interested. Either these kids aren't — or I'm a flat failure and have nothing to give. That's all!"

"You're not a failure! And there are always some who care, even in the worst classes. That is our reward — even the single one with a responsive gleam in the eye." Aran spoke with an assurance she did not altogether feel. What she had said about dissatisfaction with her own discipline was true. But never, even in her earliest days, had she lost control of a class. Never had she endured the noise through which she had heard Terry trying to teach one day when she had gone to her door with a message. After weighing the possibility of entering and quelling them with the weight of her superior authority, she had instead, to save her young friend's face, tiptoed quietly away. The insolent remarks, the open defiance which Terry wretchedly reported baffled her, though she did her best to suggest methods of dealing with them. Teaching was her vocation and she had never seriously considered another; but she thanked Heaven that she was meeting today's classes with twenty years experience behind her. If this was the experience of a novice as attractive and gifted as Terry Maxfield, she would hesitate to advise any sensitive young person to enter the profession now — at least in a city school. And with the elimination of difference between urban and rural life by means of car, radio, and television the problems of teachers in smaller centers were no longer less acute — and in some cases more complicated.

A surreptitious glance at the clock removed any hope of completing even a fraction of the work she had intended to finish. She might as well cheer Terry for the next ten minutes.

"Count your blessings, dear. If a teacher like you is having trouble, think of your poor teaching partner the week you spent with me last year. Do you remember how the class tied him in knots when he passed a board full of declensions with every word spelled wrong? And think of Eva Salter with all the English and French and a class of Social Studies in Oldbrook Continuation School. Remember, too, there's a frightening shortage of teachers — "

"I don't wonder. Sometimes I think it will be shorter by me next year."

"Right. But the lovely part is that you *can* get out. In the depression even teaching jobs are scarce. Now there are half a dozen things you can do."

"But, Aran, I want to teach! And I don't want to fail!"

"That's even better. What I'm trying to say is that circumstances have given you the upper hand — even with Nine-E. Just go ahead and be ruthless. They're trying you out. You can wear them down if you're firm. The first hundred days are the hardest. And think of the people who haven't your compensations. I doubt if you will be teaching all your life."

That last remark had the desired effect. The ripple of brightness which had been clouded out of Terry's face fought its way back and deepened as though clouds had finally blown away.

"That was what I came to tell you — before Nine-E took over the conversation. Aran, I think I can consider myself engaged."

"You think! It's a question of whether the lucky man thinks . . . ."

"Oh, I know. But I'm not nearly as sure of myself as you are of me. The — the Rupert episode left me pretty low. That's another reason I like George. He's so completely frank . . . like an open book."

"What did you read last night?"

"Well — we went dancing. I hesitated about going because I just can't be out late on week nights and face classes next day, but it was his birthday and he wanted to celebrate. So, of course, I asked him out for dinner and Mom made him a cake and he was awfully pleased."

"That was nice for him."

"Well, he likes coming to our place. He says it seems like home when his own is away down near Ottawa. Anyhow, we went to the Club Top Hat afterwards. He promised to bring me home early and we left before eleven, but we went home by the lake-shore and there was a full moon and we sat in the car and talked till almost one."

"I'm glad it was a mild night."

"I had a rug. George did most of the talking — about himself and his ambitions and his philosophy of life. He has everything planned out, Aran. It's really quite interesting. You wouldn't agree with him in a lot of things."

"Do you?"

Terry's blue eyes met Aran's green ones honestly. She shook her head with a little wise tolerant smile which made Aran feel absurdly younger than her former pupil.

"No. But do two people ever perfectly agree? And he may change his mind. I'd like him to talk to you. He would too. He admires you very much. Says you're a woman who achieves your goals."

"My soul, do I?" said Aran interested. "What are they?"

"I'm not quite sure. Something about being on the top professionally. He expresses himself in a rather involved way sometimes. I think it's the effect of the psychology lectures he is taking for his B. Paed." She smiled a quick smile of sympathy, knowing Aran's reaction, but continued with a determination which might have sounded pugnacious if Terry could ever be accused of pugnacity. "But I don't care — really. I'd rather disagree with him and know what he is than have someone like Rupert whom I thought I knew — and who didn't mean a word of what he said."

"But — " Aran caught back her words of objection. Far

31

be it from her to interfere with anyone else's romance! "You'll have to make it fast, Terry. Put me out of my suspense."

"Golly, it's three minutes to!" Terry promptly poured her confidence forth while Aran dashed to the side board, cleared off the subjunctive of *video* with one hand, her torso turned so that she gave her guest full attention, a priceless teaching habit she had learned many years before from Professor Carlisle at the College of Education. "It's just that — well, I'm included in all his plans, Aran. He kept talking about 'we' — it was rather sweet that he hesitated the first time, and when I didn't say anything he went on doing it. He was perfectly frank about the money he has saved for a down payment on a house and wanted to know if I thought I could teach for two more years after we were married so we could get most of it paid off and furnished rather than wait. He made it quite plain he wasn't keen on waiting. Oh, I must fly. Tell you more later."

She was gone with the bell. Aran, taking a standing jump, cleared "Imperfect Subjunctive" from the top of the board where she had stood on a chair to write it, and proceeded to the corridor to usher in her last class. She was at once grateful for a reprieve in which she might conceal her lack of enthusiasm for this extraordinary modern substitute for romance and critical of herself that she could not feel happier for Terry. If the girl was satisfied with George Madden then pity was obviously wasted on her. Or perhaps her clear young eye discerned virtue hidden from Aran's hypercritical and frustrated one. She used the adjectives of herself dispassionately, controlled her quick self-responsive smile and, to avoid last-period apathy, plunged into the causes of the Second Punic War with a vivid account of the grievances of Hamilcar Barca.

Three

GEORGE MADDEN, momentarily nonplussed, strode the length of the table to seat his hostess and compromised with gallantry by touching the back of his fiancee's chair and letting his hand rest briefly on her shoulder as he went back to his place. He performed these minor offices with the self-conscious deliberation of one who has determined to acquire correct habits without conviction of their essential importance. They were a concession to the place he intended to occupy in society. Also they increased his masculine sense of importance when performed in such gracious surroundings and with two attractive women. He always remained seated in his room when the school secretary or a woman member of the staff came to speak to him; he never yielded place at a door to the older girls in the school or held it open if anyone was close behind; but he had recently adopted the habit of baring his head on entering an elevator, whether it contained women or not, because of an indignant letter in the Correspondence Column of his evening newspaper to the effect that this was a hallmark of a gentleman. Full of a pleasant sense of brightening the lives of what he would always refer to as "the fair sex" in the many speeches he was going to make — just as he would presently refer to Terry as "the little woman" or "my good wife" — he drew up his chair and bowed his head just a little too far while Aran asked the blessing. He was pleased with the world and particularly pleased with the evening before him. Terry had expressed her preference that Aran's invitation to celebrate their engagement should be for them alone, so that her mentor and her fiancé might become better acquainted. So the table in the candle-lit dining room was set for three. George felt in this intimacy another indication that he had arrived. He had come to Rivercrest three years before predisposed to admire Aran Waring. One of her more enthusiastic pupils had taught him English in the High School of the small town to which he had come from the farm to take his Upper School year. As a junior on a large staff he had watched her from a distance and approved, he scarcely knew why, except that she represented a relaxed assurance at which he aimed. She was the head of her department, she was well spoken of at the Ontario College of Education, she was pro tem a senator of the University. Apart from her spinsterhood, which he deplored, she seemed to have a great deal more than, as far as he could see, she actually had. For want of a better term he attributed it to culture, the atmosphere of which made Terry's home so attractive to him. Yet even the few minutes he had spent in the Waring living room had shown him a difference. The Maxwell culture was one of solid financial background. Terry's father, a prosperous dentist, had inherited from his schoolteacher parents a fine library and some good old furniture; but Mrs. Maxfield's literary aspirations were satisfied by membership in the Book of the Month Club and her colonial dream home in the Kingsway had been furnished almost entirely on the advice of Eaton's Interior Decorator. With her son and daughter now requiring little attention she had taken to antique-collecting as a hobby and had become a push-over for a plausible dealer with any rara avis as long as it was guaranteed a century old.

A glance at the haphazard assortment of furniture which the Waring household had assembled and left behind when the other members of the family married and moved out showed him that, whatever gave Aran poise, it was not possession of things. He had heard that she was "religious" but sensibly discounted this as a practical factor in the attainment of poise — except when, in an attempt to account for her contented celibacy, he mentioned it to Terry as a psychologically recognized way of sublimating the sex impulse. As far as religion went, he was religious too. He had transferred his home church membership to the most prosperous church of his denomination in the vicinity of the school and belonged to the Men's Club there. Half a dozen men on the staff were members of the same church and he had greatly enlarged his acquaintance thereby. Besides, it was good for the pupils and their parents to see that a teacher stood for the better interests of the community. Skepticism was all right at college and, of course, there was considerable latitude in one's interpretation of even so latitudinarian a statement of faith as the one endorsed by his church. But the spiritual side of life should not be neglected. People were realizing that more in these days of possible atomic warfare. As his minister had said only last Sunday, unless man's moral achievements kept up with his discoveries in the realm of science, man might discover, like Frankenstein, that he had created a monster which would destroy its creator. George had been impressed by that sermon. It gave people something to think about. He liked his minister, a sociable, well-informed joiner who put his clerical voice and manner off with his ministerial gown, kept his finger on the pulse of newspaper headlines and the contents of *Time* magazine articles, and gave a pertinent twenty-minute resumé of some personal or social problem with pat comments from a wide and dissident assortment of quotable authorities, Loth Liebman, Harry Emerson Fosdick and Norman Vincent Peale to C. S. Lewis and Karl Barth, the whole neatly tied together by an apt-sounding text of Scripture, rarely taken in its context. He was popular with a congregation which heard him once a week, played a good game of bridge on his social calls, was badly out of his depth if any profound or spiritual question was put to him, and was considered a coming man in his denomination.

"I love shrimp cocktail, Aran," said Terry appreciatively. "You must tell me what you put in the sauce."

"Not now, please!" laughed George, showing his very fine set of teeth. "You women love to talk recipes!" He was a good-looking, pleasant boy, Aran thought, determining for Terry's sake to see his maturely shaped young face with its fresh complexion, fine grey eyes, intelligent brow and rather boldly aggressive nose as wholly attractive. He was kind-hearted too. When Reg Purvis's young son contracted polio the previous autumn he had taken charge of the two older children from school to bedtime for days and his heartfelt distress for the stricken parents at the time of the boy's death had made Aran warm to him.

"That's just like George, Aran," protested Terry with that delightful pride in her fiancé which shows itself unmistakably in pretended criticism. "He's most interested in the results of recipes, as witness the fact that he's already snaffled three of your — what did you say the ridiculous name was? Fromage fingers? — but he doesn't want to hear anything about the preparation. 'My lord, dinner is served,' is to be his cue after we are married, apparently. And he expects me to teach, too. Brute!"

"Could we change the subject? I'm outnumbered," said George. "By the way, I've always been interested in your name, Miss Waring. Was it in the family?"

"You'd better call me by it then. Everybody does." Aran began to remove the dishes. "Sit still, Terry, I can manage easily. 'The perfect hostess plans for a minimum of serving.' My name?" she resumed after a mental check at the table to see that broiled steak, mashed yams in green pepper shells, broccoli, beets and condiments were all present. "It's really Elizabeth after Mother. To avoid confusion they began calling me Aran, my second name. Every other member of the family inherited a family surname second but they ran out by the time I arrived — except for MacRobie which, thank goodness, I was spared, though I understand it was a near thing. Then Papa" — after thirty-five years she still remembered her father so and brought the name out naturally, its balanced pronunciation midway between the English papa and the American poppa — "came up with a brilliant idea. As a boy he had an adventurous, unforgettable trip to the Isles of Aran. . . . I perpetuate the memory. However, I console myself with the reflection that it might have been Elizabeth MacRobie."

"That's most interesting. Your father was Irish, Miss — Aran?"

"From Northern Ireland. Do have some horse-radish and watermelon pickle," urged Aran. She loved to talk of her father but somehow not with this young man. "Terry, will you? I hear, all over the school," she went on, hoping that the change did not seem too abrupt, "that this Easter tour of yours to New York is almost embarrassingly popular."

"You can say that again." George was easily diverted. "I had to close the application list two weeks ago. Girls have been asking about it too. Maybe next year Terry and I — You see, I had the expenses all doped out well beforehand, inquired and read up on what was suitable in the way of entertainment, arranged for enough trips to the Planetarium, United Nations, Museum of Natural Science, and so on, to give it educational appeal, and then sounded out my classes. I know a chap on the *Star* and I'm counting on a decent amount of publicity. It all helps — getting one's name in the public eye — as well as strengthening my position in the school."

"And leaving me alone our first Easter," murmured Terry in somewhat conventional protest.

"But the excursion was planned long before our engagement. Besides, you know you'd far sooner marry someone who makes plans for the future."

"What plans?"

Their recital and exposition took most of the evening in front of the living-room fire. At intervals Terry begged for music and they listened to Mozart and Haydn and to Aran's D'Oyly Carte recordings of Gilbert and Sullivan. But in the main George talked, between and above the records. There were jokes, there were questions, there was affectionate badinage with Terry, most of it in careful, if heavy, good taste. Chiefly, however, George talked, well, fluently and frankly, as Terry had indicated, about himself and a future he was not leaving to chance.

To "get ahead," "get to the top" — his favorite phrases — was the ruling passion of his life. He had no little intelligence, a remarkably objective appraisal of his own attributes, abilities and failings. As he talked, Aran saw his thickset capable figure against the background of its well-built farm home where the acquirement first of one modern convenience then of another piece of machinery did not make the prospect of bucolic life sufficiently attractive to the petted youngest of the family. She saw the father and mother, the much older brother and sisters, of whose vernacular and grammatical errors their educated young brother would never entirely rid himself, sensibly impressed by his wit, his adaptability, his interest in school. People who had "arrived," natives of the district who had left it and "made something of themselves," the local M.P., and the lumber magnate whose gift to his village of a public library commemorated his name there: these were the heroes of George's youth; and to do him justice, his measure of success was not merely money, though money was an essential concomitant.

Arriving at university with the swollen post-war enrolment, he had taken an Arts course for want of sufficient directive towards a profession and in search of an element which he felt to be lacking in his background. This quality of unsureness, this deficiency in self-confidence, constantly betraying or confessing itself amid his most assured pronouncements and unshakable determination, was his most — to Aran, his only — endearing characteristic. She could see how Terry's motherly instinct would feed on it in her own state of self-depreciation. But —

"If I had thought there was a chance of getting through in Commerce and Finance, I might have taken it," said

George with engaging frankness. "The estimated average salary of grads with a B. Comm. is twice the salary of grads from other courses. But my math was never that good. I figured, without that and without any capital to speak of, or any connections, and with the competition today, my chance of getting to the top in business was not too promising. I took a counsellor's job at Comet Boys' Camp the summer after my first year. Thought the experience would be good and I might make some valuable connections. A good many influential people send their sons to Comet. Well, Ron Selznick was in the senior staff that year and we talked a good deal. You know Selznick of the salary committee? He left teaching twice, once to go into business and once to join up, and he was going back in. Education is the wave of the future, was his pet expression. It's Canada's biggest industry. And I suddenly realized that he had something. I'd never seriously thought of teaching before, though a teacher I had — two in fact, one of them Gaye Martin, your former pupil, but chiefly old Garrow down in Winchester Collegiate Institute — made me think it would be rather fine if I could teach like him. But I had the man-of-action ideal. Wasn't it Bernard Shaw, who said: 'Those who can, do, those who can't, teach'?"

"A half-truth, like much of Shaw. But the half always stings," admitted Aran.

"Anyway, Selznick exploded that idea. He showed me that the whole picture has changed, that teachers can be the biggest influence in the community; that with schools expected to take over entertainment, recreation, religious training, character building, teachers have an importance in the public eye they've never had before. Especially now that it's a recognized profession. Look at the pensions, too, he said. Think what a doctor or a lawyer has to put away in investments to guarantee such security. Well, that's old stuff to you, of course. I don't want to bore you."

"You aren't. You are interesting me." There was no

subtle nuance in Aran's intonation that Terry's sensitive ear could detect. "From then your mind was made up?"

"Pretty well. Oh, I explored other possibilities. But I switched from Modern History to the General Course right away."

"Why on earth?" The question was surprised from Aran, and catching Terry's quick glance at her fiancé she wished she had suppressed it. His answer, however, was matter-of-fact.

"I'd have had to work like blazes to be sure of my specialist standing. I got a low second in first year. And without it, why put in four years when I could get the same B.A. in three? Much more to the point to pick up an extra post grad degree as I am doing. I can cash in twice this way, draw a salary while I'm getting the degree, and draw an extra two hundred afterwards. Besides," he went on, not defensively but as if challenging his hearers' ambiguous silence, "the Honor courses are too narrow. For teaching today one needs a broader education."

Supplied by the General Course, thought Aran. She had specimens every year, registered to teach subjects which they had not touched since High School, because the loose assortment of "requirements" which made up their course had no connection with the High School curriculum. Every year she agonized, watching possibilities for beautiful lessons doomed by well-meaning University graduates with less grasp of the topic than the brighter pupils who corrected their mistakes, suggested improvements, and under duress, restrained their mirth or impatience. Better ones there were, of course, who realized their lack of knowledge and determined to make it up the hard way by conscientious study. And very rarely there was a "born" teacher who could temporarily camouflage lack of grounding in the subject by an instinctive ability to elicit from the pupils what he did not know himself and to make what he did know sufficiently interesting by his genuine enthusiasm.

"Look at Terry now," continued George, and, as by

common consent, they both looked at Terry and conceded mentally that the sight was good. Her feet were drawn up child-fashion under her chair; the firelight caught the bronze tones of her irridescent rose taffeta dress and paled the gold of her hair. Under their glance her inscrutable expression relaxed into serenity and the intent eyes widened to a smile. Impulsively George leaned forward and put his hand over the slim one lying on her knee. Briefly Aran warmed to him again. So far even Terry had seemed to fit too smoothly into his calculations to guarantee any disinterested depth of feeling.

"As I was saying, look at Terry," he resumed with renewed, if not increased confidence. "Her head, though you might not think it, is crammed with Anglo-Saxon and John Donne and Cicero's letters and that's all to the good as far as I'm concerned. I heard chaps at College say they wouldn't marry a University woman for fear she'd know more than they did. So of course their wives are no help to them at all on the way up. Terry will be an asset to me in every way." Terry bent her head in mock acknowledgment, and Aran wondered if love made her deaf to the undertones of the compliment. "But as far as teaching is concerned, she's never had any psychology except what we get at Ontario College of Education, no philosophy, not a scrap of biology, no anthropology."

"Did. Second Year pass subject," murmured Terry. "Forgotten all of it except the prof's opinions with which I disagreed."

"Do you really believe that one learns more about human nature from a course in pass Psychology than from a thorough study of Shakespeare and the great novelists? Or more from a modern textbook on Philosophy than from a first-hand reading of Plato?" asked Aran and waited critically for his answer.

"It's like substituting Third Year Religious Knowledge for personal knowledge of the Bible," abetted Terry with sudden warmth. "There were people in that course — I took it as my pass subject instead of Third Anthrop — who got A by reading the recommended critical texts and quoting the professor's notes; one boy in particular I remember who was terribly scornful of the petty tribal Jahwe of the Hebrews, condescended to approve the Sermon on the Mount, and said when cornered — by me! — on Pauline theology that he had never read the 'Book of Paul.' "

Confronted thus, George put another stick of wood on the fire, settled back again, squared his shoulders, and told the truth.

"No, I don't, Aran. Quiet, Terry, whose side do you think you're on? Of course I believe that those who know the most . . . er . . . know the most. I'm all for Latin, for instance. I always liked it and I learned a lot from it. But the point is, in the present setup that sort of knowledge doesn't get you anywhere. It has in your case, to a point, because Classics specialists are scarce and they still require them in Toronto schools. But for men — well, take Garrow who taught me history. What that old boy didn't know about everybody from Solon to Bismarck wasn't worth knowing. He made us feel we knew them too. And he was so keen and made it so interesting, that I felt like wading through Plutarch, and Gibbon, and even Toynbee on my own. But he was a hopeless back-number. Used the lecture method most of the time, except when we read on our own and answered questions. No projects, no research, no marks for notebooks, nothing to show on Parents' Night. He had been teaching then for thirty years when I was in his class and had been passed over for Principal three times."

"Did he mind?"

"Well, it would have been a promotion. One of the Principals put in over his head is now an Inspector. Actually I think Garrow preferred teaching."

"Let us now praise famous men," said Aran. "Not least among them those who were spared to inspire us as teachers because they were 'passed over' when that sort of promotion came up. I am grateful for two without whom I should be much poorer, if the same person at all: the late J.H. Mills and the late J.D. Morrow; the latter was largely responsible for my presence in the teaching profession."

"Yes, but you see they were old-timers. Things are different today."

"Why?"

"Oh, come now," said George, shocked at this willful ignorance. "Ninety-six percent of the population goes to Secondary School today. And only three percent go on to University. It isn't sensible to sacrifice ninety-three percent to an outmoded curriculum designed for professional men. It ——"

"I wonder," said Aran meditatively, "what proportion of High School students went on to University in my far-off day. And why on earth the non-University student is considered sacrificed rather than privileged by at least an introduction to the subjects of a liberal education."

"Our concept of education has changed," quoted George glibly. "After all, we have realized that the whole child — "

"Oh, no, George. No!" moaned Terry.

"O.K., laugh if you like — you two and Hilda Neatby," said George good-naturedly. "But the fact of the matter is that people believe it — that the old system of education wasn't democratic, that in a democracy we must concentrate on making good citizens rather than scholars, that, since ninety-three percent won't go on to University, they should have a curriculum which gives them a sense of achievement, something they can finish before they graduate ——"

"But why call that education? No person is educated who considers that he has finished any subject — cooking or motor mechanics included."

"Yes, but —" riposted George, happy to use the grist thus provided for his mill. "When a pupil finishes a course in cooking or motor mechanics they have something practical. They can cook or tinker with a car. Whereas at the end of our course in French or Latin or Geometry, they haven't enough to use. All they do is forget what they have learned and it's simply time wasted."

"Do you really believe that?" asked Aran steadily.

"Of course. It's self-evident. This is supposed to be a bi-lingual country and how many of our High School graduates will speak two sentences of French when they go down to Quebec?"

"For the most part they don't get a chance. The French are too keen on answering them in English," said Aran drily. "Actually, you know, I'm a bit fed up with our self-disparagement on this matter of language. The truth is, whether because we are lazy or not, we are much more helpful to the foreigner — no, perish the thought that I should so designate les Canadiens! — I mean the actual heterolinguist, whether Canadian or not, who tries to learn English, than he is to us. His grasp of grammar may be non-existent, his accent ludicrous, his pronunciation of simple sounds like *th* and *r* unintelligible, but we praise him, apologize for our impossibly inconsistent language, and carry on the conversation with perfect and often difficult self-control. But let us air our timid vocabulary of a foreign language in an honest effort to learn and what happens? At the worst a blank stare and a non-comprehending shrug, at best the condescending encouragement one gives to a retarded child . . . something of Dr. Johnson's comparison of a woman preacher to a dog standing on its hind legs: 'It is not done well but one is surprised to find it being done at all.' "

George stared at her with rather apprehensive amusement.

"Yes, I see what you mean. But I hope you don't say things like that in front of everybody. I mean, it's not the popular attitude these days. Some people would think you intolerant, you know, Jingoistic."

Aran's laugh was unrestrained amusement and Terry's echoed it.

"Sorry to laugh," said Aran apologetically. I'm just fed up to the teeth with the use of the words intolerant and undemocratic — bigoted is another — used by people who would suppress free speech concerning any exceptionable statement no matter how demonstrably true. For instance, I'm ready to admit any mistake that Britain has made, and she has made many, in Ireland, in India, in the far East, and with her own people. But I still think that no other ruling power in history has done such a good and conscientious job and I'm by no means sure that the world will be better for the disintegration of the British Empire . . . a title which, by the way, like the Dominion of Canada, I refuse to regard as dirty words. I regard as rottenly ungrateful the peoples who have benefited by her justice and by the death of millions of her best men and refuse to acknowledge any indebtedness. In other words I agree with W. S. Gilbert, as in many things, when he speaks of
   'The idiot who praises with enthusiastic tone
   All centuries but this and every country but his own.' "

She stopped short, curtailing her impulse to be scathing on the subject of several holy cows which a conformist like George would be almost certain to revere. Iconoclasm could defeat its ostensible purpose when the destroyer enjoyed the act of destroying. Unfortunately George was ready with the wrong comment.

" 'My country right or wrong' is your motto then?"

"It is not," retorted Aran. "I reserve the right to oppose the stand of Canada or Great Britain or both — and have done, as when sanctions against Italy were repudiated and when Czecho-Slovakia was betrayed at Munich. No, I wave my flag with discretion — and, by the way, I believe we have a flag to wave. I have little patience with the 'little Canadian' attitude of those who believe that the way to induce patriotism is to scrap every cause for it that we already possess — history, symbol, and tradition. Why doesn't somebody suggest a new flag for the U.S. and a new national anthem too, in view of the fact that the words of 'O say, can you see?' are utterly meaningless to an overwhelming proportion of her present population?"

"You don't talk like that to your classes?"

"Why not? They are quite at liberty, when such matters come up, to express their views. I simply want them to hear both sides. As one boy said to me this year when I was answering a question about money-making, 'How are we going to know these things if nobody tells us?' I urge them to debate and reason, to reject 'Everybody says' or 'Fifty million can't be wrong' or 'I don't think so' as arguments."

"We loved it when Aran got going," said Terry reminiscently. "Those were our favorite periods. We tried to bring them on with irrelevant questions. One on Julius Caesar usually worked or a carefully connected query about her travels. But usually, for our imaginations weren't too fertile, we just waited for the divine spark — what is that favorite phrase of yours, Aran? It is a quote from Professor Carlisle . . . ."

" 'The incalculable emergent factor which gives zest to life.' Yes, I owe it, with a good many others, notably, 'praise with faint damns,' to him. And a great deal of common sense and inspiration. He gave us more practical help — I have a friend who has been teaching history on Doc Carlisle's notes — than all the textbooks on Science of Education and School Management combined."

"That's rank heresy," said George, smiling.

"And like much so-called heresy, truth."

"But you have to learn methods."

"Of course. And like 'good citizenship' you can't learn them from a textbook. 'A poor method in the hands of a good teacher is worth six good methods in the hands of a poor teacher,' Professor Carlisle said and I'm convinced he was right — though I think a good teacher will discard the poor method fairly soon. What is it, Terry?"

"Could we find our way back to your discussion about

courses in cooking and motor mechanics vs half-finished 'University' subjects?"

"Oh, yes," said George, feeling terra firma. "And you can't convince me that it isn't better for those who are never going in for education at the University level to have a feeling of accomplishment, a certificate that means they have a real working knowledge of something they can use in their everyday life and social contacts, than to have a sense of frustration at beginning a lot of subjects that will do them no good."

Aran looked at him thoughtfully. In spite of her recent curtailed outburst she hated to seem an opinionated woman. There were many subjects on which she held no decided views at all because she regarded her knowledge of them an inadequate basis for opinion, and when these were discussed she found it restful, as only those whose advice is constantly sought can find it restful, to listen and weigh the conclusions of people with wider information or experience. She loved Terry, as she had loved successive pupils of either sex who had responded to her teaching or needed her help; loved them, cognizant of and indifferent to the fact that she was probably "sublimating the maternal impulse," only wishing on some tired occasions that the women who did not have to sublimate it would do their job more thoroughly and leave less to her. Her love for Terry was deeper than for most of those who retained their affectionate connection with her after graduation, both because of more frequent contact and because the kinship of the younger girl's mind and sense of humor lifted their relationship to the status of a reciprocal friendship. She wanted for her, even more than for her other young friends, a happy and satisfying marriage. George was not the man she would have chosen, nor did she think he was the man Terry would have chosen. The more important fact, apparently, was that he had chosen Terry and this was the place at which the girl was incomprehensible to her; it was likewise the place at which she would not for worlds interfere. Unafraid of incurring the worst terms of psychological jargon with regard to her spinsterhood, Aran Waring had a horror of arousing the faintest if falsest suspicion that she would prefer her friends to be similarly handicapped. So, if George was for Terry, she wanted to do what she could to make her happiness more certain. If taking off her gloves and expressing herself freely at this opportunity was what Terry wanted, Aran would take them off, though with an inward sigh, for nothing reminded her of her age so surely as the fact that eleven o'clock, which seemed a decent end to her evening, was apparently just the beginning for these young creatures.

"The amount of waste in education is not one that can be nicely calculated either before or after, is it?" she began and her smile flashed suddenly at him as she continued. "Consider my eight years of piano lessons: and the result: *God Save the Queen* in one key, the opening bars of *The Pink Song of Love,* more or less correctly harmonized, and the erratic ability to play a few hymns. Pure waste? — and the case is repeated dozens of times within my knowledge with even less to show for it by people who took their lessons seriously and tried exams! Now back at last to cooking and motor mechanics. I'll grant for the sake of argument that the girls who take the Household Science option at High School will do their own cooking, and that the motorized boys will keep their cars in shape. Grant it, mind you, in spite of personal conviction that the easy solution of fast-frozen pies, ready-mixes and bake-shop or delicatessen makes a stronger appeal to the "practical" girls than to those who choose the harder subjects and therefore have the imagination to consider home-making a creative activity and not just drudgery. But how many of the men you know who keep their own cars in shape and repair minor damages have taken a course? Most of them have picked up their knowledge on their own from native interest. As for the other Science, Mother is my prize example! She taught school till her marriage and there was no Household Science Department in the Jarvis Collegiate of her day! What a curriculum! *Un Philosophe Sous les Toits* was her second year French Authors text — I know because I used her copy when I was in Fifth — Grade Thirteen to you. Likewise her History text for the same year was Hallam's *Constitutional History of England.* I'll show it to you with her name and form on the flyleaf before you leave: all nine hundred and thirty-odd pages of it, every page wallowing in inches of italicized footnotes. I know, I know. The population attending secondary school then was select, selected or selective . . . ! I'm not arguing that nor am I recommending Hallam as a High School text. My original point is simply this: that from a completely scholastic background and occupation, with no formal "training," Mother became a marvellous cook and baker — of everything from gravy on or macaroni to bread and lemon pie. All our food was homemade. Moreover, after marriage she taught herself to sew and made all our clothes, even the first little tailored suits for my brothers."

"But times are different."

"That seems to be the answer to any argument."

"Look at the difference in home background."

Aran controlled her exasperation.

"There were some fairly unsavory home conditions in Toronto then, and there are a good many very healthy ones now. Besides, some of the best homemakers I know come from homes where everything was brought from the cardboard box to the table. And our opportunities of learning at night school, cooking school, by radio, T. V., newspaper column and magazine article make day-school courses a "waste" if you insist on applying the word to any honest occupation of time. I use it only in the sense that I think it waste to teach anything in school which can be acquired by the average person on his own more quickly and cheaply elsewhere. Then you mentioned democracy. Yet the idea of segregating our adolescents with a view either to their heredity or to their predestinate toil, and differentiating their education accordingly, is disturbingly reminiscent of Plato's Republic."

"But," interrupted George, thrown off balance by this reference, "surely Plato's Republic is the ideal democracy."

Terry caught her breath sharply. Aran covered the sound in hurried speech.

"No-o-o, not exactly. Like Platonic love, the Platonic republic has given rise to popular misconceptions. Since it was an ideal state, in his sense of the word, people feel that it must be an ideal in the modern sense of any form of government which we happen to admire. I can't help knowing a bit about it," she went on, apologizing for herself and Plato, "because it loomed rather large on our Third and Fourth Years' curriculum in Classics. Actually his citizens were almost as sharply segregated according to their ability as castes in India. There was no equality of opportunity as we know it. And in spite of the weaknesses of modern democracy I feel that it is the safest form of government yet devised. I'm too democratic to want a caste system of education enforced, whereby those who may not have the opportunity of climbing to the top are forbidden ever to put their feet on the lower branches of the same tree."

"But when their education is finished they have nothing to show for it," protested George.

"They have a diploma — which is all your modern equation of one subject with another, your insistence that no body of knowledge has value of itself, makes them consider important anyhow," retorted Aran. "Rot! Sorry, George, but that statement always irritates me. According to it there is no point in reading a dozen poems of Tennyson or one play of Shakespeare or one novel of Dickens unless you can read them all. There is no value in learning to swim unless you can proceed to fancy diving and life-saving tests. The mental training of the multiplication table — especially with more and better adding machines — is negligible unless one proceeds to advanced Algebra. Don't the exponents of that argument realize that one graduates from University, if the course has been of any value, conscious of his appalling ignorance? Don't they realize that in every field there are degrees of knowledge, but that each degree can enlarge the mind and contribute to the personality? Even in the decried realm of foreign languages, one or two years of study, given an interested pupil and teacher, can be more effectual than a five-year course devised to show immediate results. A student is taken out of his own narrow circle, his own milieu; he has to project himself into the mind of another person — equally human, but using a different mode of expression; he realizes himself as part of the process of human history, not an orphan in the universe; he is driven to examine the words and terms so glibly used, and to grasp their original meaning, the lovely logical and wildly imaginative mental processes by which one word can take on new — obvious or apparently unrelated — meanings. He — I'm off on my hobby, I see. Terry, why didn't you throw something? But all the time his mind is being 'led out' — and that's what education means. His reach may exceed his grasp. Well, as a friend of Jeeves put it, rather well I thought, what's a heaven for?"

"You're wrong there. Browning said it first."

Aran decided to avoid subtleties in the future.

"Seriously, George, I meant what I said about my belief that it is infinitely more democratic to give at least the rudiments of a liberal education to every child not mentally retarded. I have friends who left school in second form — I forget to call it Grade Ten — and some who quit in fourth. Some of my University friends have husbands or wives who went to work after High School. Oh, I know that there must be deeper bases of unity; but where these people all went to Ontario or similar High Schools, there is no embarrassment when we are together, no sense of different cultural background. We all have a common language — quip quotations from Shakespeare, passages of memory work, an expression or two in French. Everyone *gets* a reference to the square on the hypotenuse or the conjugation of *amo* or 'Is this a dagger that I see' even though he would swear he has forgotten everything else. He doesn't sit with the politely frozen expression of the man in the ads advising you to bone up on Elbert Hubbard's scrap-book in order to be au fait with polite conversation."

George looked quizzical.

"You wouldn't call that last a very practical argument, would you really, now? Education is a pretty serious and expensive business if the only result is to be able to understand what gives when someone says, 'Parlez-vous francais?' "

Aran laughed, suppressing a strong inclination to snap.

"I didn't think I was offering it as the only result," she countered gently. "As for practicality — whatever that means — yes, I consider it as practical as for boys and girls to spend precious hours learning the inner workings of motor cars which may be drastically altered in ten years and into which the majority of them will never look. But this isn't a conversation; it's a monologue. It's your turn — again."

"Where you and Terry lose out" — he included his non-participating fiancee with Aran, apparently on the damning grounds of their having chosen unnecessarily difficult Honor courses — "is that you aren't speaking twentieth-century language. I don't mind admitting that there's a lot in what you say. I didn't have any of the frills myself — continuation and small-town schools didn't run to them when I went through — but my cousin up here took a course in Civics in Grade Nine; spent a couple of periods a week learning about Aldermen and garbage disposal and how to cast a ballot. He says the teacher hated it and so did the kids and anyone of them could have read the text through in two hours and got as much good out of it. But there has to be something to take the place of the University-training subjects and we have to keep kids till they are sixteen."

"Why?"

"Why? Because it's compulsory age. And anyhow, we want them to get a diploma."

"Why should it be the compulsory age? It's not divinely ordained. I'd lower it two years. Oh, well, that's another hobby-horse of mine. Go on."

"As I was saying, you two aren't on the beam. Whether we like it or not, the picture has changed. The little red schoolhouse and the old-fashioned Collegiate won't do for nineteen fifty-five."

"You don't want them to, do you Aran," asked Terry. Aran shook her head, but kept her attentive face turned to George.

"But even if everything you say is right, it doesn't alter the fact that people today don't want what you call a liberal education. They want something they can understand, something down to earth, something that shows fast results, something that the youngsters can get out and do to demonstrate that they have learned it. And they are going to get what they want; so it's up to us to give it to them."

"To us?"

"To those of us who don't want to be left behind. As a matter of fact, if we're smart we'll be a jump ahead of them. A teacher is a fool if he thinks he can retard progress."

"All change is necessarily progress? The switch from Roman plumbing to slops thrown into the streets, the change from Greco-Roman medicine to leeching for every malady from headache to anemia?"

"There you go back to the Classics again! Whether change is progress or not, the whole structure of Western

civilization rests on it. Look at advertising. It's a disgrace
to have last year's car or last year's refrigerator. And people
feel the same about the last generation's education. I'm not
saying I agree. I just say that you can't swim against the
stream — the wave of the future I was talking about earlier."

"Even if you believe it is wrong — detrimental to the children's interest?"

George laughed comfortably.

"I wouldn't take it too seriously. The point is that those
who go with it are the coming men. Those who oppose it
won't do any good and they won't get anywhere themselves.
I can't see any principle involved worth sticking out my
neck and losing my chance of promotion for."

"Aran, dear," said Terry suddenly. "We have kept you
far too late. You have to go to a meeting tomorrow morning, don't you? And George and I are going out with some
friends of his to see 'Niagara Falls'; so we'll be late tomorrow too. It's been a lovely evening and your dinner was
superb."

"It certainly was. If everybody combined the practical
with the theoretical like you do, there wouldn't be any argument," said George neatly.

Aran waved them to their car, locked the front door and,
tiredness temporarily arrested, went in search of her autobiography.

Four

The Fathers Who Begat Us

"It's not a question of going to Hell or not going to Hell. What we have to do is to find out what is right for us and do it no matter what the rest of the world does."

I doubt if any other equally brief speech, vanishing quickly from a seven-year-old's surface recollection and sinking deep into her unconscious memory, has left so permeating and permanent a mark upon a child's attitude towards life. Not only was it an epitome of Papa's character but the wisdom of his answer accounts in some measure for the gratitude which has always placed my father close after my creation, preservation, and redemption, in my General Thanksgiving.

He was sixty-two at the time and I an alternately bouncy, moody, troublesome — spoiled, the family said of the youngest, but that I indignantly deny — child. My question concerned the eternal destiny of my friends and their families who attended the movies forbidden to me. The effect of his reply was twofold: it crystallized a conviction which anyone reared in our family must, at even so early an age, accept or resent that we Christians were peculiar people with standards independent of the dictates of society; and more slowly it served to curb the tendency which I share with all positive and strong-willed human beings, to impose those standards on other people. "You're the only girl I've met," Sybil Strange surprised me by saying when we were at College, "who refuses to do something herself with-

out lecturing all her friends who do it." Non mihi, sed tibi, Papa, sit gloria!

Aran stared at what she had written. How fumbling, how undistinguished a portrait it painted of the one who, after half a lifetime's absence, was so vividly alive, all human, and distinctive a personality to her. The incident had forced itself upon paper because of her inherent revulsion from George's entire philosophy of compromise. What, as a truthful if polite hostess, she would have replied to his last dreadful apologia of all that was anathema to her in modern thought, Terry's timely and designed interruption had kept her from deciding. But was George entirely to blame? There, but for the grace of God, she might be, had it not been for her father.

Six feet tall, "the most perfect figure in Toronto" as Mother loved to quote his tailor; "a fine big man with a light foot," as the single glimpse of him so impressed one Irish Sinn Feiner that he described him to me thus thirty-two years later: that was Papa. A magnificent head, covered above the high, broad brow — or almost covered at the crown — with iron-grey hair; an oval face, clean-shaven in my recollection except for a grey moustache — Mother had persuaded him to shave his handsome brown side-whiskers early in their married life; a fine straight nose which I — alas! — did not inherit; hazel-flecked grey eyes, set deep and far apart with laughter wrinkles in the soft skin at the corners; a mouth I think of as smiling at me, or gravely speaking, or splendidly, tonelessly, singing with head flung back in church, or laughing as he paused over the dinner roast, carving knife in hand, to tell one story after another while Mother, proudly protesting, tried to stem their flow until the serving was over; a face, especially with those honest, discerning eyes, that could have belonged only to the man he was, a gentleman, and a man of God.

In happy childish anthropomorphism I prayed for many years to a God with my father's face, and am deeply certain that my transition to faith in the Invisible God was facil-

56

itated thereby. The "vast tapioca pudding," as C. S. Lewis describes the dismal concept of a modern child discouraged from such natural imagery, would scarcely have provided such a helpful steppingstone; and the inadequacy for me throughout my life of every portrait of Christ has, I realize, its basis in the fact that in some particular they all fall short of my father's face.

Is it any wonder that necessity for conformity, for acquiescing in popular trends is an alien, almost a humorous concept, to the product of a household which, in some or all of its habits and taboos, differed, not only from the majority but from every other household known to me? Most of the taboos were common to Methodist or Presbyterian families before the nineteen hundreds. Many of them have lingered in a majority of Toronto families to this year of grace. These latter belong for the most part to closely knit groups of like habits and have little intimacy with others. The fact stands that among our friends and relations, our fellow church members, and our school companions none shared the strictness of our religious observance and — odd as it seems — none ridiculed it, at least to us. Among matters forbidden or tacitly avoided, I cite: drinking, smoking, dancing, the theater; cards — not to this day can I say "I bet" without pause — ; profanity — Gee and Darn were excluded but Hang, Confound, and a refreshingly varied series of expletives eased the tension of vigorous quick-tempered youngsters in whom the process of sanctification was slow; any purchase on Sunday, riding on "Sunday" streetcars, Sunday papers, the playing of games, sewing, knitting, cleaning shoes or any labor classified as "unnecessary" on that day. To eliminate the negative and accentuate the positive is equally easy. Three services on Sunday — four as soon as we were old enough for Junior League and the boys to be taken to ten-o'clock class-meeting with Papa — were the undisputed requirement. My mother and father attended Wednesday prayer meeting without fail. And, three hundred and sixty-five evenings

a year — surely Mamma and Papa went out to dinner some-
times? — after the evening meal we had "Reading," our name
for family prayers.

Aran paused in her scribbling, and smiled reminiscently. How often she had heard parents bemoan the impossibility of achieving some desirable custom or avoiding some detrimental trend with their families because of prevailing attitudes and opinions! How many five-year-old Saturday-afternoon movie addicts, how many unwarranted, undesired television sets, how much easy capitulation to teen-age rambunctiousness found their justification in George's unwillingness to swim against the stream. If she mentioned her own upbringing, to suggest gently that conformity was not inevitable, times, she was sure to be told, were different. It was a point she was perfectly willing to concede, being as aware as anyone of the intensified pace and strain of mid-twentieth-century living. She was also willing to concede many of its advantages and improvements over the "good old days" of which any skeptic of the latest fad is deemed to be dreaming. Only none of that argument was apropos. Rightly, or wrongly, to rear a family so that, years after his death, its teen-age children would abstain from dancing in a jazz-mad age was no easier than to train children of the fifties to refuse to take cocktails before a school dance and attend necking parties; and certainly neither was easier than for the families of early-century Christians to boycott gladiatorial combats in the arena or to avoid the excesses of the Grove of Daphne. It all hinged upon the conviction and personality of the parent.

She wrote again, after massaging her scalp vigorously for some moments so that her dark silver-brushed hair — salt-and-pepper she called it in times of self-disparagement — fell around her like a mane.

My amazement grows when I regard this regime dispas-
sionately and hear stories of rebellion, resentment, surfeit
of religion among my contemporaries and later generations,
who have had a smaller measure of parental control. For,

in spite of lapses and transgressions, usually discovered and punished, it never occurred to us to doubt that Father was right. Speaking for myself, when in later years I have modified or abrogated many restrictions, it has never been in defiance or in condemnation of his judgment; always with the sense that his dicta were for our best interests while we were "under the law"; and that if we could talk it out, he would approve our reasons.

That is the distinctive factor in my Father's dealing with us: his reasonableness. Whatever we did or were forbidden, we were given the reason, made to feel that our way of life was ours, a responsibility and a privilege. More was expected of us, we felt, than of other people. And since we had more fun than other people, this seemed essentially fair.

Even our taboos fell into reasonable categories. Sunday was the Lord's day and nothing should interfere with its devotion to Him. But others had an equal right to serve Him or not as they chose; accordingly any indulgence of ours which encroached on that freedom was wrong. As no one who knew my father could doubt that God was more real and important than anyone or anything else, it followed naturally that His worship should have invariable precedence over other considerations. But His service was by no means grievous; laughter and jokes and guests were not barred; our reading — and we were avid readers — was never supervised, and if we sang no secular songs on Sunday, hymn-singing around the piano was so much more satisfactory that the family has always preferred it, though on weekdays we varied it by singing through the Irish and Scottish song books with great gusto and some melody.

Paradoxes there were many: a teetotaler, my father would not let us children sign the pledge. For our sake and the sake of example, he eschewed the theater; but he trained my brothers in recitations and dialogue and encouraged my sister and me in all forms of dramatic expression — his concession to let us see "good" pictures and plays if shown at Massey Hall was a charming bit of Irish logic.

He was a born raconteur with an apparently endless fund of jokes and stories, and a debater of such logic and eloquence that his opponents admitted his victory in every discussion. One subject alone could not be treated lightly. When the habitual after-dinner request "Get the Book" was obeyed, silence on the part of the most obstreperous was required and "Don't you know it's the Book we are reading?" never needed repetition. If his prayer sometimes seemed long to a child whose playmates were waiting outside in the soft spring evening, I shifted position as I knelt by Mother's chair, and played with the combs in her brown hair — how brown it was, though she was years older then than I am! But even a child could feel the reality of a God who was addressed with familiar awe in so beautiful a voice — the same voice that had set us laughing ten minutes earlier — natural, unsanctimonious, but with the quiet of eternal things in it; and even a child's memory was bound to retain scraps and nuances from a prayer which combined everyday practicality with lofty aspiration in splendid Scripture and Prayer Book phrases.

Each member of the family must have had an individual relationship and have an individual memory. I have been kept from envy of the others whose acquaintance extended from four to eleven years beyond mine by the singular fullness and felicity of my own. Perhaps because I was the youngest, perhaps because, with a wider gap between myself and the others, I caught all the childish diseases alone, perhaps because from earliest recollection I attached myself to him on every possible occasion, I seem to have usurped more of his time and conversation than the scant ten years of my life with him would warrant. I sat on his knee in our family unofficial pew — Papa was inexorably opposed to the pew-renting regrettably adopted in our Methodist Church — and watched the minute hand of his big gold watch move slowly past the hour mark to the twenty-after-twelve which usually brought the service to an end.

It was my father who, passing my room and hearing strangled sobs from the darkness, came in to comfort my eight-year-old grief. When he discovered the cause, that I had finished reading Mark Twain's Joan of Arc just before bedtime, he did not laugh or tell me that it was just a book or that the event had happened a long time ago. It was he who, stretched on my sickbed of an evening, made measles and chicken pox a delight in recollection by telling me fascinating stories of Ireland — stories in which history, theological controversy and personal narrative were mingled; stories which I years later verified with his brothers and sisters in Belfast: stories ranging in topic from raucous narratives concerning the acceptance of the dogma of the Immaculate Conception, a fresh topic in his boyhood, to the conversion of an ancestor of mine by John Wesley, an ancestor whose subsequent worthy life was crowned by a most impressive departure for glory on a white horse.

It was my father who refused to stand in my way when, at the age of nine, I requested Church membership, stating, when Mother urged delay, that I knew more of what was involved than most of my elders who would be admitted to membership at the same time: a statement probably true, if more disparaging to them than complimentary to me. He also, at about the same time, refused to allow me to sign a written pledge of my own composing, in which I promised to refrain from theatrical entertainment for life — except, I had gravely added, to see whether it was suitable for my children. In view of my present childless state I cannot be sufficiently grateful for his wisdom in keeping me from the choice between perjury and deprivation of the potentially glorious and enriching experience of the theater.

And it was his answer to another childish question which has removed so far, and I trust for life, the shadowy fear and puzzlement and unease at the thought of the hereafter which clouds the thinking of many, even sincere Christians. How incalculably big with consequence a small incident can be! How tragically unaware many parents are of the effect for good or evil of their answer to a trivial question!

It was a late spring afternoon, the last spring of my father's life; so I was not yet ten years old. The maples, planted by the city in front of each house of the High Park suburb to which we had moved in my infancy, were sturdy young trees, flinging their full-leafed shade half across the road which, though paved, was our undisputed playground. Traffic there was, of course: all the services horse-drawn and good for hookeying-on behind — a forbidden pleasure — with dangerous little steps on the summer wagons and clear backs in the winter sleighs. Motorcars there were — I had recently ridden in one for the first time — but not enough to spoil whole games of May I? or Red Light, played from our verandah to the one across the street, and not enough on these long evenings to interfere with a full game of baseball, my latest wild enthusiasm.

Moderation, in love or detestation, in joy or grief, has all my life been humanly unattainable to me. Through the years, from Glaucus in The Last Days of Pompei, to Rupert Brooke; from Philip Merival to Henry Lytton, from the study of Greek to High School Rugby, from horseback riding to Gilbert and Sullivan, from Julius Caesar to John Wesley — I select a few of my loves at random — I have expended a full heart in usually vociferous, always ecstatic abandon. That spring the object of my affection was baseball. Just as the game was over I caught sight of Papa's tall figure walking, light-footed and with a characteristic quick swing of the arms, down from the street corner. My heart torn with the glory of living, I ran to him, remembered not to ask to be swung up on his shoulder, for Mamma had warned me that I was too big a girl now for Papa to carry, and put to him the all-important question:

"Papa, will there be baseball in Heaven? Because," I went on, conscious of my temerity in dictating, but wanting to be perfectly honest about the matter, "if there isn't I don't see how I can be happy there."

May I digress, for the benefit of those who prate from inadequate knowledge that children brought up in a strictly religious household are terrified or cowed into belief, to say that fear played no part in my childish attitude towards God — nor ever has except an infinite degree of the reverential loving fear I felt for my father. Nor can I recall any time when I did not believe that I belonged to God and — not through my own merit but by His grace — was destined for Heaven. Hence probably the deplorable presumption of my question, based on a comprehensible concern for assured future arrangements!

I have sometimes wondered how, without knowledge of my father's reply, I should have answered the same question. By any conventional standards a rebuke was in order. (This was before the days when a parent, so confronted, dare not take the responsibility of answering without consulting the nearest expert in child psychology.) Or a kindly laugh, or procrastination to "a time when you are older." Or a cowardly confession of ignorance. Instead — I can still hear the rich quality of his voice as, hand clasped in his, I trotted, trying to match his stride with my too short legs, until, when we turned in at our familiar sidewalk to the homey refuge of the broad white-and-green-painted verandah, my fears were lifted:

"You're very fond of baseball, aren't you?"

"Fond!" The inadequacy of the word left me speechless.

"How long is it since you played your first game?"

My mind sought to penetrate a lightless past.

"Two weeks about."

"Before that, you liked playing other games?" I hesitated. That was so long ago. "Hoist the Sails, I remember. Hop Scotch? You used to have a good time playing those?"

I conceded that they had served a purpose.

"You don't miss playing them?"

"No!" The rest of the team had been called in to their several suppers. Otherwise even food would have been a weariness. 'With ashes who would grudge to part, When called on angels' food to feast' was implicit in my negation.

"Suppose," he went gently on highly theoretical ground, "that in a month or so you should learn another game as much more enjoyable than baseball as it is compared with the others you don't play now."

My imagination boggled.

"It is possible though, isn't it? Before you knew of baseball —"

Honest logic forced the concession.

"Well," he returned to the original query, "I don't know whether there will be baseball in heaven or not. There may be." The mere admission of such a possibility permantly relieved the awful sense of "other-ness" which haunts our finite minds. "But you can be sure of this. In Heaven there will be so many lovely and interesting and exciting things to see and do, things so much more interesting than baseball, that you will no more miss it than you miss these other games now."

'Let us now praise famous men and the fathers who begat us.'

Aran stared unbelievingly at her watch. It was well into Saturday morning. A girl whose body craved a nightly eight-hour sleep and who had regarded Napoleon, Edison; and such other four-hour habitués as sub- or super-human, she had never before been carried by sheer compulsion to work till such an hour. Now, of a sudden, the energy seeped out of her. She was very sleepy and experientially conscious that her present tiredness was nothing to the exhaustion of the following morning, when she was due at a ten-o'clock committee meeting at the University, and expected to be brimful of sound suggestions for bringing the possibilities of gainful employment for Arts graduates to the public's attention!

It was a pity to stop at this point. She had written more than enough, she estimated with a quick pleased grin, to convince any confirmed Freudian that she had the corollary of an Oedipus complex. Let them wait until she completed the picture with her mother! Was it possible, she wondered, to have both Oedipus and whatever-the-equivalent-for-a-woman-was-called complexes? Or would that make her a psychical Hermaphrodite? But she could not attempt a description of that dynamic, single-minded, yet amazingly complicated personality at five a.m. Tomorrow she must find time while the George-created impulse was upon her.

She switched off the bed lamp, flung one pillow on the floor, turned so that the street light and approaching dawn would not distress her sensitive eyelids, and prepared to sleep.

Five

By SATURDAY EVENING Aran, who had postponed an engagement with an old school friend, one of the "we'll do something if we aren't too tired" type, found herself wishing that she had kept it. Her morning meeting had lasted into early afternoon, her afternoon had been usurped by the unexpected descent of a former pupil with a "desperate problem," no less in need of lengthy listening and sympathetic help because both desperation and problem existed, viewed objectively, only in her imagination.

Now that she had time to write, the writing fever had passed and, as always, she could think of a dozen things to make her postpone the unutterably dreary driven moment when she must again squeeze her vagabond thoughts into the tidiness of verbal dress. There were unanswered letters waiting; her long-neglected dresser drawers were a disgrace; the deadline was approaching for four Latin papers, the setting of which she had taken on herself to spare Terry; the new snapshot album which one of her nephews had given her for Christmas was empty and a whole desk drawer bulged with multifarious snapshots. Actually she was too tired to do anything but read; reading she suddenly craved with an almost physical longing. If those pupils of hers who, groaning, chose their "supplementary reading" books by gross weight, knew what luxurious dissipation it seemed to her to be compelled to spend a whole evening reading, instead of quietly snatching brief periods for it, to the neglect of pressing duties! Preparation of tomorrow's Bible Class lesson, for instance. But how she wanted to read!

It was a crying shame that two of her Christmas books were still unread, one of them *Orley Farm* — an evening with Trollope would be most relaxing.

By an effort which she considered nothing short of heroic, she dismissed the temptations which sought to divert her whenever creative writing was demanded. The description of her family background which George Madden's weighted opinions had recalled by contrast was incomplete. Giving it spiritual and moral direction was her father, but the breeze which carried it gaily along was her mother. And how to describe her mother?

To estimate the predominating effect of my father on my early life is much easier than to attempt a similar estimate of my mother,

wrote Aran and wrinkled her nose at the stickiness of the sentence. She tried again.

An analogy could be drawn between Ancient History (sic) and Modern. In the first case we deal with an epoch which — for teaching purposes at least — came to a fairly well-defined end. We can see it in general outline steadily, if not whole. In the other we are personally still involved in the international tangles, the blurred edges of events, the fluctuation of movements and peoples, the ramifications feeling their way into an unknown future. So my father's death early in the family's life makes possible at least a sketchy summing up. His portrait stands for us as it was when we last saw him. But in the thirty-four years of my mother's life without him, in her relationship with us as adults, her character developed and altered so that, like her face in a series of photographs, while recognizable, it was never static nor capable of fixed interpretation. And her death is still too recent to allow me to write of her as non-contemporary and not conscious of what is being written.

If that doesn't discourage any potential reader, thought Aran ruefully, my work must have a hypnotic charm. Stop dithering, woman, and write. This isn't a definitive biography of your mother. All you want — have you forgotten? — is the companion picture to establish the claim that yours was a happy, normal home life — as Pooh-Bah says, to give artistic verisimilitude to an otherwise bald and unconvincing narrative.

"It is not good for man that he be alone. I will make him a help meet for him." *Mother fulfilled that function in my father's life. Just as high as his heart, scarcely five-feet-two, she loved to tell us that her weight at marriage was one hundred and four pounds to his two hundred. Her eyes were very blue and her light brown hair had been worn cropped before her marriage, much like the Italian boy-cut of today. To me she seemed very tall, and my childhood eyes were equally fascinated by the roll of hair on top of her head and by the high-throated lace blouses which, I was sure, were kept in place by pins stuck in her neck beneath either shapely ear. I never remember seeing her other than fully, neatly dressed and with her hair "done." Her horror at women who go down to prepare their husband's breakfast in dressing gown and house slippers was exceeded only by her uncomprehending disgust at those who do not prepare their husband's breakfasts at all. Mother was the practical, long before she became the legal, head of our household. She had complete control of the slender family finances, and when she decided anything, even such extravagances as my father's unwilling voyage without her to see his people in Ireland, or elocution lessons at one hundred and twenty dollars a term for the baby of the family, she won her point. But my father was the Very Important Person in the house. His tastes were considered to the exclusion of brown bread and turnips from the family table and to the occasional special treat of oysters, the only specialty I ever remember in which the children did not share — an exclusion which, considering our feeling for oysters, we felt to be no deprivation.*

In our home there was no division of authority. "Ask your father," was Mother's final word on any important question. *Differences and discussions they may have had in private. It never occurred to the family that they could have diverse opinions nor did we ever hear an impatient or critical word between them.*

Mother had been the silver-medal winner among all the school children of Toronto — seven marks fewer than Lucy Robbins who won the gold medal, she used to tell us — and both Sir Sam, her English teacher at Jarvis Collegiate, and James L. Hughes praised her as second to none among the schoolteachers of her day. Yet her admiration for my father's mind was so wholehearted that any success of her children in any field was always greeted with: "It must be your father's brain," or, "Well, I gave you a clever father."

My father's pride in her was equally delightful. She was just what a sensible doctor would have ordered for him. A streak of Scottish shrewdness, inherited doubtless from her father, made her a wonderful manager. How a large family was so well clothed and fed on a civil servant's slender income was her secret. We had a family washerwoman, Mother's clothes were made by a dressmaker, Mother had a practical nurse in the house for a month after each of her confinements. We were all given piano lessons except my brother Martin, whose explanation that his "fingers wouldn't stick on the keys somehow," if adopted by the rest of us would have lessened pressure on the family exchequer.

Did I describe Mother as single-minded? A poor word, it will have to suggest the quality which made her, then and always, content with her life. High-spirited and ambitious — she had wanted to go to University in the days when women students there were few — full of fun and with an infinite capacity for enjoyment which never flagged, yet she made her husband and family her career with unsentimental, almost unconscious devotion, making a fair show of the straitened circumstances of her married life and steadily facing a killing burden of responsibility in the first decade of her widowhood, so far from considering that life might have been kinder that she seemed to feel her-self a highly privileged woman. But I anticipate. Yet the satisfaction which the modern woman often fails to derive from membership in several clubs, two family cars, the shifting of responsibility for children to private school in winter and camp in summer — to give time for a "life and friends of her own" — my mother had to the full in a program of steady household work, social life limited to church activities and the "At home every second Thursday" of her engraved visiting card, satisfaction culminating in the family pew on Sunday, where her own efforts were re-sponsible for what she considered the most beautiful family in the world, from the boys in their perfectly detailed, homemade sailor suits, the little girls in the equally pretty dresses, work of her hands, to her own trim figure in its long-skirted blue suit and Papa in his immaculate Prince Albert.

And where, questioned Aran vaguely, coming out of this pictorial reminiscence with a sigh, does all this connect with my main theme? Mother hasn't come alive yet. She sounds like a paragon of all the wifely, motherly virtues, a sort of saccharine model for Mother's Day cards. And she isn't. What's more, she never was. She's full of dynamite and a saint only in the original New Testament sense. There I am again, writing as if she were still in the next room!

Did I say that Mother was Father's complement? I should have done. In spite of, perhaps because of, his rich vein of humor, he was, like most great-souled men, melancholy in temperament. Mother, more given to surface moods, was essentially cheerful and optimistic. Papa was gentle and, except when his principles were at stake, considerate. Mother, the most sensitive of women, was almost entirely tactless. Until recent years, if I tried the accepted family method to prevent her "pulling a boner," she retorted — and not because she missed the point — "Stop kicking me under the table. You'll ruin my stockings!"

*This somewhat disconcerting directness which marked all
her dealings was the result of her transparent honesty.
Though she could keep her own counsel, and on occasion
rebuked her more garrulous daughter with the irritating
maxim:*

Tell a little to a friend, a little to a crony,

Keep a little to yoursel' that you don't tell to ony,

*she was nevertheless incapable of dissembling either her
words or her feelings. As she was intensely critical and
given to strong likes and dislikes, it was a saving counter-
balance that her heart ruled her head and that heart, once
appealed to, was most tender and sympathetic in its self-
giving response to everyone in need. It never surprised
us to find a peddler or a beggar seated in our front hall,
enjoying a cup of tea and a share of whatever food was
available. Ice or coal delivery men drank homemade grape
juice in summer or coffee with Christmas cake at that fes-
tive season, if it occurred to Mamma that they looked tired.
The money which she saved in coppers by careful comparative shopping for groceries she was as likely to squander
on unwanted packages of needles, pairs of shoelaces, ingenious, unusable gadgets, and calendars of all descriptions.*

*The hospitality which she extended to these strangers
was open to her husband's and children's friends. Always
a moderate and self-sacrificing eater herself — "Here, dear,
I simply can't finish it," she would say, strangely replete
as soon as she saw one of us particularly keen on any
special delicacy — she had the instinct of the true "lady"
(from the Anglo-Saxon, I understand, meaning bread pro-
vider) that the offering of food and drink gives spiritual,
not merely physical sustenance. Never was a casual guest
allowed to leave without refreshment — and no hired help,
electric kettles, refrigerator-stored soft drinks, foods, bought
or ready-mixed, made that offering impersonal. So by a
devious route I came back to Mother's incalculably large
share in the warmth and interest of our home.*

Good homemade food is an integral part of the memory

of most happy childhoods. Untold numbers of fortunate children of an excellent cook can match their individual childhood recollections with mine, which are all centered in a large pleasant kitchen, with no labor-saving devices except a great gas stove; with an oblong golden oak table at which three or four could spread books of an evening for homework; with a butler's pantry adjoining and making a splendid hiding place for sundry games involving Indians (who lived one winter in a carefully constructed wigwam on the upper landing) or permitted a free circuit for anyone who was chasing anyone for any reason, unless the hapless hunted found the door entering the dining room blocked, as it sometimes was in winter, by two great barrels of prime Northern Spies. Memories of good food provided in abundance are not rare; but they are usually associated with a woman of the big motherly type, a kindly home-body, a contented Vesta, fixed as her hearth, and in a self-sacrificing, somewhat colorless way restricted to physical ministrations for her family.

Anything less like Mother I cannot imagine. My marvel in retrospect is, not what she provided so lavishly, but when she found time to do it. For not only did we seldom go anywhere without her but she was usually the instigator of anything in the way of an outing. A "regular" breakfast and a hot noon dinner for seven provided enough work for a woman's day of rest. Mother added a filling supper — foamy omelet, peas, piles of hot buttered toast, her own golden bottled peaches and a high, iced layer-cake must have been a frequent menu to stand out superbly whole in my memory — for more than seven, because we children frequently brought home guests, though only my eldest brother Phil dared to bring them unannounced; but between and among these duties she had twice walked to and from church and had taught a class of nine-year-old boys at afternoon Sunday school, after which relaxing pastime she often went for a walk with us in High Park. And her unexceptionable trimness of appearance was partially accounted for by the fact that she religiously exchanged her Sunday costume for a tidy house dress between each service and the ensuing meal.

High Park! Of all the places encompassed by Mother's zeal to go on picnics Howard's blessed legacy was the easiest of access. Spring, summer, autumn, winter, in the eight years of our vicinity to it before my father's death, no single family can have given it more frequent and varied patronage. My brothers regarded Catfish and Grenadier Ponds as their especial domain. On rafts they propelled themselves over the "bottomless" pool where, according to a legend unquestioned by us children, over one hundred British Grenadiers sleep in their unmarked graves. From its depths they drew up and brought home catfish — dead — snapping turtles, painted turtles and snakes — alive — the last three to be kept as pets, in a back-yard tank or down our seemingly expandable cellar. Mother never shuddered, outwardly — when Martin draped a snake around her neck or when an enormous brood of white rats, sired by an ancient whom we called Abraham, escaped from their basement cage and dripped for days from unexpected places in the cellar. Her tolerant interest extended to guinea pigs, pigeons, doves, squirrels and a chipmunk, at least one alligator and, for a brief period until it was drowned in our laundry tubs, a hoot owl. Before my arrival on the scene a large dog and a goat, as well as the innumerable progeny of two Angora rabbits, had kept the children from being self-centered. But the dog had been poisoned, presumably at the hands of some cyclist, for which class he always showed deep resentment by separating the seat of their trousers from the less important appendages; the goat, an animal of catholic appetite, had sought piquancy for a routine meal by entering a neighbor's house, walking up to the guest room and eating the embroidered "shams" from the pillows — we sold her reluctantly for fifty cents to a man who lived in more open country near Bloor Street. As for the Angoras, their rooted

73

opposition to race suicide finally proved too much for the Waring hospitality. We did not legally acquire another dog; but during those years a beautiful collie, alternately ill-treated and neglected by his master, attached himself to the family in general and my youngest brother Paul in particular, pulling the boys on sleighs in winter and on roller skates in summer, and keeping a watchful eye on their dangerous expeditions in the Park.

But my sister and I were not allowed in the Park alone. All our memories of it have Mother as their central figure. Mother at the age of fifty-four thought nothing of tramping out with her brood in the lemon-colored winter twilight for two vigorous hours on the toboggan slides, and back, before the evening crowd gathered, to appease our voracious appetites with a great dish of homemade pork and beans which she had left in the oven; Mother would even accept her boys' dare to go on a bobsled down the speedy half-mile run; Mother was swift on ice skates, and had undertaken in our frozen back yard to teach my father the art his feet had never learned in youth, daunted at last when, losing balance, he pulled the clothes line with him and cut his head open on the ice.

But it was our summer picnics in which Mother's genius showed at its best. Sometimes alone, on holidays and Saturdays with Papa a wholehearted companion, she led the family plus their friends, or neighbors' children who looked lonesome when the expedition set forth, on hikes from which the modern Boy Scout would demand a ride home. Half a mile up the street to the Park, down the long slope from the old Bulmer restaurant into the woods at its foot, across the unpaved road and little foot bridge, over the stream, up the hills where skiers now practice a then almost unknown sport, down again to the northerly end of Grenadier Pond where two single planks carried us over the unrecognizable boundary into Swansea; up the steep hill, past a few isolated farmhouses, to the dusty country road which carried us straight to the Humber River. There each deposited his share of the commissariat. *The boys gathered plentiful wood and made a fire; Mother, an advance guard of the barbecue brigade, boiled water, fried bacon and eggs, kneaded and baked a bannock — was ever anything so delectable as fresh bannock melting its abundant butter? — or heated our favorite camping dish. This melange was called bullion and I have never tasted it prepared by anyone but Mother: a just-right proportion of canned peas, corn, and tomatoes, well seasoned and given perfect consistency by the inclusion of broken pieces of bread and a generous lump of butter. For appetites growing during the walk and sharpened by the smell of wood smoke I can recommend bullion accompanied by thick slices of fresh white bread-and-butter as a welcome substitute for caviar and filet mignon. Frequently a pan of taffy, boiled on the improvised fireplace, provided comfort for the return journey. If the youngest member was too tired my brothers carried me for short distances chaired on their hands, or, better still, I had undisputed possession of Papa's broad shoulder; but Mother arrived home more vigorous than we now return from a drive to a prepared dinner at the Terra Cotta Inn.*

These picnics on terrain considered home ground to Westenders were a constant; exciting variations were excursions to Centre Island, Scarboro Bluffs, and that irreplaceable pleasure-ground of a bygone Toronto generation, Scarboro Beach Park. The hour's streetcar journey to this last place was itself sheer delight. Seldom has necessary journeying partaken more of the nature of adventurous entertainment; never has sight-seeing, sense of importance, and delicious peril been purchased so cheaply as when all three were blended in a seat on the unrailed edge of those open summer streetcars, perched dizzily above the sheer drop of two steep steps to the racing street, while the motorman clanged his bell and the intrepid conductor swung recklessly along the lower board, "coffee-pot" in hand. The whole affair was jolly; and after riding from Sunnyside through the heart of the city, over the brown and sluggish Don so different from our clear and rustic Humber, out into the eastern end where clapboard summer cottages were more numerous than brick, to come to the great iron gates of Scarboro Beach Park, with the day just beginning but already with the thought of lunch not far from our minds — that was Paradise enow.

To those who revelled at Scarboro Beach it has always been a mystery that the city fathers let such a good thing get away without providing its equal; we cannot imagine its superior. Even for mothers like mine, apart from the pleasure of their children, it must have been a haven and a boon. The moderate entrance fee — fifteen cents for adults sticks in my mind but whether that was a fixed rate I am not certain — ensured freedom from purposeless and questionable drifters. The enclosing gates prevented children from straying beyond bounds. Bathing was available on a safe beach. Shade trees, benches and picnic tables awaited the unpacking of sandwiches, hard-boiled eggs, whole ripe tomatoes, pies and cake. All the usual pleasure-ground attractions were there for those who had earned or saved their money; and very careful decisions had to be made between the cheap but common Merry-Go-Round, the Roller-Boller-Coaster, the Crazy House, the Ferris Wheel where you could see away out over Lake Ontario, and the wonderful boats that swung farther and farther out on seemingly fragile cables, adorned at night with colored lights till my heart nearly broke with the beauty of it. But if only one paid treat was available there was no question on anyone's part: one crowded hour of the Chute the Chutes was worth an age of these lesser amusements in which we could indulge, though in a less delightsome and secluded atmosphere, at the Exhibition Midway. Even once a year, embarkation on the little boat, the long slow funicular trip to the dizzy height where our conveyance swung slowly, painfully into position, the poised, choking, almost-but-not-quite regretful moment of seeing the blurred and beautiful world spread out below while we tilted, remained suspended — then *the flying wind and the awful glorious rush and the splash of the miraculously unsubmerged boat in the pool below — that was a memory to enrich twelve months of waiting.*

But a unique part of Scarboro's hospitality lay in the amusements provided gratis, or almost gratis. Like the privileges and entertainment provided with passage on an ocean liner, so ample pastime was available for Park guests with scarcely any additional monetary outlay. There was the Hall of Mirrors which provided, in addition to good clean fun, a psychological purgation of the inferiority complex, since anyone, after seeing himself lengthened, squat, slantwise, topsy-turvy, and otherwise distorted, was glad to accept the face and figure nature had given him. There was the Penny Arcade — not gratis but the next thing to it — where a cent brought aural or ocular entertainment of raucous and unsophisticated rowdiness. Best of all for children was or were the Bump the Bumps — another rara avis — an ingenious, sheltered floor of highly polished hardwood — the state of polish was assured by its popularity — slanting at forty-five degrees and swollen by rows of great and lesser bumps, down over which we slid to pick ourselves up at the bottom, and climb to the top, and do it over, in happy and uninhibited vigour until exhausted.

With such provision, all Mother had to do for a zestful day, besides preparing and apportioning two picnic meals and supervising our transportation, was to take along at least one friend of each "age group" so that no one of us children need encroach on the other's freedom of choice. Some of these were more or less "regular" additions to our family: the little English girl my sister Daphne's age, whose father rented the house next door from my father, and whose mother, priding herself on the spotless state of her own menage, sent her regularly off to play at our place because Mrs. Waring had other children and wouldn't mind; Muriel, my own inseparable chum; one or other of my brother Paul's select club called the Grenadier Centipedes; one or two assorted cousins. On such excursions Mother was

77

frequently alone and never seemed to be lonely. Occasionally a friend or neighbor came along, usually a younger one. Her own vigour and capacity for enjoyment was so much more akin to ours than to that of other women of her age that I suspect a female contemporary would have cramped her style.

Sometimes my father came from work in time for supper. Those were the gala occasions, for then we could stay till dark and the Beach at night was sheer fairyland. Not only were there open-air movies, where, with an odd sense of savoring forbidden pleasure, we watched the popular but hitherto unseen figures move jerkily across the big screen, and saw pies hurled with untiring abandon; but a band played, a band led by a magnificent white-uniformed creature with a great mane of dark hair and a great dark mustache. His name was Luigi D'Urbano; and the first time that I can remember being transported by music away from the tolerable earth in almost heart-stopping ecstasy was the night when, after his musicians on the stand had extended themselves in a powerful rendition of selections from II Trovatore, *a single trumpeter, concealed behind some trees at a little distance, traced the* Miserere *in notes of pure silver on the enchanted air. From that day I have never heard "Ah, I have sighed to rest me" without a nostalgic catch in my throat for the charm of that evening — the dark blue peace of the lake as a caressing outline to the kaleidoscope of the Park, the hush over the happy crowd, the throbbing band, and that ethereal wail, blending sadness and beauty into one.*

Thou art standing on thy feet above ground, Mummy.
Revisiting the glimpses of the Moon.

murmured Aran, recovering from the catch in her throat already mentioned, and the long lovely shiver with which she re-enacted any recalled experience of beauty. She should have known that isolated character sketches of her parents could not be achieved. Their characters were, in the true Greek sense of the word, the impress, the seal impression

78

of their persons; and those repeated imprints upon the deep-piled fabric of her life were indescribable unless the fabric was spread out in view. At this rate she would never get beyond a portion of her childhood.

Mother's delight in "going places," she wrote, stopping her picnicking reminiscences abruptly, *extended to a determination to take us out of town for the summer, a desire not universally or easily indulged in a largely motorless Toronto, and complicated both by its expense and by the fact that she had no intention of leaving my father to fend for himself. As his two weeks holiday did not satisfy her urge for outdoor life, she compromised by removing us to open country so near the city that Papa could come home every evening.*

A recital of places sacred to the memory of Waring summers makes strange reading in this year of Metropolitan Toronto. Ashbridge's Bay, or central Rosedale, or the top of Scarboro Bluffs in two outmoded streetcars, purchased at a bargain by my father instead of tents, afforded then more primitive camping life than is now permitted by the effeminacies of existence in Muskoka or Haliburton.

But the year which realized Mother's yearning for canvas with a month on the shores of Big Mud Turtle Lake in the Kawarthas, perhaps because it was the first tenting experience for any of us, perhaps because it was Papa's last holiday with us, became a family legend, taking on, with the absurd unpredictability of such events, the nature of a milestone, a turning point before and after which family history was never quite the same.

For me personally this is not difficult to explain. That summer I had my seventh birthday. That summer my impressions were for the first time self-conscious and whole, rather than fragmentary and kaleidoscopic. I can recollect, not only events but my reaction to them and, for the first time, my sharing in the family reaction. So, far more acute than many later events which time has obliterated, are my recollections of the long midnight hay-ride from Coboconk

Station to our camping ground, the awesome hush of the black night near an invisible lake while our tent was being erected by lantern light, and the smiling transformation of night's distorted configurations in the morning sunshine. I recall our temporary bleak dismay at the arrival of a lumber gang whose boom filled our tranquil lake with logs, as if they had spilled a gigantic matchbox into it; our surprise at the pleasant association soon set up between their encampment and ours; and the campfires where Mother's raised doughnuts and Father's Irish stories were equally appreciated and where the one or two born entertainers to be found in every such group regaled us with individual song or recitation. "The Creation of Sam McGee" (rendered with enormous gusto) is always associated for me with fire light and great laughter and a whippoorwill calling under a star-flung sky.

Such experiences, such interruptions of the planned, expected, even desired, routine were always accepted by my mother as flexibly as by a child. That they frequently imposed additional work on her never seemed to dull her pleasure in giving herself to whatever came her way with whole-souled vigor. "I'm not doing anything else when I'm doing this" was her invariable retort when in later years we raised conscience-stricken objections to prolonged labor on our behalf, and the surface simplicity of the remark enshrined the practical philosophy of an essentially happy life. Baking a cake, telling a story to spellbound children at a Sunday-school party, teaching a three-year-old to read, cutting down a dress of her own to fit my sister or me were alike exalted to importance by her assumption that they were most important, an attitude which is part of her legacy to me, even if only theoretically appropriated.

Another lesson which I have been able to learn from Mother with slightly better success is that of regarding possessions as unessential to contentment. Unconsciously — for I never heard either parent refer to it — we realized that many good and desirable and enjoyable things and privileges existed, and existed in the possession of our friends which we did not really need and could not afford. Socrates' comment on the market place: "Bless me! How many things there are that one can do without!" could have been spoken less affectedly by them.

Athough Mother was fond of a couplet,

> In Heaven above, where all is love,
> There'll be no sorrow *there,*

which she used to sing with irritating emphasis when we misbehaved, sometimes substituting for "sorrow" "meanness," "quarrelling," "sulking" or anything else apropos, she was a living evidence that much sorrow can be avoided here by refusing to yearn for any possession beyond one's means. "Remember the needs of others," Papa had corrected the clause, when he first heard her ask a formal blessing on the meal. "If we ask God to take care of all their 'wants' He would never be done." What thenceforth she asked for others she was content with herself. Paradoxically she enjoyed the least superfluity or luxury far more than those who demanded them as rights, and she never survived her surprised delight in the extras which were granted her.

"All we have to do is find out what is right for us and then do it, no matter what the rest of the world does."

I have attempted the impossible task of dissecting the soil in which such a mandate took root.

Six

"BYE," CALLED ARAN and shut the front door. The Warings had always called a good-bye on leaving, and a greeting immediately on entering the house. Homes where members of the family came in or departed in silence lacked the cheery note in her estimation, just as families, however deeply attached, seemed unfriendly or cold where the members did not mark departures or arrivals after lengthy absence with a kiss. The Waring kiss was not, properly speaking, osculation at all, merely a token embrace and the gesture of two heads by-passing each other at the shoulder; but it was a gesture, and from childhood neither girls nor boys ever parted from either parent, or from each other formally without it. So the good-bye call to Muriel was almost as necessary to her departure as opening of a door.

The click of quick heels on asphalt reminded her that the new walking pumps of her favorite Dutch boy last needed rubber lifts to replace the leather which her vigorous stride had already worn down. It was, incredibly, a month since she had bought the shoes, intending to have the alteration made. A dozen times her plan had been thwarted. Such a simple thing: to drop one pair of shoes in the little shoe-repair store on Bloor Street for the easiest of operations! Perhaps today, after school? It was the date of the monthly staff-meeting. Frequently called off when she had cancelled other engagements, it would be a command performance when she wanted the time for something else. Oh, well! Rivercrest was most fortunate in the matter of staff-meetings. Some schools had them every week. Actually, the more she heard of other schools, over the entire Dominion, the more she felt that, with all the defects which a disgruntled mood could find in it, she would rather bear the ills she had than fly to any other in an extremely imperfect and by no means rapidly improving educational system.

But that was not getting the baby a new pair of rubber heels. She might feel energetic enough to dash down to Bloor Street after the staff-meeting; but they had planned to have dinner early so that she might be fresh enough to prepare her speech for Wednesday. Tomorrow she would have no time. It was young Daphne's birthday and she must drive to her sister's for the family party, going via the Lakeshore and Eaton's in order to pick up the gift she had intended to buy the previous Saturday. Wednesday evening she had promised to revive her seventeen-year-old speech on Greece to oblige a friend whose reading club, studying Greece as its year's project, had been suddenly bereft, through illness, of this month's member-speaker. Thursday she could rest — no, dash it, she had promised Doris, when they called off their date, to go with her to the Crest Theatre! And Friday was the night of her Latin Club meeting, for which somehow she must pick up costumes from O.C.E. for a skit, work in a rehearsal of the same, run off the new song sheets on the mimeograph, supervise the preparation of cardboard squares for "Presto," the game she had invented to combine the *utile* with the *dulce* in face of approaching examination, and make sure of sufficient food and its delivery to the school. The executive of her last Club four years ago had been miraculously endowed with a sense of responsibility and ability to work by themselves. These youngsters were eager, and willing, but helpless unless she stepped in. And the energy required for the meeting itself: to keep the program running so that the executive was apparently running it; to have silence at the right times and activity at other times; to get sixty variegated boys and girls mixing easily without dividing into cliques or becoming rowdy; to engineer and control, so that the academic purpose of the Club was not submerged beneath unacademic horseplay, yet so that a general atmosphere of esprit de corps prevailed — Aran knew that she would probably achieve it, but the process of achieving appalled her in prospect and she longed for the post-achievement exhaustion. Another sign of age doubtless; but the groans of younger members of the staff facing comparative ordeals always reassured her on that score. Adolescents en masse, in or out of school hours, were a wearing proposition these days — at least for anyone who had to see things done decently and in order.

She stopped walking so suddenly that the street fell silent after the staccato of her heelfall. Halfway to school, in time for a wonder, and the milling of unproductive detail through her mind had kept her walking automatically, head forward, almost insensible to her surroundings. Now she paused and became acutely aware with four of her five senses; her long-dawn breath and slow, comprehensive glance around was like an act of contrition before she began to walk again, but this time with head up and joy in the act of walking. This scant half-mile to school she had walked, usually four times a day, for twenty years. Almost a ritual, it had never become, like much ritual, automatic and meaningless. She seldom took her car, even when tired or late, because in any weather walking had therapeutic value. And this walk, by its very familiarity and mediocrity, had become symbolic of the daily round, the common task, which Bishop Ken assured us should, and Aran Waring generally found did, furnish all we ought to ask. It was never monotonous; in fact it became dearer through the years with the enriching of associations and comparative memories. Frightening that she could take it for granted even once and miss the homey variety of detached houses in a district which had grown without planning through three widely separated eras of building: the two grand houses, survivals of Victorian pretentiousness, set back on spacious lawns in corner lots, with enormous windows and elaborate red stone trim, with balconies and absurd pinnacled turrets; the substantial, ugly, but individual houses built to hold their self-respect beside these imposing neighbors; the sloped roofs and covered verandahs of the two-story bungalow type, dating from the boom of the twenties when Crossroads changed status from independent village to Toronto suburb; the newer, straight-fronted, garage-inclusive rows built, four to six, on the corner spaces once occupied by vanished "grand" homes.

This was the background, and here was offered a choice which she made according to tiredness, or weather, number of pupils walking, or the need to mail a letter, between continuing around the crescent or traversing the two sides of an anything but regular right-angled triangle. She hesitated today, newly perceptive that the keen March morning air had in it a suggestion, too faint to be called scent, too fugitive to be noticed except by an experienced sense of smell, not physical alone for it brought with it a nostalgic wave of memories of forgotten springs, and she shivered with poignant joy, beyond reason and beyond expression. Just then the sun, which had been stroking the closed grey sky with persistent saffron rifts, forced a narrow entry; her decision made, Aran turned right, avoiding the cold shade of the crescent, and walked full into its warm glory. She noticed the sharp framework of tree branches blurred almost overnight with the swelling of sap, a prophecy of budding. The sun's warmth made the air tender to her face. She lifted her chin and felt it caressingly on her neck; then pulled the glove from her free hand and spread her fingers so that the breeze filtered through them like water. It was glorious to be alive; every spring surprised her with its recollected but never quite believable sweetness. But then so did every autumn, with its daily thickening carpet and thinning canopy of lazily drifting leaves, colorful and variegated as chivalric banners; and so did the tremulous excitement of every first snowfall and the succession of brilliantly carved or softly muted winter days. Only in the heat of mid-summer did this route have an aspect with which she was less familiar. She had always pitied people who lived where seasons were not sharply differentiated. Hibernation in Florida or the more frequent longing for it among her acquaintance she regarded with tolerant wonder.

And this walk had accompanied her through every variety of emotional climate. She had taken it in fear and apprehension; in heavy-hearted sorrow, in puzzlement, and in elation. She had "made talk" with ill-at-ease pupils who fell in with her so that neither of them could decently escape; conversed on every possible subject with young friends who waited for her or made a point of meeting her or walking home with her; she occasionally walked with one or other of the fewer and fewer neighboring teachers who also walked to school. But much of the time she had walked alone, never lonely. She had prayed many prayers of thankfulness, petition or intercession; she had composed scraps of poetry from full sonnets to what her biographer would doubtless refer to as "Unpublished Fragments": from passionate lyrics which relieved surcharged emotion to limericks and silly rhymes for party games and shower or birthday gifts. She had argued out with herself ethical and theological problems, prepared Sunday-school lessons, repeatedly thrilled to find, coming from nowhere, the required idea for a forthcoming speech. Scarcely a house was not marked by some encounter, some incident, some mental crisis.

She had set out upon it with the heady nervousness of a novice that long-past September day when Mr. Rossiter, Rivercrest's former principal, had seated her on the platform and presented her, with his incomparable zest for showmanship, to the assembled school. She had set out on it many a Monday morning, weak with apprehension at some class or problem to be faced, some difficult pupil to be foiled or won over; she had set out in heady triumph after some personal success, or in the secure assurance of some good news, or in the happy anticipation of some great event. She had hurried home along it to share with the various members of the family, and always — until last year — with her mother, the gloom or the elation and hilarity of the day's events: her shy pleasure at that first and therefore most significant of many similar experiences, when in the midst of first-term uncertainty Esther Andrews, a Fifth Form student, had stopped her in the hall to thank her for the inspiration of her teaching; her furious humiliation when, after she had spent herself in a series of introductory lessons designed to interest the most indifferent in the study of Ancient History, Henry Bliss had quietly transferred to another teacher who would, he doubtless felt, stay more closely with the textbook and get him through the examination!

She had walked the selfsame road the bleak morning after a sleepless night of surmise and dread when one of the girls with whom she had been working to produce the *Minerva,* the school magazine, was missing from home. (The youngster had been located at the border, safe and sound and rather relieved to be frustrated in an attempt to seek fame and fortune in the States after an emotional fracas at home.) She had raced along it lighthearted as any pupil, after short sessions on Rugby-game days, and in the sudden shock of mingled emotion on VE day.

On occasion a single tree, the falling of a certain shadow, the rounding of a curve would recall, complete, a memory or an incident in a phase of her life now remote, like a once-read book.

Perceptible change had given while it took away, so that a new contour before the eye of the flesh gently obliterated the old from the mind's eye. She had grieved over the chestnut trees which came down with a great corner house. Only two at the far end of the crescent now swelled with sticky buds in spring and plopped green bursting burrs in autumn. But the trim, wrought-iron porch railings, flanked with dwarf spruce or boxwood hedges, were by this time part of the familiar picture. The generation sauntering past a trim bungalow, with picture window exposing the entire living room to view, could not remember the oak-shaded lawn which had been the "grounds" of the house beside it, so guarded by leaded windows and solid door that no guess at the interior could be hazarded without entrance. She had seen the problem of sloping lawns solved by paving a rampart with flagstones, by terracing, by sinking and converting the sides into a rockery. She had seen house after house change hands and nationality. Small children, who chatted freely with her on their way to public school she heard later in the day answering their mothers in languages which her rudimentary knowledge of French and German failed to identify. She passed the house where a pretty girl, whom she had taught in the thirties, was bringing up five attractive children with confidence-restoring discipline. In a big house a little farther on, a man whom she had seen grow there from a pleasant dark-eyed boy, had met violent accidental death; the slim girl just ahead, who had followed the crescent when she turned right, had first greeted her by curling her tiny hand around Aran's finger as she stopped to make appropriate sounds by her baby carriage. But the general features of the walk were unchanged, and so was she.

A chapter in her book should be entitled: "To and From School on Foot — a Study in Moods."

The last quarter of the walk was uphill. Aran took it at a steady stride, and, pleasantly glowing, passed from the freshness into the enclosed Monday morning heat of the school.

To an outsider all modern secondary schools may seem much the same. To the teacher each has an atmosphere, as distinctive as the character of a city. If I were transported from China and placed blindfolded in the lower hall of the old wing here, thought Aran, I'd know I was at Rivercrest. It was not quite twenty-five to nine by the central hall clock. There would be time to ask if the mimeographing machine was available first period. The last week before exams was likely to be a busy one in the office.

A few students were hanging jackets and sorting the day's books at the row of lockers just inside the inner door. The majority of those who arrived before this time were serving morning detention, playing off inter-class games in the Gym, practicing marksmanship in the old basement. The main army would drift down from Braeside or up from Bloor in an imperceptibly thickening stream in the next ten minutes. Then the stream would thin again, till the sprinting stragglers arrived singly to dial their locker combinations with unbelievable deftness, sling unnecessary books in and draw approximately the right ones out (to carry one book more than necessary for the four morning periods was against the unwritten code) bang the locker shut, give a twist to the dial, and bolt to catch up with their class as it lined up for morning exercises.

From the shadows of the old wing which formed the stump of a capital T, Aran passed, blinking slightly, into the fluorescent-lighted cross-bar of the new hall. The instinct for self-preservation, abnormally developed after years in a High School, made her step aisde just in time to avoid head-on collision with a strongly built youngster, who came bearing down the hall with a singleness of concentrated purpose which seldom carried over into classroom work. Saved by her quick swerve she merely received a sharp jab in the shoulder from his zippered book-bag and recovered her purse, as it was knocked from under her arm. She stopped dead.

"Pardon me," said Aran with great distinctness.

The boy, already two yards past her, and as unconscious of social error as a speeding motorist of having hit a squirrel, was struck by the familiar sound and turned.

"Oh — Miss Waring. I didn't know it was you."

Aran sighed. She hated these pedantic interludes. Jackman had been in her class in Grade Ten, was now in Grade

Twelve, and would almost certainly not be taking Latin Thirteen. He was a decent boy, had his *R* in athletics, and had been in the running for Rivercrest's representative on Eaton's annual, High School, See Canada excursion. But when was he going to learn elementary courtesy?

"Don't flatter me, Jackman. Is that the point?"

"No, I guess not. I was in a hurry to get to Harrison's — Mr. Harrison's room."

"I still feel that you could look where you were going. And more important, apologize, no matter whom you knock down!"

"I'm sorry."

"Well, don't overdo it! But try saying that next time you collide with anybody, even with another quarterback, except in a game, of course. Bye."

She resumed her walk, the embarrassed party, as she always was on such occasions. She rather envied, but could never emulate teachers, some of them a generation younger, who were able to "talk down" to their pupils, reprimand and reason gently as with an inferior intelligence. Too acutely mindful of her own youthful reactions and responses, she had to presuppose, in a sometimes despairing effort to call out in her students, similar responses and sensitivity. But a professional pedantic gloss would be, she felt, much easier. Particularly she resented the irrational, exasperating tears which came into her eyes, especially on occasions when none of the simple connotations of crying had any relevance to her feeling in the situation. So she was forced, as now, to use the light touch or to trust silence and facial expression to speak for her. But was civilization soon to be devoid of social amenities? She remembered her youthful disgust at stories of insolent Junkers who elbowed civilians and women from the sidewalks; and she had resented in certain countries of Europe the overbearing attitude of some Churchmen on trains and on the streets. But now in Canada students, walking three and four abreast or loitering on corners, were less and less inclined to concede any right of way to other students or to older pedestrians. Aran always stood her ground or demanded it pleasantly as a matter of principle, but she did not enjoy the process.

"Good morning, Aran."

She turned to see who was using her first name, something which even the women teachers seldom did in the hearing of pupils. George Madden, smiling a little more toothily than usual to hide a pleased self-consciousness at his new familiarity, was standing, long ruler in hand, beside the entrance door. Within sight of the office George was even more assiduous in attention to hall duty than he had been when his form room was on the third floor.

"Good morning, Mr. — George," she attenuated her mode of address lest it convey a rebuke. "Mr. Sansom, I hope you don't feel too Monday-ish."

George's companion, a gentle, tired-looking young man half a head taller than George, smiled a trifle wanly.

"I always feel Monday-ish, Miss Waring."

"Monday-ish? I don't even know what you're talking about, Sansom." George's cheerful voice rose a trifle and Dr. Moorhouse, who had entered by the front door, passed them on his way to the office. "I think that Monday stuff is pure imagination."

"Then I have a vivid imagination too, Mr. Sansom," said Aran. "If it's any comfort to you, I had to force myself into the fray every Monday for years — and still do on occasion. Whereas the first teaching day of every term I'd have given anything to avoid. Even after I had taught ten years I never could imagine what I should say or do in front of a class again."

"Only I'm sure you found out more quickly than I do. Still, it's a relief to know you feel like that, too." Frank Sansom, Flying Officer with more than one hundred hours over enemy territory to his credit, looked a shade more cheerful. "George has been telling me — "

"About the fine evening we had with you. I hope we didn't keep you up too late, Aran."

Aran did not tell him how late. He had not finished.

"Terry and I went to see 'Niagara Falls' the next night. Quite a picture. And I've been trying to urge Frank — but talking about pictures, Miss — Aran, I mean, I have a couple of snaps here I promised to show you of Winchester High and your old student, Gaye Martin."

Aran carried the snapshots under the central light bar and put on her reading glasses to examine them. Meanwhile George's voice continued, though no longer for publication, positive and resonant.

"No, but seriously, old man, I think it's a great idea. You need something to change the feeling you have about Ten-E or you'll have a hell of a last term. You say they've been asking for a class party. Well, this is a natural. No fooling, I'd take any form for the background in Canadian history alone; but I've got too much to look after with this trip coming off. But if I had them in Geography — there are some marvellous shots of rock formation and water erosion and the underground caverns they found — old river beds — when they were drilling for the new power plant. And right in the picture so that it won't bore them like a documentary — "

"Thank you, George," interrupted Aran giving back the pictures.

"No trouble at all. I thought you'd like to see her."

The men were still deep in conversation as Aran turned into the office.

"Oh, Miss Waring," said Dora Stringer glancing up from the buzzer board, "we've been ringing your room. Here she is, Dr. Moorhouse."

"Aren't you the optimists! You should know better by this time. It's — good grief, it is a quarter to. And I was so beautifully early. What have I been doing now?"

"Nothing yet," Dr. Moorhouse smiled at her; "we just want you to fill in, second period, for Mr. Yeats in 318."

Spare gone. No use asking about the mimeograph. Aran was philosophic.

"Is he ill?"

"His mother died this morning. We didn't know in time to get a supply. We're still trying. You may have your spare after all."

"Oh, by the way, Aran" — there were no pupils in the office now, Aran knew without looking around, or the perfect secretary would not have lapsed into informality — "I'd better tell you now or I'll forget once exams are on. The cadet schedule is being posted in the staff rooms today. It's your turn to look after the Inspection tea, May sixth — you and Mrs. Semple. Will you take charge? You can check the book for numbers and detail any time."

"Talk about rushing the season," marvelled Aran, preparing to depart.

"We like to let you know in time," smiled Dr. Moorhouse. He had a professional habit, like that of some doctors, of referring to himself constantly in the plural so that one never knew if others were involved. "We always liked to know ahead when we were teaching. Now we've delegated the authority. It's your job, Miss Waring."

Aran ascended the Up-Stairs two at a time to save energy, slung her coat hastily on a bar in the empty staff room, and raced down the hall to open her door for three or four students already waiting. Another week had begun.

Seven

AT TEN TO FOUR on Wednesday Aran turned the key inside the front door with a relieved click, and walked with accelerated pace to the other. Normally the eighth period was one of two after which no class needed admonition to stand not upon the order of their going. Today, because she was anxious to get away, little Len Jerome, who needed special instructions less than any pupil in Nine-E and therefore frequently hung around at the end of a period to enquire about a footnote or an exception, had gravely faced her with an example in the text which did not tally with his interpretation of her teaching. That difficulty cleared away, he became chatty about a story in their English mythology text to which a Punch cartoon, thumbtacked to her bulletin board, had reference. Ordinarily Aran welcomed these signs of intelligent interest, though she deprecated Jerome's skill in introducing them always at such inopportune moments as this or at the beginning of an important lesson assignment, and admired his expression of innocent deprivation when she postponed the consequent discussion. Rudy Braun, Jerome's dancingeyed inseparable, had waited with him, also full of praiseworthy zeal and, just as Aran was guiding them firmly but unobtrusively to the door, recognized as his own a Science textbook which had been lying unclaimed in full view on her desk for five days. Their final unwilling exit was due, Aran suspected, to the fact that their presence was required in the gym for an inter-class volleyball game at four.

Aran's grin as she shoved them gently out was amused as

well as relieved. Perhaps she was soft. But of what use her claim that teaching was a profession, not a job, if bright youngsters with no idea of the reason saw her grudging them time after hours. And if these two were a bit spoiled and needed to be slappped down occasionally — and she administered the metaphorical slap when necessary, although their resilience seemed inexhaustible — one never knew what was being satisfied or what good might be achieved by such contacts. Now for home and her speech — Oh, no!

The rear door opened too hastily to her touch. Stefan Svensen stepped back, looking at her with apologetic blue eyes.

"Hello, Svensen. Is there something you want?"

"You are going, Miss Waring. I come another time, perhaps."

"It's quite all right. What is your difficulty?"

"But you were ready to go. I don't want to keep you."

"Nonsense, Svensen. What do you think I'm here for?" Aran's warmth was genuine. Any boy who did not take her services for granted should be encouraged, no matter what the urgency of her situation. And perhaps it was a small matter, misunderstanding about homework.

"I wondered if you could explain," said Stefan, encouraged but still diffident, "the Ablative of Absolute? Maybe I missed the first day when I was sick. I don't know. I never really got it, I think. Now — whenever I use one, it is wrong, whenever I don't, it requires an Ablative of Absolute."

Aran's heart sank as she led the way to the front board. Her favorite construction, with which, as she told sceptical, then wonderingly tolerant classes, she could play for hours, the Ablative Absolute was, she realized, caviar to the general. If all the students to whom she had explained it after school — and with no small measure of success, for it was a challenge that brought out her best powers of exposition — could be laid end to end, it would be a lengthy, varied, and imposing sight. Moreover, she never knew where to commence, as the self-abasement of the seekers usually disclaimed even nodding acquaintance with the construction. Nor could she tell where an explanation would lead. Sometimes a mere sentence admitted the light; sometimes she unearthed an awesome darkness regarding the primary facts of grammatical life. Where to begin with Svensen? A reasonably good, always attentive student, she was teaching him this year for the first time. In spite of his Norwegian name, his people had come from Latvia, she understood, and had been in Canada six years. Oh well, she would soon find out. She picked up a piece of chalk.

"Sit down, Svensen. You'll concentrate better if you are comfortable. And I'd copy this down, I think. She hesitated a moment. Tomorrow was the Red Cross Penny Collection. In quick succession she wrote:

"The money collected will be sent to" — no, not the Red Cross, too confusing to translate — "the office." Office, *tablinum,* will do.

"The money collected, the class will be dismissed."

"After promising money, Stefan left the room."

"After collecting the money, Stefan left the room."

There, that included all basic possibilities. In pedagogical jargon, she supposed she would be praised for making the lesson a "life situation." Help! As if she hadn't done that, intuitively, since she began to teach without knowing that such a heavy-footed term existed.

It was four-thirty when Stefan (Stephanus in the cultured tongue) actually did leave the room, his puzzled expression gradually replaced by one of pleased comprehension which Aran, too experienced to be sure, hoped would persist when he tried her especially composed drill sentences that night. And at eighteen to five, sagging slightly after a record half-mile, Aran reached the front door of her home.

Muriel Treherne opened it and Boojum, whose waggle had twitched the front curtains when she was still three houses away, arrived, after her careful leap from the window, in time to interrupt any greeting. Once her insistent paw ing and her suspicious point-to-point sniffing of Aran's hand and skirt (she had stopped in her race to pet an Irish setter along the crescent) were satisfied, Muriel began the speech Boojum's effervescence had scattered.

"Aran, what on earth has kept you? I thought you had your speech to finish for tonight."

"Finish? I have one page of introduction written. Did you ever know it to fail? A boy needing special help. And I couldn't put him off, with the exams coming next week. Glory, I'm tired. Why did I ever agree to take that club on? I haven't anything to say to them."

"You'll be fine. You always are. Look — " Muriel was a graduate nurse, as well as Aran's childhood friend, and took charge of such situations. "Dinner's cooking. You said you wanted it early so that you could rest a bit afterwards. Dash up and have a hot bath — you know, 'as refreshing as four hours' sleep' — and dinner will be ready. Then I'll take the phone off so that you won't have any interruptions. As for having anything to say, you can talk for hours about Greece with your eyes shut."

"But that's different. This has to be an erudite effort," began Aran, then capitulated. "Bless you, dear. Don't think I don't appreciate it. I'll go pronto."

And I do appreciate it, she thought, by no means for the first time, as she relaxed five minutes later in hot water, softened by her favorite Yardley's bath salts. She and Muriel had been "best friends" through public and high school. Their paths had diverged when Muriel went in training, and later when she had married Rick Treherne during the depression. Rick had died in the D-day landing. Rick Junior, with a good job in the post-war boom, had married at twenty and was now living in Yellowknife, and Muriel, again suddenly desolate, had come to nurse Mrs. Waring during her last long illness. She had been a wonderful comfort during the difficult days after Mrs. Waring's death, while Aran slowly adjusted herself, not only to grief, not only to the unique sense of being "the older generation" which comes strangely to those who have in middle life lost their sole remaining parent — she had seen its aging effect upon her brothers in particular — but to her new, unanchored independence. While her mother lived, as well as having the care, the sometimes irksome responsibility, and the comforting companionship, she had been inseparable from the focus of the family's life, an essential element both in the entertainment which Mrs. Waring had loved to provide, long after she was physically able to provide it herself, and in the hospitality which her married sister and brothers had extended to their mother. Now, although their four homes were open to her, and nephews and nieces welcoming and varyingly affectionate, the close circle of family life which had flowed about her mother in a round of birthday parties, Christmas and New Year celebrations, and more or less regularly exchanged visits, was robbed of its center. And with the center gone, Aran became conscious, with rueful surprise that she had not forestalled surprise by anticipation, that her position had inevitably shifted from center to periphery; in fact, in spite of the strong affection which bound her to individuals, she was outside the essential circles of their daily family lives.

Into the household, where she had seemed like another daughter to Mrs. Waring in her prolonged illness, Muriel Treherne had come as an answer to prayer. And with Aran's need satisfying her own need of being needed, she remained to share the management of an otherwise too large house, nursing private cases occasionally when it suited her. So Aran had been spared the harshness of uprooting added to the break in continuity of her life, and was grateful.

At six-fifteen, reinforced by Muriel's thyme-flavored beefsteak-and-kidney pie and braced by strong coffee, Aran, ready except for the dress laid out on her bed and a final brush to her hair, sat down at her desk with a page and a half of longhand introduction and an Eatonia pad before her. . . . Fifteen minutes later she was reduced, not to the frantic nervousness which always used to goad her to her best effort, but to a desperate indifference. It would sound humorous, unbelievable, that after forty-two speeches about her trip to Greece the forty-third would be harder to prepare than the first. And the others had been so varied to suit their audience and circumstances that none of them was appropriate for this occasion. Similarly, ridiculously, it became harder every year, rather than easier, to prepare introductory lessons in Latin or Ancient History. Always she was haunted by the others she had delivered and by the queer, illogical but unshakable feeling that her present audience or class had heard all the preceding lectures, so that she strove frantically for a new approach. Useless to tell herself that her formal speeches had usually been successful, unless her audiences had been hypocritically enthusiastic. She knew when she made a poor speech — or taught a poor lesson for that matter — and when she did, the praise for which she was always thankful could do little to assuage her sense of failure.

Now — she glanced at her watch — less than an hour and a half before she must leave to drive up to York Mills. And she had hoped to have a full hour's lecture carefully written so that she could deliver it without too obvious dependence on her script. But words would not come. Attempt after attempt was scrawled and scratched out on the paper in front of her. Worst of all was this mental lethargy, this lack of interest which had descended on her like a physical weight. She might as well sleep for the next hour — but in spite of her weariness she knew there was no chance of her sleeping. On a sudden impulse she pushed the chair back from her desk.

"How's it coming?" called Muriel cheerily from downstairs, hearing her cross the hall.

"It's not coming at all. My brain just won't work."

"Don't be silly, Aran. Give them one of your old speeches. You must know them backwards."

"I haven't given one for twelve years at least. And these women have been studying Greece all year. I can't just burble — " Aran controlled her rising voice swiftly. Why take out her tension on Muriel? "I'm just looking for my diary of the trip. Thought if I read it for a while it might put me in the mood."

"Good idea. In fact, if you're really desperate, read it to them."

Aran laughed and found the diary, its red leather stamped with 1938 in gold. Then, thankful that at least her introduction was secure, she stretched herself on the lounge and immersed herself in her record of that halcyon summer before the world came apart.

Boojum, who watched her restless efforts tensely, head on worried paws, signified approval of this sensible action by jumping on the lounge, prowling uncertainly for a moment, then coming to rest comfortably and unignorably across her stomach.

Belfast, London, Paris, Rome — she leafed ruthlessly over their irrelevant delights — Naples, Pompeii, Venice — ah, here the cruise began — the Dalmation shore, Split, Kotor, Corfu — now she was in Greece. Seventeen years ago! Here was the on-the-spot proof that her memories were not just retrospectively rosy. With an occasional recollective smile for the twenty-eight-year-old girl with whom she remained identified, even while she viewed her thus objectively, she gave herself up to the joy of relived experience.

Standing on the top deck in the blazing morning sun — I saw it leap up from the hills of Attica — and before me the Acropolis raises its head from the mist.

*   *   *   *

The Parthenon I cannot describe except to say that it is an incredible work of art, made of straight lines that are none of them straight — each column curved, the pediments curved, the very floor curved fifteen inches so that an effect of glorious lightness is gained.

*   *   *   *

They are utterly humanly perfect, these Hellenic temples, the calm, serenely realized work of men who have made God

*in their own image, untroubled by the conviction that He
has made them in His.*

*   *   *   *

I looked over "the ringing plains of windy Troy."

*   *   *   *

*A glorious island lifting itself from the wine-dark sea —
a sheer, tawny, golden shining island, abrupt and scarred
and bright against the sky.*

*   *   *   *

*All the long afternoon the shadows have trailed the
mountain sides . . . and the inconceivable blue of the Argolic
Gulf which was green this morning, is deepening and the
whole superb, almost landlocked bay thrills me to such ecstasy that if I hadn't been in ecstasy since I woke I might
find words for it, but as it is I can't. . . . It must be seen.
And even then I don't believe it."*

*   *   *   *

*Delphi, the place, the approach, the scenery, the atmos-
phere was beyond my imagination. Imagination deals only
in general outlines and primary colors. God supplies the
variety and the light behind.*

*   *   *   *

*Ithaca lay below, spread in a riotous series of sharply out-
lined curves and gulfs and bays, with rocky islands and mul-
titudinous hills, some with bits of cloud floating around
them. The land was brilliant, the air divine, the sea Homeric.*

The thirty-five women relaxing over refreshments in the
big living room of the Selfridge's split-level bungalow left
Aran no doubt that the graphic melange, mythical-historical-
personal, which the re-reading of her diary had evoked for
them, had been one of her more successful efforts. Their
receptive hush and appreciative laughter had been encouraging and though she had, as usual, suddenly decided that
she was talking too long and brought her address accordingly to a summary conclusion, she had not omitted any par-

ticularly exciting episode or relevant reference. The formal vote of thanks had been excellently handled, the wittily spontaneous expression of gratitude calling forth just the right murmur of appreciation and renewed applause. Now, as one after the other came up to greet her, ask discerning questions, and praise in phrases that would have been fulsome had they not been sincerely meant, Aran felt and said in pleased embarrassment, that she as well as they should be grateful for the opportunity. Some of the girls — when shall we ever call our contemporaries "women"? — Aran had known at College; most were strangers, among them her hostess, Justice Selfridge's wife, who approached her at this point.

"I'd like my guest to meet you, Miss Waring. The girls were allowed to bring guests, since this was a special occasion. But Mrs. VanLuven would have been here in any case, as she is visiting me this week."

"And I'm very glad that my visit coincided with your most fascinating address." Mrs. Vanluven's accent betrayed her origin to Aran before her hostess added, "Mary is a New Englander. You've probably heard of her husband, Dr. Carl VanLuven of Queenstown University."

"I was just telling Inez that I wish Carl could have heard you." Aran wondered quizzically if she would have warmed instantly to this slim brown-eyed woman in the carefully understated woven wool dress even if she had not been making such pleasantly flattering remarks. "My husband lectures in Economics, you know, but he's deeply interested in anything historical. All your literary references — the way you introduced them naturally into your personal experiences — I think it's a shame that so few of us heard you. At home we have tickets for a travelogue lecture series but I've never enjoyed one as much as this."

"Oh — " murmured Aran deprecatingly.

"It's quite true. I never realized before that we have come to depend far too much on pictures. With your words we didn't need pictures — and it was a far richer, more evocative type of pleasure. No, don't be embarrassed. Inez was saying the same thing a few moments ago."

Inez corroborated the statement. Aran basked pleasantly and at the same time was amused at herself for basking. At such times she could almost hear her brother Paul, her mentor after their father's death, saying, as he had always said when she took herself too seriously, "Come off it, Aran, come off it," or repeating to restore her sense of balance a family quote, the description given her at the age of eleven by the Ouija board: "Aran is a dear little girl but she loves praise and has a hasty tongue." All right, Paul, all right! A schoolteacher can do with a bit of this occasionally.

She had assured Muriel of her intention to come home as soon as she delivered her speech. In the congenial and stimulating atmosphere she remained until nearly midnight.

Eight

"HELLO," SAID ARAN, entering the Women's Staff Room with an armful of examination papers. "Hilda, Nasmith would like to speak to you. Something about a page of yesterday's paper that he forgot to hand in. He seems to be in a state of wild alarm."

"Good. A little wild alarm a few weeks before the exams would have been better for Nasmith and the rest of Eleven-D." Hilda put down her blue marking pencil and went out to the hall.

"There are your precious Nine-E's, Terry," continued Aran, unloading. "Fair exchange — here is my Eleven-D History. Did they find it too long, Joan?"

"Some of them tried for overtime. Most wrote pretty well to the last minute. Your friend Nasmith was finished by ten-fifteen."

"Have you the Nine marking scheme, Aran?" asked Terry. "I went down to your room half an hour ago to ask you about it but you weren't there. I didn't think you were supposed to preside this morning."

"I wasn't," said Aran absently, looking in her box for mail. "One Royal Bank letter, one offer to sell me Consolidated Gold Stock, one — sorry, Gerry, Javanik has left school. If you want *Daughter of Time* back you'd better telephone him. Hilda, you look annoyed."

Hilda Wright had re-entered, closing the door with more emphasis than was necessary to ensure privacy. Her fine grey eyes were hot with indignation.

"I am annoyed. Look at this" — she held up a full page

of paper — "Nasmith found it in his French notebook when he picked it up today after the History exam. Must have shoved it in there with the rest of the question papers yesterday, he tells me, and will I please mark it. It's the second question sheet with blanks for correct forms."

"Do you think he did forget it?" asked Terry.

"He swears he did. Frankly I doubt it. There are too many correct answers compared with the rest of his paper. And yet Nasmith's no fool. If he did take it home he has had the wit to make several mistakes — even to cross out a correct form and put an incorrect one in."

"That's either honest or diabolical," commented Aran. "I shouldn't think Nasmith's genius quite capable of such finesse."

"I don't know. He's one of those boys who will go almost any length to put one over. He works twice as hard to avoid working."

"What are you going to do about it?"

"I told him it was against the rules to consider it. But if I don't he'll go to the office. This sheet will make the difference between a pass and a failure, of course. And Jim Britton is counting on him for the Senior team next year."

"I always hate to doubt anyone's word, even Nasmith's," mused Aran.

"Yes, but if he is telling the truth, it was stupid and careless. When is he going to learn to follow instructions? It's bad enough to read Nasmith's beastly writing without this extra trouble."

"Speaking of trouble" — Dorothy Simpson, the gym teacher, had come in during the last remarks and stretched her sturdy athletic frame on a couch by the window — "what has poor Frank Sansom been doing to get himself hauled over the coals by the Higher-Ups?"

"Sansom?" Aran paused in her leisurely preparations for departure. "So that's why I had to preside in his room the latter part of the morning."

"What did they tell you?"

"Nothing. Miss Stringer just called my room, asked if I was busy, and said they needed someone to take over for Mr. Sansom for a while. When I relieved him he didn't seem to know anything. Just said he had been called to the office. I kept expecting him back before the bell rang."

"He left the Chief's office just before I came up, looking awfully sick." Mrs. Simpson's square, dimpled face was serious. "The girls don't know anything more than I do. I've been helping down there during exams, you know. This morning, about ten-thirty I'd say, Jeffs, Dr. Addison's secretary at the Administration, arrived and went in to see the Chief. About fifteen minutes later the Chief came out, looking his most military and said, 'Miss Stringer, ask Mr. Sansom to come down at once.' Dora said she thought he was presiding. 'Then get someone to take his place.' That was where you came in, Aran. The men who weren't on duty seemed to be down in the Wreck room. At any rate, Frank came down, was admitted to the Presence — or the Presences — without any ceremony and there he stayed. Unfortunately the inner office is fairly soundproof and we were typing and running off papers, but the voices did not sound like a friendly chat."

"And that's all you could find out?" enquired Joan. "Really, Dorothy, what do we pay you for?"

"My only clue — obtained in a rare moment of silence — those girls in the office are beastly conscientious and professional — is the phrase 'Niagara Falls' and something about Frank's form. Frank hasn't turned Movie Guide for his class and advised them to see 'Niagara Falls,' has he?"

Aran wondered at her sudden sense of unease; then she remembered. From her perch on the end of the oblong oak table, she could see only Terry's profile as she sat on the couch in front, but she felt the alert tension which kept that usually mobile face expressionless.

106

"I give Frank Sansom credit for more sense — and good taste," drawled Hilda Wright, still brooding over Nasmith's alternative shortcomings. "What on earth would he do a thing like that for?"

Terry flushed. Her voice was not quite under control. "Have you seen it yourself?"

"I certainly have not."

"Then how — ?"

"Terry, dear," said Hilda, who had been fond of Terry as a pupil and occasionally forgot that she wasn't one still, "I don't need to see a picture with Rana Raynor to know that my classes should stay away from it. Only, if I told them, they would go in swarms. They would anyhow," she added with unusual moroseness.

Aran looked at the lines around Hilda's beautiful mouth and forgot for the moment her sympathy for Terry. She admired and liked Hilda Wright more than any other woman on the staff — and she liked and admired most of them. With an excellent mind, generous, high-principled, humorous, Hilda combined teaching ability of an unusual order and enjoyed considerable prestige throughout the province. And it's people like Hilda, thought Aran furiously, who are becoming so disgusted with teaching conditions that they are leaving the profession — if they come into it at all — or if they are Hilda's vintage and mine, are looking forward to retirement. She remembered Hilda's predecessor in her department, who had left Rivercrest ten years earlier to begin at a lower salary in a Government position 'where she had gone from one promotion to another. "It's too hard, Aran. It's too hard," she had said with unexpected tears in her eyes when Aran had pleaded her excellent teaching and popularity in the school, in a vain attempt to make her reconsider her decision. The various pressures upon Hilda were turning her into two Hilda's: out of school her warm-hearted, witty self, although constantly tired and rather dispirited, in school a thorough teaching machine, aloof and unbending. Aran sighed involuntarily and realized that Terry had risen, with the air of Alice braving the Queen of Hearts.

"Well, I saw it and it's not a bad picture at all. The photography of the Falls is marvellous. Of course, there is Raynor and her vital statistics but — " she broke off abruptly. "I'm going to telephone, Aran. I'll come down with you."

They descended the stairs together in silence, Aran uncertain whether or not to let Terry know that she was aware of the cause of her distress. For that matter, did Terry know of George's suggestion to Frank? Had George possibly brought her in to corroborate his praise of the picture? In any case, it might be better for their relationship if her own unintentional eavesdropping remained a secret.

"Are you phoning from the office or the booth?" she asked to make conversation.

"I thought the booth, unless Miss Stringer is alone in the office." Terry had not yet graduated to the Christian-name stage with most of the staff.

The lower hall was completely emptied of the brain-wearied cohorts who had milled around in post-exam frenzy fifteen minutes earlier. Just as they neared the telephone booth they heard the private door of Dr. Moorhouse's office open. With the half-formed thought of avoiding a meeting at the juncture of the halls Aran paused.

" — a most humiliating thing to have happen." Dr. Moorhouse's voice came around the corner together with the click of his key in the lock. "We thought we could trust any member of our staff to show more discretion. It puts us in a singularly bad position. After all, how can we know what goes on unless we are informed? Yet when a complaint is laid, in the last analysis we have to bear the brunt."

"Yes, indeed; I do appreciate the difficulty of your situation." It was George Madden's voice, deferential, subtly virtuous. "And of course, what you have told me won't go any farther. It is good of you to ask my opinion. Mind, I'm quite sure Frank didn't realize. . . ."

"He should have realized. He is a man, not an irresponsible student. A teacher must consider the effect of his actions on the whole community."

The men emerged into the hall and turned towards the elevator.

"Of course, of course. Well, as I said when you asked me, Sir, it certainly isn't a picture I should take a class of mine to see."

In the silence that followed, Aran forced herself to look at Terry and tried to smile a casual good-bye. She felt the smile freeze into a sick photographic grimace at the hollow frightened pain in the long blue eyes. Terry knew that she knew. No word had to be spoken. There was no word to say. She touched the girl's arm quickly, muttered something that made no sense, and hurried down the hall, craving, like a diver too long below the surface, the fresh air and the healing ministration of her homeward walk.

In some dread Aran anticipated her next encounter with Terry. For years the girl had come to her frequently, if not invariably, in emotional crises and moments of decision, and she had no reason to believe that this would be an exception. For if ever anyone had looked in the grip of conflicting emotions and confronting a vital decision, Terry Maxfield, as she stared at the retreating back of her betrothed, had been that one.

Surprisingly the encounter did not come. She did not see Terry that afternoon; there was no telephone call that night. When they met in the staff room next day several others were present. The remaining days of Easter examinations passed with casual comments on papers, pupils, marking. The younger woman looked strained and tired, Aran though, but that was not unusual at the end of one's first — or twenty-first — winter term.

Surprised but relieved, Aran left the move to Terry and forgot the unpleasant business, except when some reference to Sansom's disgrace brought to her mind, accompanied by a wave of mental nausea, the two Maddens: George, cheery, successful, slightly patronizing, giving his defeatist friend a helpful hint; George, deprecating, deferential, using his friend's fall as a steppingstone to higher things.

By the mysterious grapevine, which can never be depended upon to disseminate the needed or beneficial information, a more or less accurate account was soon circulated through the staff and student body, in spite of the suspension of regular classes and activities. Mr. Jeffs's son, one of Sansom's form, had not been sufficiently impressed with the educational features of the film and most of his friends had seen eye-to-eye with him. The youngsters had behaved reasonably well on the whole under the uneasy chaperonage of their teacher and his quiet wife; but enough remarks had gone around, then and later, regarding the more obvious attractions of the picture to embarrass some of the girls and set too many of them talking. The affair had been discussed at one bridge club and at a bowling club before Mr. Jeffs brought it before his chief and came to Rivercrest to administer rebuke. Several parents who had not even bothered to ask where their children were spending that Friday night, added telephone calls of righteous indignation. A garbled report of the office interview was pieced together. Frank Sansom's prestige, never high with the student body because of his austerity and ineffectual discipline, dropped irreparably; while with the staff, who had found his reserve a barrier to intimacy, it was held in the curiously questionable abeyance of a man already condemned.

Of George Madden's share in the matter not a word was said. George himself said nothing, although he spoke of "poor old Frank" in the men's staff room and had told him privately that it was a damned shame. But Frank gave no hint of it, nor indeed a word in his own defense. He performed his duties perfunctorily, absented himself from the staff room — unnecessarily, for the men teachers liked what they knew of him and felt that he was a victim of a mistake in judgment which any one of them might have made and got away with. School teaching may give a veneer of smugness to the small. A good teacher is always willing to concede: "There but for the grace of God go I."

To most of them, Aran not least, the whole thing would have been ridiculous if its implications were not so grave. Considering the emancipation of the younger generation — the types of book and magazine available on every hand, the pictures which they viewed uncensored at local movies or over television, the social contacts and habits encouraged in the interests of "normal adolescent behavior" — for a man of Sansom's scholarship and war record to be treated like a child and have his moral judgment called into question by those in office, and consequently to be pilloried in the eyes of the school for being the misguided cause of their seeing a mediocre picture which most of them would have seen anyway; it was one of those preposterous dream-like absurdities which, an outsider would believe, could not happen. Unfortunately it had happened. And in the peculiar unofficial organization of the modern democratic school system nothing could be done about it.

Aran, who hated to admit that nothing could be done about injustice, sought a remedy and was baffled. No positive or public action had been taken against which protest could be made. That any number of tolerated abuses were, in her opinion, more detrimental to juvenile welfare did not make up for the fact that this particular event had focussed public disapproval. The only mitigating factor, that Frank Sansom had acted on George Madden's advice, did not lessen his, Sansom's responsibility. If she divulged her knowledge — gained inadvertently — it would only involve George in his friend's discredit with the principal and put her in the position of a talebearer, without righting the wrong. She considered the idea of inviting the Sansoms for dinner, pointed though she felt the gesture to be, in view of the fact that she had only a vague idea which of the younger women who came to the annual tea was his wife. To this end she tried unobtrusively to engage him in conversation in the hall, but he had shrunk back into his shell and there was no way of forcing her good will into his unhappy retreat.

So, since Terry was apparently fighting it out alone, Aran remembered to pray for her, and was grateful to be spared the strain of an emotional interview. Piles of examination papers, from the single token sheet of a repeater considerate enough to spare his teacher pages of nonsense and, like Socrates in one respect, knowing that he knew nothing, to the fourteen closely written pages of her best Ancient History student, were guaranteed to occupy the mind and time to the exclusion of much else. Especially this year she marked in a determined, if losing, effort to complete the marking before Good Friday, for she was taking part in a panel discussion at the Ontario Educational Association, intended to visit friends in Detroit when the O.E.A. sessions were over, and yearned to have at least a day of the week's holidays completely free. A rapid marker, she held grimly to her schedule, with the commendable result that, when school closed on Thursday, she had only the two sets of papers written that day to cloud the horizon.

In the back-to-school flurry, with papers to be given out, marks entered, averages calculated, and reports prepared, staff room that swirled lightly around these matters, with occasional eddies about the shows Dorothy Simpson and her husband had seen in New York and the tan Hilda and Joan had acquired on the sands of Bermuda. On Thursday morning when Aran arrived most of her colleagues had not yet dispersed to their rooms, and Dorothy, who had no form room, was glancing through the *Globe and Mail*. Suddenly she straightened in her chair.

"Listen to this, girls. I thought all our vacancies for next year were filled. 'Toronto Board of Education requires for September — and so on — for Rivercrest Collegiate Institute a Science Specialist — man preferred.' Joan, are you leaving without telling us?"

"No — I'll tell you all right, and well in advance. But I bet I know who is."

"Frank Sansom?"

"Who else? All the regular resignations were in over a month ago."

The door opened to admit Terry, radiant in a new dressmaker suit of mushroom pink, her golden hair swept back in a shining pony-tail, her eyes shining — in fact, an unmistakable glow of excitement about her whole person.

"Terry, you look lovely," said Gerry Black, the librarian, with the ungrudging admiration of a thin elderly spinster for all that her own youth had never been — an attitude more common perhaps among teachers than in other walks of life.

"Smart suit," commented Dorothy. "I tried on one something like it in New York, but it made me look like a house, and not too well constructed a house at that. Terry, George has been a bit pally with Frank Sansom, hasn't he? Does he know that he's leaving?"

Terry who had turned slowly around at Gerry's direction to exhibit the detail of her suit, stopped in the act of pulling off her gloves. The shine faded.

"I don't — no I didn't know — " she began but at that moment Dorothy caught sight of her bare hand and swooped.

"Oh, Terry, when did you get it? Girls, look what our baby has."

Among women no age or profession is proof against the evocative fascination of an engagement ring. Until the bell scattered them belatedly to their form rooms, the cries and comments and questions and good wishes were undistinguishable — except perhaps in the general quality of enunciation and felicity of verbal expression — from those in any office or for that matter in any one of their upper forms. Aran was the only one who noticed that the pristine shine had not quite returned to Terry's face.

Nine

MURIEL AND ARAN had just finished dinner that evening when the telephone rang.

"That will probably settle the question whether we go to 'Spring Thaw' tonight or next week," prophesied Muriel, and she was right. They had not reserved seats and had been undecided whether to risk picking them up at the last moment; so when Terry Maxfield asked rather hesitantly if she might come over for a while if Aran wasn't too busy, Aran took the request as an omen.

Dr. Maxfield's combined home and office was less than two miles away and Terry arrived in her father's Dodge before the dinner dishes were washed. Boojum met her at the door with the ferocious outsize yelps which made Aran periodically regret her payments for burglary insurance. Once over the threshold, however, Terry was received, as Aran consoled herself a burglar would also be, with leaps of joy and the performance of her single and not too original trick. When Muriel, having asked to see the ring and made the appropriate comments, shoved the two out of the kitchen, Boojum accompanied them upstairs to the den and leaped up between them on the wide lounge.

"You've had the woodwork painted," Terry observed idly, stroking Boojum's black-and-white coat with unnecessary deliberation.

"Just after New Year's. Don't tell me you haven't seen it since. No, I suppose we weren't up here the night you brought George for dinner."

"I don't think we were. Time goes so quickly. Aran, do you mind if I remind you of something?"

"I hope I won't. What is it?"

"Once when we were just becoming friends — when I was at College, I think — you showed me a lovely piece of old lace. Do you remember what you said?"

Aran smiled.

"Daphne brought me the Spanish lace from her wedding trip. It was over a hundred years old then. And I saved it to wear at my wedding. Of course, I remember I said that I should gladly let you use it if you wanted when you were married."

"I'd love to if you really meant it."

"Why shouldn't I mean it? I hate hoarding. My one married niece had her costume planned before I thought of it. Deirdre Lane wanted to use it but she was married overseas in uniform. It will look lovely on you. I'll get it out."

She went rummaging in a drawer and brought back to the den half of what must have been an heirloom mantilla, a delicate maze of roses creamy with age, clingingly soft. Terry took it in reverent hands.

"Aran, it's wonderful of you. I couldn't afford anything like this, even if it were obtainable. I'll be awfully careful of it. You really don't mind?"

"Don't be silly. I should have remembered it myself in time but I didn't think — or I thought it was a bit previous."

"It isn't really, you know. If I weren't having the reception at home, I'd be far too late in making arrangements. As it was, I just reserved the church for the time I wanted. June the twenty-ninth is a popular day."

"June the twenty-ninth?"

"Yes, I thought I'd told you. No, you had gone down the hall when Joan asked if we had set the date. We did, the night George came back from New York. May I try this? Would you wear it lengthwise over a little headdress, so? How does it look?"

Aran glanced from the real face to the mirrored face.

"Lovely. You're the person to wear it, Terry. It isn't possible for everybody. With the tailored type — like my cousin — it's not good at all. But it becomes you more than anyone I've seen — except, of course, myself!"

"Let me see you in it. Please."

Aran caught it around her dark hair like a pushed-back hood. The effect was transforming.

"Aran, it's beautiful on you. You should be wearing it."

" ' 'Tis true, 'tis pity, and pity 'tis, 'tis true.' " She gazed for a moment smiling at the bride she had intended to be, then laughed and, lifting the lace folds carefully, tried the same effect on Terry.

"That's perfect, I think. But it depends on your dress."

"I know. That's why I came tonight. I'll have slipper satin I think — the off-white shade nearest to this. If it were winter, ivory velvet would be lovely. And I had thought of setting the lace in a panel in tulle dyed to match, but this way — Aran, could I dispense with more of a veil altogether — if I have a court train — and just have this caught somehow to give that hooded effect?"

"I don't see why not," began Aran, and stopped speaking.

Terry had been trying the effect from side and rear with the silver hand-mirror Aran had brought her. Now, upper lip caught between her teeth, she was staring at the wide-eyed, lace-framed young face, staring intently, as though seeking something she could not find. Suddenly her face broke up. She swept the veil from her hair, thrust it into Aran's hands, and collapsed, crying quietly, on the lounge.

"Terry, Terry dear," said Aran, then waited. The pain of seeing Terry cry never lessened with recurrence. It affected her with physical poignancy like the bleak future-less grief of a child. The girl hardly ever cried, according to her own statement; when she did, Aran seemed to be the invariable witness. So she had watched and waited, pitifully praying, when Terry had lost her scholarship as the result of her first year University exams; so when Rupert

Halsall had left for Europe without proposing; so, almost frightened for the girl in her broken-hearted despair, at his untoward return.

I wonder who said that it is easy to bear another's pain, she thought, seeking in unspoken words relief for the constriction in her own throat and the weighted tenseness of her compassionate muscles. He could have this job here and now. Poor Terry! Last time she cried because she wasn't marrying Rupert, this time because she is marrying George. And no wonder! It's exactly how I'd feel if I were going to marry George Madden. But then I wouldn't — not on any consideration. Maybe — ?

Terry's sobs, the more racking because of her efforts to control them, continued. Boojum, who had watched the wedding preparations with commendable tolerance seeing that no one was paying any attention to her, was shocked at this alteration in the atmosphere. She sniffed the shaking shoulders, pawed Terry's back gently, then, unable to evoke a response from that side, jumped off the couch, leaped up at the far end where she could see the averted face, and, waggling her distress, began to lick a tear-wet cheek.

Terry laughed brokenly, gave Boojum a convulsive hug — which she bore with fortitude in the good of the cause, wiggling free as soon as the unpredictable human's arms relaxed — and fumbled blindly for a handkerchief. Aran sat down in the nearest chair, waiting.

"I suppose," said Terry at last, looking obliquely at her and failing in her first attempt to smile, "you want to know why I did that."

This was no time, Aran decided, for banter. She spoke soberly.

"Have I ever wanted to know, or asked you, anything that you didn't want to tell me?" — insist on telling me, she thought of adding, but refrained.

"No, never. I didn't mean that. But — well, I suppose

you know whether I tell you or not." Her voice was harsh with strain. "I don't want to marry George."

"Then, for goodness' sake, don't marry George," cried Aran, but Terry interrupted her with fierce inconsequence.

"But I do want to — and I'm going to. Only sometimes I get overwrought. I can't explain it. And it's no use arguing, Aran."

Aran was silent.

"I'm sorry, dear," said Terry contritely. "I didn't mean that either. It's only — "

"Terry," interrupted Aran firmly, "I've just said — and meant — that you needn't say anything. Take the lace and run along — or stay and we'll talk about whatever else you like."

"No. Please, Aran. I want to talk to you. That's really why I came. I want you to know how I feel. You've been so good to me. And you must wonder. I should hate to see you think badly of me. But I didn't mean to cry like that. This year's teaching has worn my nerves down. In fact, the way I feel now I wish I had resigned and applied for a position at Riverbend Public School. But George said that it was safer to teach two years here and get my permanent certificate first. If I have to teach after that — and maybe I won't — I shall ask to be transferred to about Grade 5. It isn't the teaching I wanted to do but I have my Public School option and it won't be as hard as this. Anyhow, Mother says my crying doesn't mean a thing. She says lots of girls do it, even the day before they're married."

Not a particularly good sign, even then, but a very different matter. And Mrs. Maxfield ought to know, thought Aran. Mrs. Maxfield had been holding the terrors of spinsterhood over Terry's head — most unnecessarily in view of her daughter's attractiveness — since she was fifteen. Even College, and certainly a teaching career, she had opposed as detrimental, if not fatal, to a girl's chances. Aloud she said, because something was expected of her,

"When you said you didn't want to marry George, you

just meant that you were in a bit of a funk at the idea of growing up. To coin a phrase as you did a while ago, 'Time goes so quickly.' Is that it, Peter Pan?"

Terry made a better job of this smile. But it was short-lived in her effort to answer.

"Not even that exactly. I really meant that I don't love George — or rather that love isn't what I thought it was.

"But, Terry, how do you know? Why don't you wait?"

"I'm nearly twenty-five," said Terry with the determination of one who knows that her words are heresy. "The number of suitable men gets fewer every year. And I do love George. It's just that I'll never love anyone as I loved Rupert." She was silent for a moment. Aran again recalled the desperate days of her attachment to the brilliant young professor from Scotland who had been briefly attracted to her ardent youthful beauty, and, tiring of her obvious devotion, or belatedly conscientious, had returned from vacation overseas with his Scottish bride, the summer after Terry's graduation.

"And since I can't have him," she continued, "I've been looking for the best I can get."

"And it's George?" There was nothing in Aran's voice but inquiry; yet Terry's answer came with a touch of defiance.

"Yes. He thinks the world of me. He is lots of fun and has ability and we'll get on. We want the same sort of home, I'll never have to worry about him, he'll be kind. . . ."

"I think that's all very true," said Aran. Not by look or by intonation would she give voice to the feelings seething inside her. Perhaps her very restraint spoke. Perhaps Terry knew her face too well to be deceived by its mask. Or perhaps the girl's own thoughts, echoing hers, had to find speech.

"I know what you are thinking, Aran," she began again, flushing in her attempt to speak calmly. "You are thinking of some of the things George thinks that I don't agree with, and of Frank Sansom and what George said to Dr. Moorhouse. Oh, he had told me before anything happened that you were there while he was talking to Frank. But you know how I felt. I may as well tell you that I nearly died that day. I had George take me out after school and I broke off our engagement. I could hardly bear to speak to him. I didn't even cry, I was so angry."

"That's when I do cry," commented Aran. "And George — "

"He was terribly upset. I never knew how much he cared for me till then. He begged me to reconsider. And he explained about Sansom. There wasn't anything he could do, he said. Dr. Moorhouse and Mr. Jeffs had already pretty well gone over him with a steamroller. And George said today that it's a good thing he has resigned, because he wasn't happy in teaching anyhow. So in a way it's a blessing that it happened." She faltered under Aran's incredulous eyes. "Oh, I know. That doesn't let George out. But he has a right to his own code, Aran. He said that, if he had told Dr. Moorhouse that taking the class to the pictures was his idea, he would have done no good to Frank and he would have ruined his own chances."

"How did he know," queried Aran casually, "that Mr. Sansom hadn't told the Chief?"

"Oh, Dr. Moorhouse, simply fuming, met him just after Sansom's interview, asked him if he had seen a picture called 'Niagara Falls,' told him what Frank had done, and asked him his opinion. George says he was completely on the spot. Moorhouse was so sure that *he* wouldn't do such a thing."

"Still, what if Sansom had told later?"

"Frank wouldn't, George says. He'd just take what they handed out and wouldn't implicate anybody else. It's his idea of loyalty." She suddenly realized how her words must sound and her voice rose sharply. "I mean he was in trouble already. There was no point in getting George involved. After all, he wasn't compelled to go to the picture! And George had only meant to be helpful. He is just practical.

There is no point in sticking his neck out, losing his chance of promotion — "

She stopped, remembering that she was quoting almost verbatim. Aran wondered just what principle George would consider worth sticking his neck out for. Silence would have been one thing. But a straight lie — and a sanctimonious disclaimer of his own brain child? Terry was speaking again wearily.

"It's no use our talking about it. I see your point of view and I see George's. He was considering me really, and our future, he says. But I thought you'd wonder and I wanted to explain. What do the French say? *'Tout savoir est tout comprendre; tout comprendre est tout pardonner.'* I guess that's how I feel about George."

"That's fine."

"You don't really mean 'that's fine' at all! You don't understand how I can go ahead and marry him."

Aran lifted her eyebrows. For a moment Terry felt as she had in class years before at her infrequent rebuke.

"When I said it was fine, I meant exactly that. What I understand has nothing to do with it. Whom you marry is a completely personal matter for you to decide. If you want to marry George, if spending the rest of your life with him is the greatest good you can imagine, if you feel towards him as you want to feel towards your husband, if the thought of life without him is impossible to face, then I say, marry him, and I'd say it if I thought him far less estimable than I actually do. It's hardly fair to pour all this out to me and then blame me for what I don't say, Terry."

"Of course it isn't. What I mean is, I want you to understand that I know perfectly what I'm doing. I *don't* feel towards George as I always wanted to feel towards a husband — as, for instance, I felt towards Rupert. I should miss him badly if I lost him now but I could spend my life without him — yes. There are things about him I'm not proud of. There are things I'd like to be different. But in spite of that, I'm going to marry him, because I want to get married. Is that — can't you understand that at all?"

She was wistfully anxious for approval.

"Yes. Yes of course I can understand wanting to be married. Glory, so do I! What I don't understand is why, when you feel like that, you don't wait until you meet someone else."

"How do I know I ever will? After all you — " she bit the words back.

Aran grinned broadly. "Say it, dear. I waited. And look at me now!"

"Aran," said Terry earnestly, "believe me, if I could be like you about it, I would. But I can't. I don't want to go on teaching all my life. I lie awake nights wondering what I should do if I had nothing else to look forward to. And it isn't just teaching. Diane, who has a good job in Mastersons' Publishers, feels just the same. I know married women go on working, though I don't want to. But they have somebody to share it with. They aren't lonely. I'm afraid of growing old alone. I'm afraid of being an extra woman in the family — never being asked out except to all-women affairs. Even at home I've seen how an unmarried daughter is despised or taken for granted. Everything centers around the children with families. Besides, I want — a normal experience. I don't want to be considered unnatural or an 'unclaimed treasure.' And I want — I want terribly — to have children. So that is why I'm marrying George. And there are awfully good things about him too . . . . I might have a far more romantic attachment and find it wouldn't last. Mother says I'll never have to worry about George. He'll always be faithful to me."

Probably true, thought Aran, though an oddly calculating consideration for a prospective bride. Respectable matrimony is an essential factor in the respectable advancement which is George's goal. That is Terry's safeguard. Unless, of course, by an unforeseen change of circumstance some other woman should become more practically valuable to him. Shame on me! He isn't bad, just weak, with those possibilities of an ugly show of strength which are the bluff of a weakling unbolstered by principle. Of his willful choice George would never want to hurt anyone; to protect himself and to attain his goal, he could be more ruthless than many a stronger man. Bad enough, if he were always a subordinate, but suppose . . .

Suppose this aesthete made omnipotent.

The words Stephen Phillips had put into Seneca's mouth, concerning the potential danger of young Nero, were not completely apropos but she knew why they had crossed her mind. Suppose George — and other Georges — made principals of schools, leaders in the administration. Was a time coming — there were enough danger signals — when education would be in the hands, not of "scholars and gentlemen," but of ambitious time-servers, with no code but expediency?

She forced the dismal prospect from her mind. Terry was looking at her anxiously.

"Will you try not to despise me, Aran?"

"My soul, I don't despise you. I think you are exceedingly sensible."

"Aran," said Terry, smiling more naturally than she had done so far, "I have heard your ideas often enough to know that 'sensible' in conduct, like 'practical' in education, can be a Bad Word. Is that the way you mean it now?"

"Not exactly." Aran hesitated. "You do realize that even marrying won't ensure the future you want?"

Terry set her chin decisively if not obstinately.

"I realize that nothing is certain. But one has to take some chances. And even if I were head over heels in love I couldn't be sure. Look at the marriage of the ultra-romantic sort which break up these days."

Aran felt that she had delivered her soul on that score. Perhaps she was wrong about George. Perhaps marriage with Terry would effect a change. There was nothing she personally wanted much less than the responsibility of disturb-

ing the existing arrangements. Even if Terry should be unhappy, she would apparently prefer the unhappiness to the
dreadful emptiness which she had sketched out for herself unmarried. But the child had come to her, confided in
her, broken down before her. Surely there was some word
she could say which might recur to her help in future need
— and there might not be another opportunity like this one.
She felt her way.

"You want to be married and you are going to marry
George. Right. I won't say I understand exactly, because
I doubt if we ever do really understand another person's
motives unless they coincide with our own. But since it
will bring you what you want, I shall dance — well, do the
equivalent — at your wedding with the best will in the
world. There's just one thing that puzzles me and it has
nothing to do with your marriage to George. It concerns
what you said about yourself: your loneliness, your fear,
fear that every day will be like the preceding day, fears for
the future — "

"Don't you have them?" interrupted Terry. "Aren't
you ever lonely, aren't you afraid? Or weren't you?"

"Yes, I have been. Yes, I sometimes am — usually in the
middle of the night," admitted Aran. "But for enjoyment —
don't you get any fun out of yourself, out of *being* yourself, I mean?"

She realized that she had put it badly. But she knew
of no other way to explain something which needed no explanation to her. Terry shook her head.

"No, I don't. I get fed up with myself most of the time."

Aran tried again, this time more hesitantly as she probed
deeper. About a realm in which she felt natural and at
home, she hated to use words which might sound smug or
suggest cant.

"Forget it, then. But, Terry, you are a Christian — and
by that I don't mean that you were confirmed at the age of
fourteen! I can understand anyone having fears, or feeling
lonely. I have and do, briefly. And the worst of them are

concerning things that never happen, such as what I should do if faced with the stake or other refined modern cruelties. No, the worst are completely indefinite, not fears, but fear. Those are the birds which Luther, who must have had a few, could not prevent flying overhead. But a Christian doesn't let them nest in his hair." She forced herself to the point. "I mean, when you are lonely, or fearful, what about Christ? Doesn't He remove fear? How can you feel lonely with Him?"

Her last words were too earnest to cause embarrassment. Terry's blue eyes met her green ones warmly, but without any answering light.

"I know what you mean, theoretically, but I don't know it in experience. I'm afraid He doesn't mean anything to me — in that way. That is," she said hurriedly, "my faith is a comfort to me. I'm sure that if I should lose George, or when Father dies — or if I had a baby and lost it — I shouldn't feel the hopelessness and bitterness that non-Christians do. And I don't expect to be afraid of dying. But I don't understand how the thought of Christ can keep you from — well, from being blue. And it certainly doesn't make me want children less or not plan to have them. If I were going to do something I thought was wrong, it would stop me, but this isn't wrong. George is a Christian too, after all." With which somewhat ambiguous conclusion she rose hastily. Aran felt that her decision was taken. A door was sliding to between them. But it was Terry and not she who made a last effort to establish communication before it closed. "Perhaps I shall have it some day, Aran, if you go on praying for me. Boojum — " with the word the door clicked — "you are without doubt an uncannily knowing pup. I doubt if my black skirt will be improved by your solicitude but my feelings certainly were."

The recovery of her surface gaiety carried the brief remainder of the interview off on a wave of chattiness. Aran, turning back from the car — for Terry at the last moment had left the house without the veil — stood for a moment in the green April evening and wondered how long the brightness would remain. Or had the outburst been the last, a final protest of the ideal against the actual?

> *Thou art mated with a clown*
> *And the grossness of his nature*
> *will have weight to drag thee down.*

Was it kinder to pray that this would happen, or that it would not, with the anguish and the self-disgust which must so ensue? She tried to shake off the tangling web of such questioning as she entered the house. Tired as she was with the distress and discomfort of the visit, the younger girl's arguments and decision had stirred her to introspection. Why, in the final analysis, had those arguments no real weight with her? Why had the equivalent of Terry's decision been — not just untaken but so impossible that it had never really needed consideration?

Ten

MURIEL AND BOOJUM went for a walk. Aran prepared for bed as a futile safeguard against further activity. Then with a faintly guilty expression, as though she was taking herself much too seriously, she removed from her desk drawer the pad, which had rested there since her second spurt of biographical writing, and placed it with her pen on the bedside table, just in case. But the thought of writing was, as usual, intolerable. Much better for her sleep and for tomorrow's classes if she could read herself into a pleasant state of relaxation. Fortunately a new Wodehouse had met her eye when she was downtown on Saturday. She picked up *Pigs Have Wings* and thanked Heaven, not for the first time, for that indefatigable contributor to the joy of nations, whose "later manner" was the polished fulfillment of the promise of his youth.

Or was it? she asked herself after fifteen minutes. Yes, the fault was certainly not with Wodehouse. She had read the first chapter while standing waiting for Muriel in the Book Department — her favorite meeting-place downtown — and her uninhibited enjoyment had so interested a nearby browser that he had bought a copy of the book on that sole recommendation. But for the time the undertow of question and answer, of argument and reminiscence, was too strong to let her mind drift with the rippling current of the story. She shut the book, with an apologetic pat for the apocalyptic pig on the dust cover, and took up her pen.

Prematurely, she told herself presently, looking at the inartistic doodling which now decorated the still waiting page:

the Union Jack, the monograms of her initials, the unrecognizable cartoon of Boojum, her stumpy tail drawn in five different positions to suggest its perpetual motion. And Freud could doubtless make something of that, she marvelled. Certainly a primrose by the river's brim was quantitatively and qualitatively more than a yellow primrose to him. What ingenuity he and his disciples had — like, in another sphere, the indefatigable women who, professionally or socially take one glob of assorted tea leaves after another and pour consistent, and often uncannily accurate, interpretations into the drinkers' wide-open ears. Whereas she, with her mind so teeming that it would not admit diverting thought, could bring nothing to birth in words and resorted instead to futile scrabbling.

That was the trouble. Terry's plight, her words, herself as the symbol or epitome of an attitude towards life, had struck too many chords in rapid succession. They could vibrate simultaneously in the aoristic shadowy outreaches where memory and impression blur into wordless thought. But to separate the individual themes and translate them into recognizable and recapturable notation, that was a task for intelligence through the divinely lucid medium of words.

"And I sometimes think I'm not very intelligent," she confessed aloud ruefully, smiled to realize that she didn't mean a word of it, and, raising her eyes from the pad, caught sight of herself consciously for the first time in the dresser mirror at the foot of her bed.

Her reflection stared back at her. Final preparations for sleep not yet made, lipstick and hair still in situ, it was a more appetizing reflection, she granted, than the one that would greet her in the cold morning light — if she ever took time to study it from this position before rolling out of bed in the fog of sleepiness which was always densest around seven-thirty. In the soft golden glow from bed and dresser lamps, from this distance, her nylon-and-lace nightgown revealing the youthful throat and shoulders which she had always considered her one perfect feature, she could almost push the years aside and see herself at Terry's age. Not twenty-five!

> *"She'll very well pass for forty-three*
> *In the dusk with a light behind her,"*

she murmured, wondering briefly why jokes about age, and the frantic struggle to avoid, elude, deny, wish away, or philosophize on it now touched her so little. Even on that, of course, she could not dwell; immediately it became another instance of "The lady doth protest too much methinks." But it was simple fact that at no time in her life had she yearned to revert to any earlier period, not even to recapture the ecstatic joys of that period, which she could live again almost at will in a memory which was for her less memory than re-enactment, a memory that blessed without burning.

The age of twenty-five, for instance. At those words a major note had sounded above the minor chords of recollection. She knew why. Silly thing to do perhaps, but she was making no headway as it was and there was just a chance that visual aids — Help! how those jargon terms became part of everyday speech and even thought — might "give an assist to the activity of production."

This time her rummaging was more prolonged. One storing place after the other uncovered nothing but such an outlandish assortment of patterns-that-might-be-used-again, speech manuscripts, saved birthday bows and ribbons which always vanished completely when a gift was to be wrapped, place-cards of forgotten banquets, menus of Captain's dinners, the Bible given her by her father and mother at the age of seven, a taper which she had carried in the Catacomb of St. Sebastian, newspaper clippings of long-past amateur dramatics, and envelopes of unrecognizable snapshot negatives, that she resolved for the twentieth time to devote a week, if necessary, to reduce them to order. By this time a half-whimsical desire had become an imperious requirement. Fortunately Muriel returned with an effervescent Boojum to whose a-temporal mental processes half an hour was always equated with an age. The latter licked all that was exposed of Aran as she crouched to examine some small books below the bottom shelf of the bookcases in the den, then tore to her basket in the bedroom, and collapsed like a spent force. The former inquired the object of her search.

"Your 1935 diary — that red-leather one? Seems to me I came on it the other day. Aran, what are we going to do about these back numbers of *Punch*? We'll have to move out of the house soon if you don't make up your mind."

The remark was not irrelevant. From a substantial walnut magazine rack presenting to the world a solid array of the problematical periodical she neatly extracted the bulky little volume into which Aran had poured her surcharged enthusiasm of her first trip overseas, and presented it, with the air of a conjuror whose rabbit has not failed him. Aran hugged her.

"Bless you, Muriel, bless you. How on earth did it ever get there? Now that I have it, goodness knows why I wanted it so urgently. But, bless you anyhow."

She returned to bed, feeling rather as the mountain must have done when it saw the product of its enormous gestation. She would never get anything written tonight. Why had she not recognized this driving insistence on a non-essential as just another of the devious ways by which her mental laziness put off the anguish of writing? However, now that she had the thing, thanks to Muriel, she might as well look up the one entry for which she had sought it. She turned the pages rapidly, strenuously resisting the temptation to read the glowing account of her pristine discovery of England. Those voyages of hers were the only occasions on which she had ever kept a diary, apart from two diligent accounts of her twelfth and thirteenth years which she occasionally re-read to keep a sense of perspective, when the silliness of the modern teen-ager provoked her overmuch. Ah, here it was, her twenty-fifth birthday spent in London; and in the morning before the account of the day's celebration — "1066 and All That," she and her mother had attended in the evening — she had saluted the day with this paean:

I Praise God

That, except for the fulfillment of love, I have known superabundantly all the joys of life:

"Wow," commented Aran wryly, and read on.

Laughter.

Intense enjoyment of the beauties of nature.

Rapture in listening to music.

Wild excitement of traveling.

Awed delight in viewing antiquities.

Heady pleasure of popularity.

Throbbing satisfaction of acting.

Physical intoxication of swimming, riding, walking, skating, skiing.

Genuine pleasure in eating.

Rare comfort of family affection, as a whole and in every individual relationship.

Wistful happiness in good memories.

Gladness at reunions and anniversaries.

Irrational excitement of passionate affections.

Keen delight in intellectual achievement.

Assurance of God's love and of Christ's redeeming Presence.

I have lived — Vixi

(And I retain my sense of humor?)

Aran was relieved, as the parenthesis reminded her that she had written the youthful eucharist with the same pleased discomfort as she felt now and in willful defiance of her unwritten code that to "take oneself so seriously" even to oneself and in private diary was not quite "sense-of-humorish." The phrase made her smile because, like so many strictly family expressions or jokes, like the favorite quotes between herself and Daphne or herself and Paul particularly, it was a family colloquialism.

Not — "sense-of-humor-ish," she began to write, *laid under taboo a dissident assortment of activity and attitude: a multitude of quite innocent words, such as "betrothed" and "spouse"; any discussion of sentiment or — save the mark! — sex; any cant or glib religious phraseology; and much sin! Many of the people who over my lengthy lifetime have been afraid they were shocking me, or deplored my state of chastity, or tried to impress me as devilish or daring, would have been chagrined if they could have realized that to me they were being boring, and lacking in sense of humor. It is part of our inheritance to feel that sin is a horrible and ugly reality and we, apart from the grace of God, as ugly sinners as any — never that it is a glamorous and desirable, but forbidden, fruit, and those who persistently indulge in it the genuinely courageous and honest of mankind. For its helpless victims we could feel pity, more, sympathy; for those who gloried in it, nothing but contempt.*

In maturity I have become, I trust, less Pharisaical than the statement sounds. Experience has taught me more of the underlying motives, the frustrations and fears which produce a parade of self-satisfaction in conscious wrongdoing; taught me also to loathe the "respectable" sins against which this calculated swagger may be a protest. But although evil has drawn me and involved me in prolonged and desperate struggle, it has never been qua evil, or because it and those who yielded to it have seemed more interesting than goodness and God. And anyone who should know better and yet is juvenile enough to feel proud of "being bad" just seems funny to me — or pathetic, which is not so very different.

Probably some of my bewilderment about Terry is connected with this very catchword. My first impulse is to say: But she has too much sense of humor to marry George — and yet to many people the remark conveys the impression that George is some kind of joke or that they don't

think the same things funny — both of which conclusions
are true, but neither is exactly what I mean.

No, that won't do. I must put it another way, in fact
in a threefold way. I cannot understand how — not why —
Terry, feeling as she does about Rupert, can marry George;
I cannot understand how Terry can marry George; I can-
not understand how Terry can marry George.

She stopped abruptly, realizing that this was not the chapter of an autobiography she had intended. But the challenge to see if her own motives, her inner compulsions,
would bear translation into words and her own scrutiny in
written form made her continue.

Feeling about Rupert as she does. Almost two years
since she had the slightest reason to think that he cared
about her at all — and, to do the man justice, he was very
decent in his conduct towards her — and yet at the Alumni
play in January the poor kid hardly knew what was happen-
ing on stage because he was sitting three rows behind us.
Just before Easter, when I asked if she was going to the O.
E. A., she asked if I thought he would be there! I know
her feeling can pass and should pass. But how, with that
feeling, can she go into the arms of George Madden!

Of George Madden! I know, I know. A good-looking, up-
and-coming young man without any vices, who will get on in
the world and make her a fine husband! But of so much
coarser fibre in nature and mentality than Terry that the
discrepancy will always be as obvious to the perspicacious
as a loafer matched with a spectator pump. And George has
enough determination and ability to ensure that they will
spend their life with those more perspicacious than he. And
so Terry, whatever she feels in private, will be, in public,
like some other wives I know who cannot be sure of their
husbands. Sometimes they apologize for them, sometimes
they become belligerent and contradict them, talking down
everything they say. Sometimes — and this will be Terry —
they are just silent and gracious, but one can feel them
watching to see what he will say and squirming when it

is the wrong thing, and suffering — oh, dash it, do they suffer or do they become numb? But how can they overcome their original suffering enough to marry?

Aran shook her head, genuinely puzzled, as she thought of the George in her life when she had reached an age more desperate by several years then Terry's. On the whole a better person, if a bit less intelligent, she appraised him in retrospect, much more handsome in a clean-cut, collar-ad style, less capable of dissembling. Tad had been like George in his social climbing and imperviousness to hint; he also was frankly and flatteringly aware of Aran's superior attainments. She recalled the discomfort and boredom of dates which she had tolerated in order to have an escort or to avoid hurting his feelings; recalled the night in his car when over an almost intolerable period — she still remembered how cold her feet had become — she gaily and almost successfully parried his determined efforts to propose — trying to the last to save face for him. But though she had jokingly calculated the worldly advantages — Tad had done well in business since — she had never for a moment considered marriage a possibility. *For one thing, I couldn't bring children into the world to have Tad for a father,* she murmured. *How will Terry answer to hers for George?*

The ludicrous picture of Terry arraigned before a jury of her children showed her, as suddenly as if a blind raised had revealed a lighted room, the conclusion that most interested people — always presuming that the situation held any interest — would draw concerning her own refusal to marry. Adulation of her father had made it impossible to marry anyone for whom she — and the children she had always hoped to have — could not feel the same adulation. Considering the explanation — with or without the psychological implications involved — she conceded dispassionately that it contained more than a little truth.

Undoubtedly my difficulty in finding The Man — always taking completely for granted that I can have him if I find him! — is due, at least partially, not to dislike of men but to liking of them; not to the postulate of an unrealizably high ideal but to my happy relationships with men better than the common run. I enjoy the company of women and of men, but men by and large have influenced my life and thinking far more than women. As youngest of the family I was constantly in the company of older men: my brothers and their friends, Daphne's large number of concurrent adorers — how barbarous this "going steady" of youngsters seems to us of the Twenties and how immoral our gregariousness seems to them! Whether they were all superior to my own contemporaries I cannot judge; certainly they gave me a more sophisticated standard of comparison. But childhood with my father, and the partial replacement of that relationship by Paul who was most like him — beginning when Phil and Martin were in the services — erected a preliminary hurdle of character and personality too high for most men to surmount. Then "you want the innocence of eighteen with the sophistication of forty-five," Daphne told me once, and we agreed that the requirements were a bit unreasonable.

But that is by no means the whole explanation, though it does indicate why time and time again, from my first soulful devotion at the age of eleven to an eighteen-year-old chum of my brother, through a series of attachments carefully concealed, brief in duration and varying in intensity, to an amazing assortment of men attainable and unattainable, ranging from two years my junior to thirty years my senior, my mind ruled, if it did not immediately quell, the emotional tumult of my body. Never, in spite of the thrills and fears, the excitement and yearning and absorption of these innocent affaires de coeur — in which by and large I conducted myself with praiseworthy adherence to a noble New Year's resolution which I made at the age of twelve: "Always remember that it is better to win a man's respect then his liking!" — did I deceive myself, or rather did I receive the sure assent in my innermost being, that this was the man I wanted to marry.

135

This is not to say that such a person does not, or did not exist: merely that I have not met him or that, if I ever did, circumstances have prevented our recognition of the fact. After all, Daphne, more brilliant than I and as fastidious — indeed much of my youthful hypercritical standard regarding men was learned from her — nevertheless met the one who measured up to it when she was twenty, chose him from her enchanted gaggle of suitors, and has gone on with devoted husband and lovely children to the life I should have loved but have never coveted. But how did Daphne get in here? My charming, versatile, warm-hearted sister, who prayed for me to be born and helped to bring me up, who invented stories and games for the two of us, and whom I resemble so much, yet with so great a difference, deserves a book to herself. This is my experiment!

I said that I did not envy Daphne. Although I admired her more than any woman and to the exclusion, by comparison, of many women, I loved her always too much to feel jealousy. I am healthily normal enough to rejoice at my own successes but only if they were equal to hers and not at her expense — and they seldom, if ever, were or are. But I cannot understand people who, unless their words are insincere, actually covet the career, the experience, the personality, the appearance of someone else, wish to be someone other than they are. Boundless ambition I can sympathize with: to achieve great things — but still in one's own person! In perfect humility I state that I have never wanted to be anyone else; girls who regret that they are not male, men who wish that they had lived in another century, or had been born in another country are a cause of genuine wonderment to me. It is logically the equivalent of that other horrible and incomprehensible wish: that one had never been born.

The charge of smugness risked by this attitude I deny. Far from being self-satisfied, I see the desirability of improvement, physically, mentally, morally — but improvement and perfecting of the features and qualities which make the in-

dividual me, I should have preferred my eyes larger and stronger, my complexion idealized, my mouth more clearly defined — three cheers for lipstick! — my figure slimmer and firmer. Time and energy fail me for the enumeration of faults and failings which must be overcome in order that potential qualities and virtues, some latent or dormant, may have room to grow — in other words, that I may be as lovely and lovable on all occasions to other people as, at rare times, I seem to myself! But of what use to live at all if there is no joy in being and in being oneself? And if there is some dreary sense in such an attitude for atheists, how illogical an absurdity for the Christian. Why look to eternal life if living here has not been a potentially wonderful experience? (I am not speaking now of those who by accident or man's brutality have been prevented from realizing even a modicum of normal living.) What is the glorious hope of the resurrection of the body if you have despised that entity here and now?

Perhaps the "sense of destiny" to which I referred earlier and which in every stress and sorrow and seeming disappointment has kept life meaningful and strangely exciting is simply this: that I was created for a purpose, the purpose of finding and realizing and being, to the glory of God, myself: that in Christ alone this purpose is realizable, partially in this life, perfectly afterwards; and . . . .

And with this sense of destiny, Aran wrote doggedly, conscious of the abysmal failure of her halting sentences to translate the deep, wild, nameless joy of the experience itself, *how can I — or anyone — compromise in a matter which concerns the personality and the personality of others so vitally as marriage? Far from my attitude being a "sublimation of the sex impulse" the contrary act is a prostitution of the sublime, a giving of "that which is holy unto dogs."*

What a nasty name for George, she thought aloud. Boojum stirred in her basket in protest at the reference, and came over to the bed, with the remarkable tripartite waggle which suggested that she might come apart in sections. Aran ignored the first minute of her pleading, as she stood with forepaws resting on the bed and a look of agonized entreaty, though she could have easily leaped the distance. Then, to prevent complete disruption of her efforts — for Boojum, though so clever that they had to spell words such as "walk" and "vet" in her presence, had never been able to understand the basic negative — she lifted her prayerful twenty pounds to the bed and watched her grave imponderable gyrations to the final slump of complete satisfaction.

I must try to make it clear, she said to herself, resuming:

My last question, How can Terry marry George, has nothing to do with George himself, impossible though I may feel him to be as an object of wifely love. It is concerned entirely with her feeling, or lack of it, for him, and with her motives in marriage. God keep me from being high-falutin' and arrogant. Thousands have married unwillingly, under compulsion or with unselfish motives; men and women for the sake of their helpless children, royalty from a sense of duty, others — mostly women, poor souls — as the helpless, unconsidered chattels in economic or family compacts.

Nor would George's limitations and gaucheries matter, she thought, if he inspired in her a love which covered them. Myrna King's Grant is an animated golliwogg to all appearances; Reg Purvis passed over Doris to adore Jane. a girl who could have gone unmarried to her grave without our special wonder (there's a mixture of Tennyson and Shakespeare for you!). There are innumerable examples of men and women "with a face that only a mother could love on pay day," to quote Muriel, and/or with unremarkable personalities, who have yet called out in someone deep and intense, or quiet and contented, love — I need be with Myrna and Grant or Reg and Jane only a short time to feel it.

There must have been many cases, too, among those forced or arranged marriages, where the discovery of acquaintance and a shared life engendered real love. That again is not the case with Terry. She has discovered George and she

138

doesn't really like much of what she has discovered. She is under no compulsion. She doesn't love him. And yet she is marrying. That to me is the mystery about which I can't argue because my feeling is so strong that it seems instinctive. Even on the superficial plane it kept me from what my mother would call "familiarities" — and a better word than necking, too! — at times when physical attraction was present and powerful. How can a woman divide herself, separate body from mind and spirit? Nor do I mean what an otherwise sound theological writer dismisses as "a storm of emotion." Heaven knows I have been a seething volcano of emotion over more than one man, and felt admiration and affection for others whom I still couldn't marry or even experiment with in preliminary indulgence — because I didn't love.

But surely, she wrote hastily, leaving a topic which would elicit from the Freudians their most assured and pat pronouncements, *I can appreciate her motives, having had most of them myself. Unfortunately, as Terry is intelligent enough to know, marriage is no guarantee that she will actually achieve the more praiseworthy aims. I doubt if companionship of the sort she will have is really less lonely than loneliness; children are probable but by no means inevitable, or a sure solace; a dozen contingencies could make her go out to work to the end of her days; and the awful prospect of being invited only to all-women gatherings — a fairly frustrating experience sometimes — could be hers at any time in the event of George's death. So the only certain advantage is that she will be a married woman, thereby escaping the charge of being "unfulfilled" which, as a threat, is the modern substitute for the damnation of hell.*

The difference being, continued Aran with some relish, *that whereas we have no idea how many were saved by the earlier threat, we cannot know how many have been damned by the current one. As one under the curse of unfulfillment myself, I shall not be considered an unprejudiced commentator: in fact anything I say will unfailingly be used*

against me. Still I protest that my right to attempt an ob-
jective consideration of the condition is at least equal to
that of a "fulfilled" individual of, say, twenty-five, who is
experientially as unqualified to examine my state as I
hers, or for that matter, his. It is even a possible hypothesis
that in twenty years of unfulfillment a degree of fulfillment
may be attained at least the equivalent of six months or a
year of fulfillment."

Boojum changed position. She had been lying on the
1935 diary which now came into view. Aran glanced again
at the exuberant items in the scrawl which had changed so
little.

"All the joys of life" . . . . and every year repeated or intensified some of them or added new variations to compensate for some lost. "Except the fulfillment of love" —
does that liability cancel all other glorious assets, even if
the "fulfillment" were in every case, and not in a minor
fraction of their number, the experience of love that it can
and should be? Like the sentimental superstition which
supposes that the act of giving birth transforms a selfish,
shallow, ugly-tempered woman into the haloed venerable
of Mother's Day cards, this new phobia would drive women
to any cheaply substitutive mating, preferably but not necessarily legal, to escape some incalculable, certainly untrace-
able, abnormal warping of their nature.

In every other sphere the factor of circumstance is rec-
ognized without derogation. We all know men who would
have made excellent doctors or teachers or actors, given
the education or training; women who are "born" nurses,
deprived of the necessary qualifications. More pertinently,
we know fathers and mothers who are completely devoid of
parental feeling, and men and women who have been de-
nied the privilege of being the good fathers and mothers
which they are fitted to be. Whatever the "spinster-ish" or
"unfulfilled" qualities are: prudishness or prurience, inhibi-
tion and inability for self-giving, fussiness, frigidity and
neurosis — all inhere in many married women of my ac-

140

quaintance. And the fulfilled or married virtues: tender-
ness and understanding, tolerance and humor, patience, gen-
erosity and courage are present, in great or small degree, in
as large a proportion of unmarried as married women.
Hilda Wright, for instance, or Joan Easson: is there some
magic in a week's marriage with George which will make
Terry more womanly, more well-rounded a character than
they are? The truth is that they haven't met the men they
would gladly have married: perhaps they died in either
war. Perhaps they did meet, and the men were already mar-
ried: or, before the attraction was strong enough, some other
more predatory females swooped down and took possession.
And that being the case, they would not — could not, if
they are like me — accept a George, much less "go after"
one, because they could not live with themselves if they did.

Aran lifted pen and eyes from the paper and stared at
the mirror without seeing it. She had not written, but surely it was implied, she could not write dispassionately, yet
in the first person, of the passion and longing, the purely
bodily craving which was never satisfied in virginity. Why
need she write, when so much had been written that every
virgin of either sex was regarded as a perpetually suffering
holocaust, or an addict to perversion? The actuality, in her
case at least, was infinitely more merciful. The times of
need were bad, certainly, but so were other moods uncon-
nected with sex; they did not last and it was not . . . not . . .
sense-of-humorish to exaggerate their importance in the
rich, varied pattern of daily sensation. They did not become worse with denial, and for the Christian they were never
intolerable. She had reassured, on both points, a young
couple — it was an amazement that they should come to
her together and have confidence in her answer — who were
torn between intense desire and a wistful yearning to wait
for the sanction of marriage. Besides, as no youngster could
know, but as she had learned from friendship with people
of widely divergent character and standards, physical indulgence for its own sake did not satisfy; it merely fed an ever-

leaping flame. She knew those who indulged in it without conscious regret and were insatiate, either pitifully or horribly its prey; those who yielded against conscience reaped self-disgust without tranquillity.

I don't condemn Terry, Aran resumed her writing. *I have no right and less desire. She has never had the relationship of blended love and respect and intuitively similar thinking that I had with Papa, or later for years with Paul, to let her know what a great man is like. Her mother has always talked of men as if they were another, slightly inferior, race to be humored, worked upon, put up with — but acquired at any cost. As for fears and fear of the future, she hasn't had, as I had all my life, a mother who, faced with the most pressing of financial obligations, said time and again in an emergency: "I'll tell the Lord about it," or, when one of us expressed apprehension: "Never be afraid of anything but sin." What a woman! Unable to swim and caught in a driving storm in the middle of a Haliburton lake the second time she had paddled in a canoe; in a tent with Daphne and me at midnight, on a beach backed by pathless woods, with the tent pole swaying in the wind and hailstones beating on the canvas; rowing us down a river in dark and mist to the same lonely camp; at seventy-two climbing into the crater of Vesuvius with eager curiosity while lava fell around us. . . .*

Aran cut her reminiscences short. She had written herself to exhaustion. How to sum up?

I have always wanted to marry, and taken for granted that I should. There is no "closed-door" feeling about it. Even now I would gladly. And I have always wanted, not sentimentally but really, to have children, five by preference — as much as Terry does — with the difference that I never wanted them to compensate for what I hadn't, but to share what I had.

"Dost thou still retain thine integrity? Curse God and die!" Strong words, but they represent with queer accuracy what I should be doing if I made Terry's decision. If, to

quote the motto, "the world moves forward on the feet of little children" — a beautifully ambiguous statement — it is probably well for the world that there are many Terrys. If I question progress dependent on such action, I sound like the French grandee who "did not see the necessity" when the peasant said: "Sire, we must live." But for me — and many other women — to be capable of love, ready for it, honest about, though if need be never experiencing it, is to retain an integrity which we should lose by the very act of compromising with second best, in a vain effort to achieve wholeness.

Well, thought Aran almost too tired to close the pad, "Vether it's vorth going through so much to gain so little," as Tony Weller said re matrimony! Aran Waring you are a chump! You should tear up this evidence of baffled emotions. If anyone else read it, the title immediately suggesting itself would be Sour-Grapes. . . . So be it!

With an amused spurt of energy she wrote: *The truth, and, if not the whole truth, at least nothing but the truth: So help me God. Amen.*

Eleven

"SOMEONE AT THE DOOR, Miss Waring."

"Yes, I heard," answered Aran absently. A polite but urgent request from the office for vaccine test cards arranged alphabetically, boys and girls separate, "and could you send them right down please, coming just as Eleven-B took their seats, had necessitated lightning change in procedure. The lesson on Comparison of Adjectives was scheduled, but she had altered her preferred method hastily in order to gain the requisite few minutes without letting the beginning-of-the-period interest sag. "See who it is, will you please, Roberts?"

Even as Roberts lumbered obligingly to his feet, Aran drew Stockton, Anita, from its plausible but erroneous hiding-place between Stauros, Dimitri, and Van Every, James E., and, driving it neatly home where Pike, Maryella, rubbed shoulders with Uvanov, Tanya, glanced up and saw Dr. Moorhouse's unmistakable profile of crisp grey hair and clipped grey moustache through the open glass panes of the door.

"All right, thanks, I'll attend to it," she countermanded, setting the cards down carefully. If the Chief wanted to speak to someone in the class he would have phoned for him; if he had an announcement to make he would have knocked and walked in; ergo —

Opening the door she was confronted, not by one grey-haired man but by two. The stranger's hair was thick and straight, brushed smoothly close to his head like a fitted iron-grey cap. The unexpected tan of his face suggested a recent trip to Bermuda or hours of golf.

"Sorry to disturb you, Miss Waring," said Dr. Moorhouse with more of genuine apology in his voice than the conventional phrase usually contained. It made Aran wonder a little. "May I present Dr. Goodchild? Dr. Goodchild, Miss Waring."

Aran smiled and found herself shaking hands without knowing if she had initiated the gesture. The name conveyed nothing to her, nor did the face, plain in the large-jawed pleasant way which Cary Grant and James Stewart have made more popular than "regular" features.

"Dr. Goodchild is President of Queenstown College, Massachusetts. He is in Toronto on business. And this is where I owe you an apology, Miss Waring."

This is where Eleven-B owes me an apology, confound it! thought Aran, acutely conscious of the merry babble of voices in the room behind her. They were a well-behaved class, in the main; they had probably finished the assigned work, there was no reason, under the present regime, that they should keep from conversation, and the fact that they were not deterred by the proximity of the principal argued consciences void of offense; her discomfort at the difference between what actually happened when a class was left alone and what ideally should happen, was, she knew, out of all proportion to the magnitude of its cause. She considered stepping back into the room and trying the combined effect of the word "Class" and as deadly a glance as she could assume — effective treatment if she were to stay with them but likely to lose its efficacy after thirty seconds absence. Or she could rap a sharp warning on the door and hope for a momentary lull. But a warning of what? "Threaten once, then act," Professor Carlisle had told her class at O.C.E., and she had tried to adhere to this simple-sounding but profound maxim. But what punishment had Eleven-B to fear but a class detention, in which the innocent would suffer mildly with the guilty — she not least among the innocent! — for a quite unintentional offense. She ground her teeth quietly behind pleasantly smiling lips and waited, with an eager puzzlement of raised brows, for her principal's explanation.

"Dr. Goodchild wrote, asking if I would arrange to have him observe the teaching of classics at Rivercrest during his time in Toronto. I received his letter the day I left to chair the first Principals' Workshop. As I remember, I was unable to inform you that day, though I wrote that we should be glad to oblige him; and I forgot to leave a memo to that effect for Mr. Howells. I am just back a day on the job myself and have hardly had time to catch my breath. So, I confess, it came as a shock to me when you entered the office this morning, Sir," he turned smiling to the guest, "and I felt I should explain that Miss Waring knew nothing of your arrival till now."

"It's a shame to come in on you unexpectedly like this, Miss Waring. Are you sure that I won't be disturbing you?"

Aran saw no point in demurring. On a technicality she had the right, she supposed, to refuse the entry to her classes of someone not officially permitted, though Dr. Moorhouse's assent probably qualified as official permission. But, regardless of the disfavor she would incur, it never occurred to her to show resentment. It was, after all, an honor. It wasn't the stranger's fault and as for her Chief. . . . There were schools in which the principal could listen in at will and undetected to any unsuspecting teacher. Dr. Moorhouse had heard her teach once, years ago. Now he knocked, and, on occasions such as this, apologized. What more could any teacher want? Well to have worn her new shantung coat-dress, perhaps, instead of her indestructible grey worsted suit; to have rearranged the week's lessons so that Ten-A would be doing something next period more spectacular than review sentences.

"The loss will be yours, Dr. Goodchild, but at least I can't be suspected of preparing 'model' lessons."

"I'll leave you in good hands then," said the Chief, with relieved cordiality. "Miss Waring, I have arranged that during your spare Dr. Goodchild will see Mr. Madden's exhibition gym team. Otherwise he will be in your room for the day. You'll bring him down to my office at lunch time, will you please?"

He departed by way of the Down stairs. Aran hesitated a moment. Student teachers and occasional exchange visitors were usually already seated when the classes arrived. Inspectors went and came like the tent-folding Arab. But a University President could hardly be directed to enter by the rear door and help himself to a seat. She marvelled rather that the Chief had not arranged a more elaborate program. She had better do the honors and it would be too bad for the class if they did not respond!

"Shall we go in this way? Rivercrest classes aren't honored by such distinguished visitors every day. How did you happen to choose our school?"

He smiled down at her.

"It was no accident. Mrs. VanLuven returned from Toronto full of praise for a wonderful speech she had heard."

The query posed by her mind at the name of Queenstown was answered.

"Mary VanLuven is a great friend of my wife. Carl and I were at Yale together. She knows that the state of the classics in our present University and High School system is of great concern to me. So when I was coming up to Canada it seemed a good idea to see what I could of the situation here. And her recommendation left me no choice as to school."

" 'O Canada, I stand on guard for thee,' " said Aran smiling. "Alas my poor country! Well, under the circumstances I don't feel like apologizing further."

She opened the door, paused a second to let the fact sink in, and led Dr. Goodchild into a quickly hushing class, noting with relief that the only people out of their seats were two boys, who had lingered to adorn their declensions with elaborate and, in one case anagrammatical, signatures. Eleven-B rose to the occasion — bless them, they usually do, even now! she thought — looking mildly impressed at the visitation of a dignitary — some of them considerably interested in his novel bow-tie, his college pin and his large fraternity ring which their uncannily discriminating powers of observation noted. They stood rather sheepishly to greet him at Aran's almost imperceptible gesture, and settled down with the commendable response to being under inspection on which she had usually been able to depend.

Something else on which she could count was her own spontaneous quickening to the stimulus of an audience. A receptive — or even a quiescent — class was enough to call out unpremeditated aptness of illustration or allusion. The addition of a stranger seldom failed to accelerate the flowering of her mind from the seminal facts to be imparted. Pure extrovert, or plain show-off, she told herself with unembarrassed enjoyment, as the tendency manifested itself now in an unforced quip, a happy series of examples, an inspired explanation to clear up a pupil's difficulty, and a crushing, but not brutal riposte when one of the "they'll do it every time" boys considered the presence of a visitor an auspicious occasion to pose a covertly insolent question. She brushed aside the discomfort which assailed her at these moments, for fear the visitor, whether inspector or student-teacher, would think that she was making a special effort. About the class she did not worry. Those who could discriminate between good and poor teaching would also realize that many of her best lessons wasted a good deal of their sweetness on the desert air. And as far as Dr. Goodchild was concerned, there was no virtue in repressing apt remarks which she would make, if she thought of them, when he was not there. He seemed to be enjoying himself, and even the forms over which she shook her head dumbly as they filed from the room did not detract from his frankly evident admiration. He lounged beside her in the hall between periods, commenting and questioning with considerable acumen. She found him witty and well-read, perceptive and honest. Whatever his business in Toronto, he had given up the day to observe her teaching and expressed himself as quite content to leave

Rivercrest with its other excellencies — his own phrase — unobserved. All in all, the visitation gradually became less of a trial than a pleasure as the day went on.

Of course, she admitted, he was tasting the sweet without the bitter. The appalling errors on which her quick glance fell as she looked over their homework merely offered an opportunity for her to display varied techniques of correction. Grade Thirteen's flattering enjoyment of her flight into Gilbert Murray's *Trojan Women* apropos Virgil's description of the sack of Troy did not hide from her the failure of repeated efforts to convince most of them that Latin poetry could be translated without a crib. And Twelve-B, its collective lethargic mentality at saturation point in the seventh period — always her worst period with them — was past caring about the presence of the President of the United States, much less of a mere University President who was probably an egg-head anyhow. Usually good-natured, if passive, they were disposed to resent any effort to stir them into co-operation — except, of course, Drina Lampman and Olga Svensen, Stefan's equally diligent sister, and big John Black, who played brilliant basketball and refused to let that fact, or the covert pressure of an indolent group keep him from taking an interest in schoolwork.

Even their efforts could not drag a Monday afternoon Twelve-B through a paragraph of Livy, and to restrict questioning to them was too obvious an admission of defeat. Aran tossed a metaphorical coin whether to stop teaching and order them to work out a translation in the remaining half of the period, the effort to be collected and marked as term work — that would be tails — or to make one more effort to arouse them to consciousness of Livy's masterly handling of a dramatic moment. Heads won.

"Close your notebooks, class," she said crisply, "and for goodness' sake put down your pens." She hesitated a moment, then walked over and raised three of the five windows with a long vigorous shove, letting in a wave of fresh May air. "Take a few deep breaths — I know it's an effort but you'll find some effort is unavoidable as you go through life. Right. Now don't exert yourself but just let Livy talk to you for a few minutes. I swear if you do, you'll understand. This *is* a language, remember, and some ancestors of most of you spoke it. Come on back to us, Jeffries. I knew I ran a risk when I opened that window. Thanks. You'll be outside, most of you, in less than an hour (a very short time if you realize that this was written approximately 1975 x 365 x 24 hours ago and yet shows human nature as clearly and far more subtly than most of the plays you watch on TV). Just listen while Jeffries reads it for us."

Jeffries had not read five of the sonorous words in a dismal, unintelligible mumble before Aran realized that, regardless of ostentation, she should have carried out her original intention.

"You win, Jeffries, you win — pro tem," she interrupted. "Good grief, man, could you recite the multiplication table with less expression? Doesn't it mean *anything* to you that this is the language of Antony and Caesar, of Scipio and Justinian? No, evidently not. Well, this is approximately the way it should sound. 'Immo Arreti ante moenia sedeamus, inquit, hic enim patria et penates sunt. Hannibal emissus e manibus perpopuletur Italiam vastandoque et urendo omnia ad Romana moenia perveniat, nec ante nos hinc moverimus quam, sicut olim Camillum ab Veiis, C. Flaminium ab Arretio patres acciverint.' Now look at the first section which we have already translated. Flaminius is fed up with a delaying policy, fed up with waiting for action, sure that the old fogies are wrong. Besides, he feels that they are being made to look like fools and he wants to infuriate his men to the point of acting against all Roman discipline. This is where we come in. Roughly he is saying: 'Hannibal can devastate Italy; Hannibal can slip through our fingers; Hannibal can make us a laughing-stock; Hannibal can reach the very gates of Rome. And what do we do?' " She glanced at her book to recommence the Latin reading without abating her forensic fury. The class was at last mildly interested.

Book in her right hand she flung out her left in a spontaneous dramatic gesture. 'What' I ask you, do we do? Nec . . . .' "

Twelve-B's howl coincided with her lightning realization of the sound of the word. Thoroughly awake at last, they laughed with reiterated enjoyment which no telling of the joke afterwards would ever recapture. Dr. Goodchild came perilously near rolling in the aisle. Aran leaned against the blackboard in helpless mirth. The class, since the joke was on her, felt warmer in a patronizing affectionate manner than they had all period. At the point where one or two would have prolonged the merriment by deliberate raucousness, she took charge again.

"Twelve-B, if you were half as keen on understanding the work assigned as you are to pick up the slightest double entendre it would be a better world for teachers. And the moral of that is, said the Duchess, digging her sharp little chin into Alice's shoulder, we shall have to add this to Wednesday's assignment. Can't let Twelve-A get ahead of us."

"Latin is by no means a dead language to your students," said Lemuel Goodchild, strolling to the front of the room as Aran returned from the hall after dismissing her last class. Her smile this time was a sceptical one. She had heard the remark for twenty years and though it always gave her pleasure she was no longer convinced by it.

"Entertainment isn't education, I'm afraid. And you see how much zeal or even interest in learning I have been able to arouse in Twelve-B after eight months."

"You give much more than entertainment, Miss Waring." Aran hoped that he had not thought her disclaimer rude. "The interest in your Grade Ten, the type of questions and discussion you evoked in your Senior Grade, and the masterly way you compared and contrasted the Renaissance with Periclean Athens: you can't dismiss that as mere entertainment."

Aran's flush was not primarily of pleasure. That history lesson had been her one "contrived" period of the day, the result of a hasty decision and a hasty alteration of lesson material during her brief noon hour. And though she agreed that it had been a masterly effort she felt rather ashamed of her contriving. She almost confessed it now.

"I'm afraid I use any excuse I can find to get back to the Greeks — or the Romans. When I began to teach Ancient History we had five periods a week in Grade Twelve for just that. Now we have four in Eleven to teach everything from Pre-History to Europe in 1759. I can't teach History in great swathes. I've regretfully asked to be relieved of it next year."

Their conversation might have lasted much longer had not Dr. Moorhouse appeared a few minutes later to escort his guest to the Track Team display which a shower earlier in the day had disrupted. Dr. Goodchild said some things as he took his leave which Aran thought it would do no harm for Dr. Moorhouse to hear. And the two men departed.

"Another day, another dollar," she said aloud, quoting her brother Paul. Not one of his best, she realized, remembering a time when she had referred so constantly to his authority that when she concluded an obviously Scriptural quotation with the remark, "as Paul says," a bright Sunday-school pupil had quipped, 'St. Paul, Miss Waring?' How long ago that was! And how ridiculously short a time it seemed, with days like this, yet infinitely varied, slipping into years. She picked up her notebook and noticed the file of cards beneath it. Amazing that they had not called again from the office. And was it pure coincidence that there had not been a single interruption by telephone or message all day? In any case something to be thankful for. Would that, she wondered, come up for discussion on the forthcoming TV panel in which she had been asked to participate?

Twelve

LEANING BACK in a chrome-plated chair, Aran submitted, amused and curious, to the deft, impersonal ministrations of the TV make-up artist. Two chairs away a tall, svelte, capable-looking woman to whom she had been introduced in the reception room as the President of Toronto's most progressive Home and School Club, had already been "done." Through her lashes Aran glanced at the finished reflection in an attempt to estimate what her own result would be. "Close your eyes; fold your lips together" — a huge moist sponge passed over her face, back to her exposed ears, under her chin, to the plastic cover protecting her dress — "now open your mouth. Just yourself, you say, I guess your brows will do as they are. Want any mascara?"

"Anything you think will give me a touch of glamour."

An answering flicker stirred the reflected mask two mirrors along, but the technician was not amused. Obviously, Aran thought, her twenty-two years considered such advanced age (even if her cool experienced young eyes could be deceived into deducting six or seven years as Aran's kindlier friends did) as far beyond glamour. Especially in one who showed such shocking disregard of appearance as to let grey hairs thread the dark unchecked — a streak of silver off the brow would be smart! — leave eyebrows following the bone contour, and fingernails their natural color.

"That's not usual for this sort of panel. But mascara will help your eyes to look less blurred" — a murrain seize this synthetic robot! — "under the lights. Look up! Don't blink. That's good enough."

A swift application of the brush, as effortless and automatic as the dropping of conventional parsley on a table d'hote entree, a facile flick removing the plastic cover without disarranging the dress, and Aran was shoved off the assembly line.

"Sooner fix your hair yourself." It was a statement, not a question, and, cigarette box already transferred from her white uniform pocket to her slender, exquisitely groomed hand, the girl disappeared.

The mirrored face, like, yet unlike her own, transformed by the heavy pancake make-up into a sort of wax-works replica, crinkled into a grin, and Aran realized with relief that the effect before the unsparing camera would be better than she had feared. At least the wear and tear of the year-end was less discernable around eyes and mouth. Mrs. Poynter smiled too.

"She doesn't help the morale, does she?"

"An understatement, that. I doubt if the ordeal ahead will daunt me at all now."

"Have you been on TV before?"

"No. On radio twice, a much less complicated — "

The door opened to admit a lovely wood nymph of a girl whom Aran instantly recognized as Television's own Elissa Train, darling of the fans, interviewer par excellence, and now producer of her own program with an audience-rating to make American stations look to their laurels.

She smiled at them with bright indifference, sat down to a corner mirror evidently her own and, unlocking a stage make-up box, proceeded with a facial improvement, less a routine than a ritual. Aran remembered her early appearances and the almost nightly increase in attractiveness as she had experimented gradually to obliterate weaknesses or distortion in her features and to emphasize her more alluring ones. Both women felt suddenly amateurish and unsure in the presence of this professional poise. Mrs. Poynter took out her purse mirror, studied her profile for a moment and touched the swirled ends of hair at the back of her head.

Aran, conscious of her own mannerism, practiced relaxing her jaw pleasantly, then widened her eyes to a look of perceptive repose and hoped that she would neither "hang her eyebrows on her front hair" nor deepen the furrow between them by unconscious frowning in moments of intensity. "You're playing Miranda, remember, not Goneril," Daphne had cautioned her once in that connection. Actually the youngest Waring had received so many kindly corrections for gaucheries that she wondered how so many bad habits had lingered!

"Are you ready, Miss Waring? It's time we joined the others, I think. Now how do we go? Turn right through the reception room and along the corridor to the third door on the left."

"That's it. You're on 'Everybody's Agora' aren't you?" Elissa Train looked at them in the mirror. "Best of luck."

Aran smiled back, at her and at her own feeling of pleased acceptance. Another aspect of the phenomenon C. S. Lewis had discussed in *The Inner Ring!* How every group, every profession, had its circle, those who had arrived, those who knew the ropes, those who talked, and in some cases invented, its special language or jargon. And on their own ground at least, they were the priests and priestesses who could admit or exclude the uninitiate. In several groups she had been Inner Ring herself, but unconsciously, until a realization of the admiration, the pleasure, the gratitude of someone outside made her realize, feeling absurd and surprised, that she, Aran Waring, was to some individual one of the Important People. When on her Class Executive at College, she had entertained a former High School friend for lunch at Wymilwood. The girl, a nurse-in-training, had always been insouciant, dashing, popular, far more than she, and it had not dawned on her until their parting that the rush of unfamiliar activity — it was just before the Vic Bob — the frequent interruptions for excited planning, the questions *she* must answer, the directions *she* had to give, were to her friend part of a strange impressive world from which she was excluded and in which Aran played an important part. A year or so later a second instance had occurred. Aran had achieved her first small success in college dramatics, eliciting disproportionately kind press notices. After the second performance a starry-eyed, stage-struck youngster, several years her junior, had come timidly back stage, obviously thrilled to meet the star and little guessing Aran's embarrassed and depreciating thrill at the novel adulation. The girl had since achieved a professional career of some distinction in England and Aran never saw her name in the papers without a moment's whimsical retrospection. So now the women, not unimportant in their own fields, were duly impressed by their moment's encounter with local TV Royalty, who in her turn would probably feel similarly humble in the studio of an international stage or opera star. God must think we're funny, thought Aran. I do hope He gets a laugh out of it sometimes!

Seated a few minutes later behind an oblong table, the oblong table on which from the security of her own den she had watched many celebrated arms lean, she felt the treacherous mental gauntness of panic, as if supports had been suddenly withdrawn and nothing kept her from falling. Once she had climbed the fire tower at Dorset, examined the unfamiliar gadgets with interest, and the far sweep of undulating horizon with exhilaration until, turning, she saw the square hole in the floor and the endless steel spiral, awfully hollowed, which was her only means of regress. She had felt then that she could not possibly, possibly, step over into that circling void, and the forest ranger on duty had dispassionately pointed to the coil of rope which was kept for the express purpose of lowering those similarly paralyzed. In the end her will had dominated her cringing body, but it was a horrid recollection and valueless to reassure her in this new ordeal.

Like the upward climb the project had sounded adventurous and fun when, a few weeks before, a C.B.C. producer had telephoned. Was she the Miss Waring who taught at

Rivercrest Collegiate? She was. She had made, he understood, some statements in her section of the Ontario Educational Association which had been reported in the papers. She was afraid so. Not accurately reported, she might have added, with a connective omitted, a grammatical error inserted, and the punch line botched, but the gist had been correct. One had to be thankful for small mercies in dealing with the all-dominant and unanswerable Press. At the other end of the line Roger Heywood continued:

"We'd like your assistance on a program which should be of national interest. You probably know the series 'I Object,' and how it is conducted?"

She did. It was one of the few programs she watched with some regularity and in which she took vigorous and unofficial part when the statements objected to were of interest to her.

"Well, in general this will be along the same lines, but with two differences. The statements to be defended or opposed will deal with present-day education and all members of the panel will have some connection with education. Then, in view of the importance of the subject, we shall have a full hour, twice as long as the usual time for debate. Fortunately, at this time of the year some of the regular features have suspended operations till the fall, and we feel that the weakness of such programs is that time runs out when the topics are far from exhausted."

"Just in what capacity am I supposed to act?"

"In a private one. It is understood that all the panel will express their own views and that no person or body will be implicated by whatever they choose to say. You may feel perfectly free."

Arrangements had proceeded smoothly from that point. Aran had seen no reason to refuse. The subject was one to which she had given considerable thought, to put it mildly, and if she rejected the opportunity someone else might seize it to air views which she cordially disliked, or might leave unsaid things which should be stated. Her anticipation had been pleasurable and, although she had not mentioned the event to any but one or two special cronies at the school, a sufficiently large number of friends and relatives were already — at that very moment — sitting in well-known living rooms, watching the tag-end of a suspense thriller, in order to see her debut. As for the unknown audience, the frighteningly *unseen* audience, the audience not held together by physical contiguity so that the electric thrill of sympathy or laughter or anger could run through them instantaneously and re-communicate itself to the speaker, but separated into thousands of oddly assorted units, chatting and criticizing, its interest failing in the words spoken because of a crease in a sleeve, a mannerism magnified. . . .

She felt herself slumped in her chair, straightened her shoulders, saw her hands as abnormally thickset and veined under the experimenting lights, withdrew them to her lap, and told herself that she must do none of those things once the program began. "Cut them off at the wrists, Lytton. Forget that you have any hands," she remembered W. S. Gilbert's advice which she had so often repeated to herself and to young actors.

She couldn't go through with it. A prepared speech she could handle, even an individual interview, but not this: a free-for-all discussion which was not free at all, since the M. C. could direct the questions and limit the time, and since a woman speaking with any earnestness would seem to lack femininity, and speaking at any length would sound opinionated! Indifference was an advantage at such times, an attitude of gentle tolerance, of wise superiority to passionate convictions. She was not indifferent on this subject; she had passionate convictions. And she could not bear the responsibility of losing support for them by unconsciously antagonizing her audience. Default would be better.

In the nick of time, as in so many crises in her life, she remembered to pray, and was again wonderingly shamed and grateful at the instant flooding of peace into her disquiet. Her heart stopped pounding in her ears, the choking sensation left her throat, she swallowed naturally, and became conscious, wondering how much she had missed, of the technical advice which the Panel Director was imparting.

"When that far light is on, you are all visible to the audience. This is your special light, Mrs. Poynter; yours, Dr. Sacheverell; yours, Miss Waring; yours, Mr. Pomfret. Don't stare at the lights. Just remember that when the camera is focussing on you, your light will be glowing. Please don't put your hands in front of your faces when you speak. We shall follow no set order. After I introduce you individually and state the proposition, anyone may begin. If I see that someone is ready I shall mention him by name. If not, I may put a leading question to one of you. Now — time, Jack? Right. When he raises his arm we are on the air. Quiet for Dirk's lead-in. There — "

Jack raised his hand, two men across the room did mysterious things with mysterious pieces of equipment, Dirk, the dimpled idol of the youthful fans, strolled into his orbit on the other side of a maze of cameras and began to talk with the hesitant, unrehearsed familiarity, endearingly his own. Aran took the last moments of respite to glance with a look of friendly interest at the other persons stranded briefly with her on this uncharted island of experience.

Mrs. Poynter at the M.C's left looked as panicky as Aran had recently felt, though she responded jerkily to her smile and gesture of encouragement. There was no need to encourage Dr. Sacheverell. A round blond man, an authority in child psychology, he had appeared on TV almost as often as the M. C. and over a more prolonged period of time. Mr. Pomfret, who had angles where Dr. Sacheverell had arcs, was a recent appointee of the Department and a strong advocate of "progressive" education. This was Aran's first sight of him and she hoped that his views had been misrepresented. As for the M.C., Roger Heywood was a genius at his job. Pleasant without being fatuous, quick-thinking and diplomatic, he could be counted on to fill in or efface himself, to sum up gracefully and to intervene with good-humored authority when tempers ran high. She met his eye at that moment and caught its signal. The main light had flashed on.

" 'The present system of education enriches the student's life and sends him into the world better equipped to meet its challenges than any yet devised,' " he summed up a little later when the panel had been individually presented, and each had made the face by which, presumably, he or she wished to indicate his character to the public. "We have identified the quotation, and agreed to certain definite limits. We are referring, as the noted Canadian Educator did, to the school system in Ontario below the University level. We have side-stepped Miss Waring's etymological difficulty over the word 'student' by establishing that 'student' for our purposes means those who are educated — very well, Miss Waring — exposed, to the system until school-leaving time. Fortunately no one has asked us to define 'the world' or 'challenges.' Now, to quote the motto of my Alma Mater, the University of British Columbia: 'Tuum Est,' which means, if I'm not mistaken, 'It's up to you.' Is that a correct translation, Miss Waring, and quite appropriate here?"

He passed the question to her and Aran, already answering, was suddenly conscious of the light which told of a focussed camera. Her reply struck her as likely to sound insufferably pedantic but she had to complete it or stammer weakly.

"U.B.C. challenges every student as an individual, Mr. Heywood. If you are doing likewise, the motto is most suitable. If it is up to the panel as a whole, 'vestrum est' would be more accurate."

Heywood caught the ball neatly.

"You've been more fortunate than I, Miss Waring, if you've ever found one of these panels acting as a whole. However, now that we have given this discussion a fittingly erudite launching, I shall get down to business by asking Mr. Pomfret whether he challenges or accepts the statement."

Mr. Pomfret's answer was unequivocal if couched in impressive circumlocution.

"Even apart from my respect for the speaker, who Education-wise is an unquestioned authority in Canada today, I would personally concur wholeheartedly with the statement. Furthermore, I scarcely regard it as debatable. Statistically and in a dozen ways it can be proven that it is one of those things of which the Constitution of the Great Republic to the south says: 'We hold these truths to be self-evident.' "

Aran stirred restlessly. The M.C. turned to Mrs. Poynter.

"I scarcely feel qualified to challenge the opinion of two such prominent educators. Certainly our young people are given a wonderful chance to develop their personalities by the enriching program of extra-curricular activities."

Mrs. Poynter's daughter was president of the Girls' Athletic Association and had won a prize recently in her school's Camera Club contest, Aran had learned in their few moments together. She was going into Soc. and Phil. and had no trouble with her schoolwork. Naturally her mother saw the sunny side of life.

"Dr. Sacheverell," Roger Heywood appealed to the veteran who had been listening with an expression of remote benignity, "have you any comment?"

It was a rhetorical question. Dr. Sacheverell always had a comment, and frequently a perspicacious one.

"No one has mentioned the qualification which saves the statement from my stricture." His strong measured voice, suggesting as it did unlimited experience, impartial judgment, a wealth of proven rather than theoretical knowledge, gave weight to the discussion, after Pomfret's high-pitched pomposity and Mrs. Poynter's nervous ingratiation. It italicized the next words as unmistakably as print: " '*Any yet devised.*' With that rider, I let the praise go unchallenged. Without it, I should be forced to deplore the lag between our Ontario system, particularly in secondary schools, and the findings of psychology. We have a long way to go before our system is freed from the curse of regimentation, of competitive examinations, of outmoded learning techniques, a long way before each child, particularly each adolescent has access to his birthright of expert psychiatric assistance. But I am not impatient. Like Galileo I say, 'But it does move,' and realize that this is true even with Boards and Departments of Education. We have come a long way from the three Rs and compulsory time-tables, from the dreary inculcation of facts, and the mechanical monotony of meaningless memory work." He paused as though a little surprised by his alliteration. Aran knew that her time had come.

"The count stands at three in favor of our first quotation," observed Heywood. "This is a most agreeable panel. Or perhaps — Miss Waring, will you let it be carried unanimously or provide a little healthy opposition?"

The light in front glowed. Aran began, slowly because she usually spoke too fast, quietly because she knew how easily earnestness could be misconstrued as animus.

"In spite of my ancestry, I'm not Irish enough to oppose for the sake of opposition," she managed to say lightly. "I have never argued against anything that I believed. But I don't believe the statement to be true at all."

She stopped deliberately, although she had intended to say more. Long ago, quite by accident, she had discovered the efficacy of letting her opponent use up his ammunition. All the panel looked at her expectantly.

"Yes," said Heywood encouragingly. "Aren't you going to tell us why?"

Aran smiled her prettiest smile, very feminine, she hoped, a trifle appealing, straight into the camera.

"Is that — is that really up to me?" she asked hesitantly. "Doesn't the burden of proof lie with those who make or support such a sweeping statement? There must be thousands listening to us who were brought up under the system decried by Dr. Sacheverell and who feel, humbly enough, that their lives were as rich and their training to face the world's challenges as great as that of the modern adolescent. We should like to hear some of the ways in which Mr. Pomfret can prove this superiority, at least one reason to include it with life, liberty, and the pursuit of happiness, as a self-evident truth. Personally — though I may be stupid — I've never understood why memory work is considered a Bad Thing, or why competition is an evil in scholastic matters alone, but recognized as valuable, if not essential, for improvement in athletics, music, and business. And, as a teacher who decries regimentation above all things — and considers it more rampant in our schools than before — I'd be very grateful if Dr. Sacheverell would explain why he thinks it is decreasing."

Eyes wide and honest, she waited. The far light showed that the unseen audience could watch the five faces, although she looked at the Director alone. Then Mr. Pomfret's voice bit the silence on a high note and she knew that she had drawn blood.

"If Miss Waring recalls the geometry which she learned under the system she admires — and she must since she enjoys memory work — she will remember that an axiom is a self-evident truth and that no one is obliged to prove an axiom. In spite of Dr. Sacheverell's charge of slowness on the part of the Administration — a much easier thing to accuse than to remedy when you are dealing with the taxpayers' money — " evidently that had rankled too, "I cannot believe that any progressive-minded person needs proof of the vast strides which have been made in Ontario Secondary School education in the last twenty years. Slow at first, perhaps. We had a whole generation of teachers of the old school to re-educate, some of them past education — " was it fancy or was there a conscious slur in those words? — "but accelerating every year."

The Director glanced at Aran.

"Miss Waring?"

Aran controlled herself nobly. The more she let them say now the more sympathetic her audience might be later.

"I should still like to hear my other questions answered. And, if Mr. Pomfret will forgive my saying it, isn't he confusing change with progress?"

Apparently this was another self-evident truth. Mr. Pomfret stared at her, momentarily wordless. Fortunately Dr. Sacheverell, like the younger Pitt, never lacked a word, the very word, for any occasion.

"Perhaps I should assume responsibility for my own statements, though I did not feel that they required clarification. We decry memory work, Miss Waring, whether of the multiplication table, dates in history, or set pieces of poetry, because to us the child is the measure of all things. The inculcation of facts outside the reach of his mental assent is meaningless. No information which is beyond his experience at any stage has value. So also our objection to a compulsory time-table. The impulse to learn must come from within the child himself. The individual's needs and preferences must dictate the course of study selected."

He was not through his speech but he paused, doubtless to let the new ideas sink in. The pause was enough for Aran.

"If you'll pardon the word," she said with cheerful candor, "I think that is straight rot — about facts being useless unless related to experience. And since attainment of objective truth probably enjoys a low rating among the new education aims, I shall say that your premise is demonstrably false to my personal experience. Are a child's mental horizons never to expand, except at the sometimes pitifully slow rate of his environment? What about the stimulus for his imagination and ambition? It's like that other tosh — fallacious theory — that classifies words and books in age-groups, and rebukes a youngster — my own nephew was one — for using, naturally and correctly, a word outside an arbitrarily fixed limit. Is the wonder and the glory — the infinite power and joy of words and their discovery — to be denied or postponed because an individual's immediate associates struggle along on the minimum working ration of five hundred?"

There was no immediate answer. Roger Heywood, glancing at Dr. Sacheverell, saw him, for the first time in his experience, struggling to replace a flush of anger by his usual pontifical calm. Opposition he had faced in plenty, but one of his pet theories had never been called rot before and he did not like it. Heywood, on the other hand, was finding the discussion to his taste. On an impulse he decided to give Aran the chance to hang or justify herself.

"You object to others making unproved statements, Miss Waring," he said blandly. "Perhaps you would explain your own words 'demonstrably false to personal experience.'"

"Is it in good taste to give a personal example?"

"I shouldn't let a question of good taste hamper me if I were you." Dr. Sacheverell's face had regained its repose but his resonant voice had a cutting edge. Aran flushed, hesitated, and plunged.

"I'm sorry. I apologize for using the word rot — unfortunately it was the only one that occurred to me." She turned from his unresponsive face to Heywood's and noticed that her individual light had replaced the collective one. "Well — at the age of twelve, at the suggestion of my English teacher — bless him — I read Kingsley's *Hypatia*. That book introduced me to a world, an age, a philosophy, a series of concepts and ideas, and to historical facts which had no connection, no parallel in my life, which in many ways revolutionized my thinking. The main features of the story I followed, some phrases and sentences and descriptions I automatically memorized. Most of it was beyond my comprehension, but it fascinated me. And repeatedly in my life, from my recognizing thrill at finding, soon afterwards, a painting entitled "Hypatia the Philosopher" in a collection of the world's art treasures, through phase after phase of education, culminating in a visit to Alexandria — that reading was an incalculably enriching experience, at once a stimulus

165

and a treasury. Surely that is what formal education should do for the young — not wait till they stumble into each new experience, less significant because isolated and unadorned, but unveil — give a preview if you like — so that the imagination is stirred to discovery and when the discovery is a personal experience, he can say: 'So this is what was meant. Others have felt this. I am not alone.' " She broke off, dangerously close to tears.

"I think we should come down to earth now." Mr. Pomfret's emotions had not been similarly stirred and his thin high voice was sarcastic. "Miss Waring in her ivory tower of Greek and philosophy — natural enough dwelling for a teacher of dead languages — forgets that our democratic concern is for the average child, the sturdy normal citizen, the one who may never have the means — or the vacation — to take a trip to Alexandria." He paused, conscious of scoring with the taxpayer. "Our responsibility doesn't stop with the brilliant, the scholarship candidate, the *small* percent who continue to University. We owe it to the ordinary child to equip him for life, to help him to find his niche in society, to cultivate his individual talents."

"To enable him to make the necessary adjustment from adolescence to maturity." Dr. Sacheverell, differences forgotten in face of the common foe, took over. "Under the old regimented system, inherited from the days when a small fraction of the community entered High School at all, the average child conformed or went to the wall. Miss Waring and her fellow theorists forget, I fear, that we have a responsibility for every child in the community until he graduates from some form of secondary school."

"Why?" The camera flicked back to her on the arrow-swift word, but she waited for her answer. The battle was joined irrevocably and as usual, though she hated quarrelling, her spirits rose at an open fight. Two against her, perhaps three — Mrs. Poynter was undeclared but obviously not strong as opponent or ally — only succeeded in driving all nervousness away.

> *"Your courage rise with danger*
> *And strength to strength oppose."*

She found herself singing inwardly, and it was with happy, almost mischievous eyes that she faced the camera.

The desire to answer this outrageous question was unanimous. Roger Heywood gave Mrs. Poynter the prerogative.

"Why, Miss Waring, in a democratic society free education is the right of every child regardless of financial standing. Surely you agree with that?"

"The Universities charge fees still, I believe."

"That is true but — "

"Hasn't every child in a democratic society equal right to free University education, regardless of financial standing?"

Mrs. Poynter was nonplussed. The merciful camera flicked after a moment to Dr. Sacheverell.

"Theoretically, of course, that is true. And we never shall have a truly democratic system until University fees are paid by the state. But that Utopian condition has not yet been realized."

"And when it is, will a University degree become compulsory?"

"Miss Waring is facetious," said Mr. Pomfret icily. The temperature of his voice was in inverse ratio to its pitch. "A High School diploma is not compulsory."

"I'm sorry. I understand Dr. Sacheverell to say that we were responsible to see that every child in the community graduate from some type of secondary school."

"I did."

"Then why not from University?"

"But, Miss Waring" — Mrs. Poynter could answer that one and felt that her Home and School Club members would be expecting more of her than she had so far contributed — "not every young person has the intellectual capacity for a University course."

"You mean for our present University courses? Then why not lower the standards and introduce other — practical — courses? Why in a democratic society should any child feel the frustration and bear the stigma of going through life unequipped with a degree?"

"I agreed to take part in this program," said Mr. Pomfret with crushing dignity, "under the impression that it would be a serious and enlightening discussion. Since one of us seems bent on treating the whole matter frivolously I consider that we are wasting our time."

Aran turned and faced him squarely. She had forgotten about the lights, the cameras, the far-flung audience.

"I have seldom been less frivolous, Mr. Pomfret. My questions are a sincere effort to clarify our concept of what constitutes democracy in education, a term which I did not introduce here."

"Then it seems to me that they could be better worded for the purpose."

Aran's eyes appealed to the Director for a decision.

"I think the opposition has a right to her answer," said Heywood judiciously. "The word democratic has been used and her views have been disparaged — indirectly, it is true — as undemocratic. Perhaps you could come to the point more succinctly, Miss Waring."

"I shall try. If it is our democratic duty to provide a High School diploma for every child — and to this end we are justified in lowering standards, raising marks, providing substitute subjects, indefinitely lengthening the period of time during which credits can be obtained — why should we not do the same to help them to a University degree? If on the other hand we concede, as Mrs. Poynter has done, that large numbers have not the type of intellect — shall we say? — to benefit by University work, why do we not make the same admission with regard to their capacity for High School — at least for Middle and Upper School work?"

"I think, Miss Waring, you have lost the thread a little there." Dr. Sacheverell interpolated with the kindly complaisance of one who always held all the threads of thought firm and unentangled. "You forget that the compulsory period of education ends at sixteen" — Aran was likely to forget it! — "an age when the majority of our adolescents are in Grade Eleven or Twelve. Since we have kept them at school till that time we must obviously offer them something to show for it, some token of achievement. To drop out before attaining this is detrimental to morale and the Administration has shown a praiseworthy concern over the high drop-out rate in our schools."

Mr. Pomfret accepted the olive branch. His gratification was short-lived.

"Then why keep them till sixteen?"

"That is the legal age."

"Why should it be? It is fifteen in England. It was fourteen here. In some European countries it is twelve. Why not eighteen? What is sacrosanct about sixteen?"

"Was not that age selected in 1919" — Mrs. Poynter was on sure ground, remembering a recent Education week program in her club — "because a bright student could graduate at sixteen from the old Fourth Form with a diploma, and any student could have his Lower School certificate? And surely, Miss Waring, it is a safeguard against an intelligent child being needlessly deprived of the benefits of education?"

"That is quite true, Mrs. Poynter." Aran was genuinely glad to agree, if momentarily, with anyone. "And it was a disinterested and idealistic act. But it was an experiment. No one foresaw or could foresee where it would lead. And there is nothing retrograde, if the prolongation of an experiment leads to disaster, in revoking it — or whatever one does to an experiment!"

"Miss Waring," said her right-hand neighbor (at least they were all addressing her now instead of referring to her in the third person — all, that is, except Mr. Pomfret), "if you are suggesting that we lower the school-leaving age, I may as well warn you that you are talking impossibilities. Our economy is simply not geared to absorb that number of adolescents."

"Dr. Sacheverell!" It was Aran's turn to look shocked. "Were you not predicting free University tuition? Surely we are concerned with education, not with economics! The same economic bogey was raised when the abolition of child labor was suggested, but the economy survived. We cannot talk of the welfare of the child one moment and business interests the next."

"Miss Waring would discover, if she occupied a less sheltered position in the economic system," said her left-hand neighbor irritably, "that compromise with business interests is necessary for state education. Her salary — "

"Perhaps," Dr. Sacheverell deliberately interrupted to elevate the discussion, "I should have approached your objection from another point of view. Just what disaster is resulting from the present age that you suggest lowering it?"

"That has been made abundantly clear." Mr. Pomfret had not taken kindly to interruption. "Surely we realize by this time that we are up against the academic mind which is interested only in the academically brilliant, the intellectual high-achievers. You and I, Dr. Sacheverell — and Mrs. Poynter too" — he drew up a common front — "are concerned about the whole child, the average child who has as much right to the development of his potential as those with an I.Q. of 140. They are the ones we look to to fight our wars, the fathers and mothers and citizens of tomorrow. They — "

"And have I no concern about them?" Aran's voice always dropped with feeling. It came steadily now on an organ note, hushing her opponent's falsetto indignation. "Why do you think I decided to teach and continued to teach? With whom do I spend the greater part of my time five days a week, and much time out of school besides? Of course I'm concerned for the brilliant — it's time we showed some consideration for them instead of apologizing for them as egg-heads, encouraging a system which treats them as pariahs, except for a few moments at Commencement, when we sandwich five minutes praise in between hyperbole over the Rugby team and a 'relieving' number by the 'normal' adolescents in the orchestra. But, by and large, the brillliant student has the stamina to take it — that is part of his brilliance, the courage to disregard mass opinion. It is the average student who is suffering, who is regimented by prevalent standards and attitudes as no compulsory time-table ever regimented him, who is being robbed of his chance to benefit by his opportunities, deprived of the very birthright which democracy gives him. Not concerned — " she broke off, realizing that her hands were clasped, white-knuckled in front of her, that her throat was taut and her breast heaving. She recovered, and by a second cheated Mr. Pomfret of his chance.

Sorry. Next time I shall borrow a soap box. But I mean every word of it."

"Come," said Sacheverell, almost benign now that she had betrayed herself by this show of emotion. "Perhaps you have personal reasons for taking a somewhat jaundiced view. None of us is above the influence of personal feelings and considerations" — What in thunder is the man insinuating, queried Aran wordlessly; age, neurosis, failure at school? — "but any statistical survey of our healthy, normal, well-adjusted High School graduates making their way into business and society will weigh pretty heavily — yes overwhelmingly — against such a biased and slightly hysterical assessment."

Roger Heywood hesitated. Seldom had a discussion strayed so flagrantly from the set lines of courteous, if hypocritical, verbal exchange. But as a showman he admitted its interest. He wanted to hear Aran defend her position and he wagered mentally that the vast majority of the audience wanted it.

"Are you going to let that last remark pass, Miss Waring?" he inquired, avoiding Dr. Sacheverell's incredulous eye. "Or are you prepared to defend your — what was it? — 'biased and hysterical assessment'?"

Aran had herself firmly in hand.

"I'm delighted to defend what I regard rather as a dispassionate and carefully considered understatement. If I speak with some intensity it is because I regard teen-agers as persons and not as case histories in a filing system. My attitude has been established gradually from years of careful, and unwilling, and supervised, observation. I should have considered it rank heresy even ten years ago."

She paused.

"Could you explain what you mean by your 'attitude,' Miss Waring?" asked Heywood quickly, as Sacheverell was about to seize his opportunity.

"I'll try. The basic element is this: a conviction that compulsory education is defeating its own end; that what costs nothing is considered worth nothing; that when a youngster regards as a right what can be of benefit only as a privilege, not only does he cease to benefit by it but his very attitude is detrimental to his character and outlook. That is, I think, the underlying cause of symptoms which I have noticed becoming more widespread over the last twelve years.

"Why do you think the change dates from that time?" The. M C. timed his intervention as smoothly as the endman in a Minstrel Show and Aran caught her cue.

"Until that time Junior Matric Departmental exams and the Depression still exercised a sobering effect, and the era of easy money had not created a group of students financially almost independent. One symptom is the deterioration of the scholastically 'good' class, the class which was once rewarding to teach, which had fun and took a keen interest in its work. Year after year those classes, with rare exceptions, are becoming more inert, indifferent, willing to do only the minimum amount of work and, preferably, to have it done for them. Instead of healthy competition for high marks, there is a wary concern lest they be considered 'brains' and complete satisfaction with the average. Worried parents have told me about their anxiety over this indifference, and I am by no means speaking for myself alone when I assert that we must expect less and less of the students, if our class 'average' is not to fall below the 55-65 required! But the conviction that school is something from which they will ultimately emerge with a diploma to ensure a better wage or salary, regardless of mental development or honest work; lack of interest in knowledge for its own sake, embodied in the indignant 'Oh, that was last term's work' or, 'Aren't you going to test us today? We'll have forgotten it by tomorrow' — as if any subject is to be crammed for a test and discarded; and the cynical 'What's good about it?' which reflects their point of view on things of the mind: *that* is my reason for concern — because it is such pitiful, *unnecessary* waste. I don't need Dr. Sacheverell or Mr. Pomfret to tell me that this is an adolescent attitude which maturity will correct after they leave school. In some cases that is so; unfortunately, in many, it is by that time too late. I know there are many exceptions above and below the average. It is the deterioration of the average which distresses me. I consider an illiterate with a wistful respect and desire for knowledge in a healthier state than a High School graduate who wonders 'why the heck anyone would read a book.' And we have many of them."

There was a brief pause. Mrs. Poynter looked troubled. Mr. Pomfret — it was his settled expression since Aran began to speak — angry, Dr. Sacheverell urbanely amused, as though he listened to 'a tale of little meaning though the words are strong.' Before anyone could answer Roger Heywood intervened.

"We were right when we felt that this program could run an hour without difficulty. At this rate we shall not have time to discuss more than one or two of our remaining quotations. Summing up, then, we have a majority opinion in favor of the present system with a strong minority vote against. Now for our next quotation." He glanced at several slips of paper in his hand, looked speculatively at the panel members, then read: " 'Among the tasks facing educationists in the next decade, the one which dwarfs others into insignificance is that of recruiting teachers to meet the unprecedented boom in the Secondary School population. The entire community must have a share in this objective.' Can anyone identify this quotation?"

No one volunteered. Such remarks had been made and repeated so frequently, and in so many forms, that any one of a number of people might have given utterance to this version. After the stormy tension of the past half hour the lull that set in threatened boredom. Aran kept silent because she had talked too much already, did not know the answer anyhow, and was a bit incredulous that Heywood should have selected, a second time, a statement which could be used to good account later. She had always liked the genial but never insipid M. C. Tonight she regarded him with grateful affection.

She admired, too, the experienced deftness with which he rescued his crew from the doldrums. A question here, a quip there, counting on the pardonable willingness of the two men to become vocal after their prolonged silence, and, to the accompaniment of the hearty, general, quite reasonless laugh to which radio programs have long inured the public, he succeeded in seeming to elicit, while really disclosing, the name of the author: surprisingly, not an educationist but a prominent barrister in an after-dinner speech entitled "Canada's Role in the Next Half Century."

That much established, Heywood passed the question courteously to Mrs. Poynter, whose share of the limelight had so far been disproportionately small. Unfortunately for her eagerly watching friends, Mrs. Poynter had been elected president more because she was one of those desirable, dependable women with a genuine love of committee and executive meetings than because she held any strong opinions on matters educational. She both liked and resented Aran, without the slightest desire to associate herself with her as the target of Mr. Pomfret's thrusts or Dr. Sacheverell's urbane disparagement. However, she did her best.

"I'm afraid I sound like a yes-woman," she said brightly, remembering to move her head so that her quite pretty profile with its "personalized" coiffure was turned to the camera, "but I cannot object to that statement. The other day I was shown a statistical graph of the rise of our school population from 1940 and the curve was simply fabulous by 1960. And surely every public-spirited citizen should feel responsibility on a matter which affects our children so vitally."

" 'With all respect, I do object,' " quoted Dr. Sacheverell in his most pleasant vein, "not to what my charming neighbor has just said but to the quotation itself. Periods of apparent crisis come and go. They must not distract us from our main purpose or make us sacrifice our bridgehead."

The panel looked its gratifying mystification.

"I mean, of course," he went on rotundly, "that the child, not the teacher, is our chief concern. Moreover, the second part of the statement: 'that the entire community must take its part' — whatever that means — in a task requiring the efforts of trained and specialized personnel is a dangerous suggestion. It is like saying that, in the event of an epidemic, the entire community must take a hand in the selection of physicians."

"But Dr. Sacheverell," remonstrated Mrs. Poynter gently, encouraged by his courteous reference, "it is very well to say that the child is our chief concern, but how can schools go on at all if we have children but no teachers?"

Dr. Sacheverell smiled wisely, as though he knew the answer if he cared to disclose it. Before he could utter more arcana, the Administration decided that it was his turn.

"Your theories are excellent, Doctor, but they must bow to facts. Your comparison of present-day conditions to an emergency like an epidemic is correct enough; but the comparison ends there. No one is saying that the general public will *train* doctors or teachers. Our legal friend was stating the need for citizens as a whole to realize the dearth of teachers, to support the efforts made to attract them into the profession."

"Granted, granted." Sacheverell conceded the point with the lightness of a man concerned with more important things. "It was a quibble, I admit, Mr. Pomfret. No one can fail to see the importance of teaching personnel. It was the primary importance that I questioned — the apparent emphasis on quantity rather than quality."

"Quantity *and* quality are both of the essence," said Pomfret with the moroseness of a man whose professional problems are lighty dismissed. "I doubt if the public has any idea of the crisis we are facing. In the realm of science and mathematics alone so few specialists are entering the ranks that we may soon be unable to give instruction in Grade Thirteen. As has happened to a large extent in the United States, the Universities will have to take it over, a task for which they are by no means staffed. And if that is not losing a bridgehead, I don't understand the term."

"Apparently we attach a different meaning to the phrase." Dr. Sacheverell's forte consisted in Olympian imperturbability. He had been stirred from it earlier in the discussion and did not intend to display such human weakness again. "Your concern is only natural, dealing as you do with the present structure, the externals of the school system. My interest being in the essence of education, I feel that such a crisis may bring about a welcome revolution, which could not be accomplished otherwise for a generation. The whole super-structure of Secondary education may have to tumble about our ears before the reactionaries are persuaded to let us build a better system, an adolescent-centered system, to which staff, curricula, everything else, is subsidiary."

Pomfret looked at his erstwhile ally with the annoyance of a relay racer, whose teammate, instead of passing the torch, has kicked him sharply on the shin. Aran, renewing her vigor for the fray, enjoyed the spectacle quietly and watched for an opening. It did not come immediately, but some preliminary clearing was done by the Director.

"We are wandering too far from the question," he cut in upon the wordless exclamation, high-pitched like the cry of a querulous gull, with which Pomfret was beginning to denounce Sacheverell and his treacherous hopes. "We are, after all, dealing with the need for recruiting teachers, not with what may eventuate if the need is not met. Mr. Pomfret, as the member of our group most closely associated with the efforts already being made, perhaps you will tell us just what is being done and what more, in your opinion, can be done."

Mr. Pomfret complied, on a lower register, with the request. His resumé included both steps already taken and projects dear to his own heart. Among these he emphasized special summer courses and in-training programs to facilitate production of teachers, propaganda favorable to the profession, and vocational talks to High School and University students which stressed the long vacations and security of a teacher's life, compared with the steady grind and competitive uncertainty of a business career.

"Teaching has too long been the Cinderella of the professions," he commented, not originally but surprisingly, Aran thought, in view of his covert slurs earlier. "The public must realize that we shall attract men into the profession" — he did not mention women — "only by offering them greater financial inducement. In these days children whose fathers drive Lincolns are not going to be impressed by teachers who can only afford — " he hesitated, suddenly aware of the unseen audience waiting to swoop at an insult — "a jalopy," he ended, weakly enough and changed the subject. "You ask me to suggest what more can be done. I am strongly in favor of imitating our American cousins and a few Canadian Universities in the establishment of teachers' courses at the University — a specific three-year course, in which Educational Psychology, School Management, Methodology, the Philosophy of Teaching, Recreational Planning, Audio-Visual Aids are the major subjects, and research projects are carried out — as Lab work — on the various subjects of the Secondary curricula. Thus two years could be eliminated from the period of training, the prospective teachers would be saved unnecessary work, much of it on subjects which they are never called to teach. Moreover, those who enter the course direct from High School will be less likely to be diverted to anything else."

Unfit to do anything else — or that either, thought Aran in disgust. She opened her mouth to say so but Dr. Sacheverell's approving resonance drowned her utterance. Her light flickered as his glowed.

"A suggestion with which I wholeheartedly concur. The art of teaching — of questioning — of eliciting from within — of making the classroom a window on life — of suggesting (or better still having the students suggest) real-life projects on which they can work in teams — of making every class a research laboratory: that is the task of the future teacher. It doesn't matter if one knows a sonnet provided one has mastered the technique of teaching the sonnet. Teaching" — he put his plump hands to his plump chest — "is not a matter of this" — he pushed his paws towards an imaginary recipient — "but of this" — the hands, palm inward, beckoned from the victim to himself. "It is not pumping in but drawing out. I couldn't agree more."

"Miss Waring," Roger Heywood cut in upon this reconciliation, "you are the only person actively engaged in the profession. Have you any comment to make? Is there anything you can suggest to induce recruits to your ranks?"

"Yes. And yes." Aran stopped and laughed. "I'm afraid not even that double affirmative will make *me* sound like a yes-woman, though. First — and only in passing because otherwise I should talk all night — let me say that I view the last suggestion with unmitigated horror. Consider what it has done to American education. I grant that at a certain stage or type of learning there are skills which one learns only to impart. Even then, the person who knows them best and who has a genuine interest in them will be — if he is a teacher at all — a better teacher. But in the sciences, the humanities, it is" — her voice broke on a note of intensity and continued in the quiet of tremendous earnestness — "it is almost sacrilege to say that methodology is of any importance at all compared with love of one's subject and a warm desire to impart it. Such an idea is wildly absurd to anyone who has known real teaching."

"I trust, Miss Waring" — she was conscious of a purple glow to her right as Dr. Sacheverell, still smiling, grated the words — "you have no intention of entering the diplomatic service?"

"I haven't. And I understood that we came here to say what we believed. I concede your right to that and I am doing likewise. To revert: that is why I teach: because the subjects I teach have enriched my life and I want to pass on that enrichment. And the teachers for whom I thank God are those who knew and loved what they taught and transmitted that feeling, together with much that was not on the curriculum. How deadly to have little teachers, who know no more and and care to know no more of a subject than the flat requirements of an examination! As for this business of drawing out — how can one perpetually draw out unless something has been put in?" She paused with what she feared was an unladylike snort.

"Perhaps you could leave that question," said Heywood hastily, trying to keep his face and his voice sober. He had one or two scores to settle with Dr. Sacheverell and had not taken a great fancy to Mr. Pomfret. Time was running dangerously short and he could not allow Aran to monopolize what remained, but the men had had a fair inning. "You have some constructive suggestions, I understand?"

Aran's eyes lost the light of battle and became luminous with feeling. How much sympathy she had lost, how much antagonism aroused by her logomachia, she could not estimate but here she must make her appeal. She was not speaking for herself, even for the fifteen to twenty years of teaching which could be more painful or more pleasant for her. She was speaking for Frank Sansom and Terry, for Hilda Wright and Roy McLean, for Stan Aldwych and Rheba Shore, two fine intelligent young teachers whom a certain Ten-D class some years before had boasted of driving out of the school in a single year, for all the potential "born" teachers, who loved their work and wanted to love their classes. More, she was speaking for those classes, made up of individuals whose minds could be filled or left vacant, surely guided or left rudderless. Her voice and her face were almost empty of expression as she began, in her effort to transpose her meaning to her audience without the interference of her own personality.

"I have suggestions which I think are constructive; otherwise I shouldn't dare to say anything destructive — and I must do that at first. I agree with much of the effort which, as Mr. Pomfret has told you, is being made, although I deplore the undue emphasis placed on money as a means of attracting the right people, the genuine and gifted teachers. It is humorous, but inevitable, that until the supply failed, teachers were stigmatized as covetous and lacking in dedication, for their long struggle to achieve a salary which is now unamimously considered inadequate to attract the 'best,' the specialists. I am not indifferent to money — nor have I ever been unconscious of the benefits enjoyed by teachers almost alone of those earning a like amount. But I believe that infinitely more important than money in attracting and holding the sensitive and intelligent, the widely educated and fully developed people who should be teachers, is improvement of the conditions under which we teach."

"You mean 'teacher-load,' fair division of extra-curricular activities, adjustment of the size of classes?" interrupted Mr. Pomfret. "A sub-committee has already drawn up and submitted a memorandum on those points, which has been sent to all High School Principals."

"No, I don't mean quite that." Aran was sorry to reject this contribution, even if it was somewhat impatiently given. "That is important, I know, though I have taught classes of forty-five with more pleasure and less strain than some of twenty-two, and a full time-table with extra periods after school than another with one or more spares in a day. And, depending entirely on the situation, extra-curricular activity can be a delight."

"Then what do you mean by improvement of teaching conditions?" Pomfret's fingers drummed the table until a gesture from Heywood arrested them. Aran went on steadily.

"Perhaps I can explain by saying that in no other profession is one — particularly the novice — subjected to so many indignities. I am not minimizing the difficulties of the lawyer, the doctor, the architect — much less of the clergyman or the nurse! But in general they have something to say about conditions under which they work, or the conditions are dictated and modified by representatives of their own profession."

"Miss Waring," said Pomfret, third-personal again, "is apparently unaware — in the ivory tower I mentioned earlier — that committees of teachers are now deciding on their own courses of study, setting their own standards, meeting in workshops and panels to pass resolutions regarding their problems."

Aran turned and fixed him with a long disconcerting stare.

"I think," she said in a tired voice, "that it would be safer to waive that question. I have worked in a workshop, I have discussed on a panel, I have helped pass resolutions. But I was referring only secondarily to that, or even to the dictation of Boards, the interference of parents in purely scholastic matters, the sniping of an uninformed public. I was referring primarily to the indignity of being every year on trial, not before a jury of one's peers, but before a mob of youngsters who know very little, appallingly little, except their power as a mob and their rights, as adolescents, to immunity from punishment for their actions."

"Would you prefer the alternative, Miss Waring," asked Dr. Sacheverell, "of the cowed and colorless classes of former school-days at the mercy of a sarcastic sadist?"

Aran could not help laughing.

"Some of you who refer to my ivory tower should come and see what classes are really like these days. Why that should be an alternative I fail to see, or why, in correcting what was wrong and brutal in another regime, we should throw out the baby with the bath — or, to change the metaphor, throw the teachers to the wolves."

"It is difficult to argue against exaggerated and sweeping statements."

"I am not exaggerating and if my statements are sweeping it is because the conditions they describe are sweepingly prevalent. May I finish — " she asked Heywood pointedly — "my contention about the young teacher on trial?"

Heywood nodded, but Pomfret cut in impatiently.

"My use of the term 'ivory tower' has been criticized. I do not know any other way of describing Miss Waring's mental environment if she is unaware that the incompetent in any profession go to the wall, and that a basic essential of the competent teacher is the ability to control and guide his classes. If he cannot interest them or appeal to their reason he has no right to stand before a class" — he remembered that the modern teacher is supposed seldom to situate himself at this traditional post — "to be in a classroom at all."

Aran sighed. The hands of the studio clock were at an alarmingly scissor-like angle and her point was yet to be made. Her incisive voice brought the camera focussing again upon her.

"I don't want to bandy words. I am discussing fact, not theory. Of course a competent teacher keeps order; of course a good teacher can interest and appeal to the reason of classes — under normal circumstances. I am saying — and it is time it was understood before the conditions outlined in *Blackboard Jungle,* the germs of which are already disseminated here, become prevalent — that the circumstances under which we teach today in High School are *not* normal. When a member of another profession is engaged or hired he is not sacrosanct — but he is allowed to demonstrate his capability of doing his job. He does not first — and repeatedly — have to convince the clients that a job needs to be done, that he knows how to do it. Under 'normal' circumstances, pupils believe that a teacher knows his subject, until he clearly demonstrates that he doesn't; that it is to their advantage, or at least their responsibility to learn that, if they don't learn something undesirable will result, even if the undesirable result is only the deprivation of that rejected opportunity. Nowadays those circumstances do not obtain. Pupils who may never have passed an arbitrary examination consider themselves competent to decide what subjects have value — "

"I thought the decline in the study of the Classics had a bearing on Miss Waring's discontent," interpolated Sacheverell smoothly.

" — how those subjects should be taught," continued Aran, not deigning to reply, "what should be the contents of their courses, privileged to ask irrelevant questions (to which they do not wish to hear the answers) concerning the entire school organization and syllabus. Dozens in Grade Nine have what is generously estimated as Grade Five or Six reading ability; yet they and their seniors are free with such remarks as: 'You're a very young teacher; if you co-operate with us, we'll act all right with you,' or, 'That's only your opinion; we're both individuals and my opinion is as good as yours,' or, 'You'll have to pass us because it won't look good for your teaching reputation if a lot of us fail,' or, from Grade Thirteen re English, 'Why can't we read Sinclair Lewis for novels and a modern Broadway play? We want to know our own world.' I quote at random and, Dr. Sacheverell, none of these remarks was made to me!"

"But surely, Miss Waring," said Heywood, "there are disciplinary means of dealing with such pupils?"

"What means do you suggest for the young teacher? All the remarks quoted have been comparatively pleasant and ostensibly reasonable. They merely suggest the opposition to be overcome before a teacher can begin trying to 'interest' and to 'appeal.' The continual, almost unconscious noise, the restlessness, the inability to concentrate or to grasp abstract ideas, the 'I dare you to interest us' attitude which from a few individuals affects a classroom, I say nothing of these. The 'discipline' problems are real enough but they can be solved by a determined teacher. Unfortunately many novices teach in schools where there are no real solutions within a classroom. Detentions are too numerous to matter and can be evaded; extra work can pile up similarly, and of course, any form of corporal punishment is taboo. And if he expels the delinquent from his class, it is considered a sign of incompetency, of 'failure to deal with his own problems.' So the poor victim faces the dilemma of endangering his reputation with the Principal or enduring a rapidly worsening state of disorder and insubordination in his own room. In a school where the Principal's office is feared and the classroom teacher is upheld, the situation is much better. But — and here I do speak for myself and for others who have no particular difficulty with discipline any longer — it isn't the large or particular problem. It is the general lethargy, the unwillingness to be interested even in the lighter and less difficult and amusing aspects of learning. They even require 'pep halls' to make them take an interest in Rugby! Almost every extra-curricular activity has to beg or exercise pressure for membership and attendance. What fulfillment can a teacher, with a genuine sense of the importance of learning, find in a future of this undignified frustration?"

"And the solution?" asked Heywood, "or have you any to suggest?"

"Lower the school-leaving age, using the money saved to ensure the continuance of those who will profit by it. Put teeth into discipline and examinations, requiring students to meet certain standards or quit. The slower but diligent learner could easily be provided for: he would have far more chance, anyhow, in classes where interest and application are not held up to ridicule by those who know that they will be shoved through with a minimum of both. Cut down the number of choices so that the able pupils are not allowed to select easier subjects instead of those which require effort and which later they may regret. That is my point," she said passionately, "I am not concerned only for the teachers, although my heart bleeds for those who are beginning to teach now. But the students, those who are capable of so much more than we are expecting of them or allowing them by our slackness, those who find classes dreary which could be a delight, those who are graduating without the glow of achievement or the thrill of honest work, those whom we are sending out robbed and impoverished of the richness that we could give them — they are, believe me, my first concern!"

She broke off. The hands of the clock pointed to the time at which they had been warned that the M. C. would sum up. Heywood opened his mouth but the next voice was Pomfret's, high, thinly humorous.

"Miss Waring, typically, is in a preferred position to pontificate concerning the upbringing of children, being, in spite of undoubted maturity, the only unmarried person in our group."

There was a brief brittle silence. The general light was on and Aran felt the eyes of the world on her face, as arrested and helpless at the crude innuendo as at a physical blow. Heywood's light went on but he must have made an unseen gesture to the camera man, for suddenly she saw hers glowing. With the sight came release from the rage which held her taut, and she laughed with genuine amusement.

"With which Parthian and poisoned shaft Mr. Pomfret hopes to end all argument?" she concluded lightly.

There was little disposition on the part of panel members to fraternize before leaving the room. Mr. Pomfret engaged Mrs. Poynter in conversation, Dr. Sacheverell was genial with the technicians, as became a man who had been in the studio as long as any of them. Both men showed a certain austerity towards the Panel Director, who seemed unperturbed by their coolness. Aran, having collected her purse and gloves, found him lingering at the table and held out her hand.

"Thank you very much, Mr. Heywood — for everything," she said gratefully.

"I should thank you for your most stimulating and sensible contribution. As far as I'm concerned, after what you had to take, I felt — how would you say it in Latin? — 'Meum erat.'"

Thirteen

THE REACTION to Aran's television debut was at once better and worse than she had expected. From the blur of conflicting thought and weariness in which she somehow arrived home, almost unconscious of driving her car, she walked into an enthusiastic chorus of congratulation by Muriel, Doris, Paul and his wife, and several other TV-less friends, with Boojum barking in mad excitement at the furore. Telephone calls from Daphne, and Phil, and a half-dozen others bolstered her morale till midnight. The rest of the night, though almost sleepless because of the quivering surge of nervous exhaustion, was pleasantly short.

The reception of her efforts at school was peculiarly anti-climactic because in a sense there was no reception. She could feel, rather than hear, accounts of the program spreading from the pupils who, or whose parents, had watched it to those who had been otherwise engaged. Several youngsters said either shyly or knowingly: "I saw you on TV last night, Miss Waring"; one, "I liked the dress you had on"; another, "My uncle says you look just the same as when you taught him." When she entered Eleven-D, the preternatural suppressing silence directed her gaze at once to the side-board where, above the caption "Miss Bleeding Heart," a large chalk scrawl of that organ dripped with appropriate gouts. Aran grinned, commented on their excellent taste in entertainment, and apologized, amid groans, for erasing the effort. Eleven-B, always willing to take time out for argument, asked her to explain Methodology, and then wanted to know if they were the class she referred to as lethargic and lacking in interest. As the forms passed her end of the hall between periods, she caught covert glances and could hear the occasional reference: "last night," "TV," "Eggheads." And some of her Grade Thirteen lingered after the period to express alert and discerning opinions on the discussion as a whole, alert and discerning to Aran's mind, at any rate, because they completely endorsed her expressed opinions.

The reaction of her colleagues was as desultory. Only three of the women had TV sets and the rest were dependent on the accuracy or bias of the report which inevitably trickled through from some witness. The non-participant in any such public effort can never realize the strain involved for the participant and the craving for some evidence of approval from one's fellows, even when opprobrium and hostility have not been incurred. Aran's appearance of assurance, her swift counter-thrust, her apparent, and in a sense real, enjoyment of speaking blinded all but her intimates to the dread in anticipation, the strain of action, the aftermath of distressed exhaustion, when a word of criticism depressed intolerably, and a pat of approval could move her to quick grateful tears. Hilda Wright expressed her quiet agreement with everything she had said and disconcertingly thought it a pity that the views had not been set forth by a man instead. Dorothy Simpson reported her husband's pleasure that Pomfret had met his match. Two others "heard that the program had been very interesting." Terry, in the longest personal encounter since the night of her confidence, was enthusiastic about every aspect of Aran's performance, and fearful, with a fear doubtless inspired by George's cautious reservations and opposing sympathies, that she had invited trouble by her fearlessness.

From the men, surprisingly enough, she received more and heartier commendation. Several spoke jokingly about the Television future available for her if she decided to give up teaching. One young progressivist, whose toes, she felt, had been trampled rather hard, told her, with the broad simile which makes any attempt at retaliation boomerang, that she must be getting old — he *loved* teaching. Aran replied equably that she *was* getting old and had tried to make it clear that she loved teaching too. Since the young man in question was already pulling wires for a job in Teacher's College, she discounted the slur — but it was not pleasant to hear. It made her more grateful for the four or five men whom she admired most, who came to her room or stopped her in the hall to shake hands and thank her in strong and sincere terms for her forthright courage. The fact that all used the word courage intimated to her their feeling that fear of trouble would have kept many who shared her views from such unfaltering vigor of expression.

No perceptible trouble ensued. True, Dr. Moorhouse studiously avoided any comment, though Aran's conscience was crystal-clear of any intention of blaming him for a general situation in which Principals and teachers may alike be the victims. Perhaps the suggestion by a member of his staff that there was any room for improvement in the entire educational system could somehow be construed as bringing discredit upon his school and could reflect unfavorably upon him. If so, she was sorry. If so, nobody could offer constructive criticism but one who had a personal axe to grind. No testimony had value except that of an experienced, successful, and resilient teacher like herself. Surely that was obvious?

Meanwhile, the event which had stirred scarcely perceptible ripples in her own school was washing the general public with waves of interest. The volume of Aran's mail swelled with letters from friends, old acquaintances, and total strangers. These, for her eyes alone, were almost entirely laudatory; not so, many in the daily Press, where for several weeks the program became a cause célèbre. Every participant in the panel, including the director, came in for some measure of praise and blame except Mrs. Poynter, who, when mentioned at all, was held up a model of womanly behavior for being agreeable and saying nothing. Aran, her "revelations," her "diatribe," her "thought-provoking and reasonable suggestions," her "pitiless indictment," her "unbelievable effrontery," her "courageous exposé" was the pivot upon which the epistolary discussion turned. The morning paper and one of the evening dailies produced an editorial each; the Press of smaller centers in Ontario issued pithy pronouncements pro and con; while the farthest wash of the wave stirred up, through the Vancouver *Sun,* a request for another Royal Commission to investigate the conditions implied.

One of the first letters called for "disciplinary measures" to deal with the "betrayer of the sacred trust of our democratic school system." Several referred to the unfitness of a woman holding such rigid and obsolete views to be entrusted with the care of the younger generation. Another charged her with base ingratitude for maligning the children of the taxpayers who provided her bread-and-butter. As a public servant, she was graciously reminded, the least she could do was to keep her mouth shut. If she was dissatisfied with her job she could always resign. Within the first week a prominent official granted an interview, in which he emphasized that the members of the panel acted as private citizens and that the Toronto teachers, as a whole, were neither responsible for nor in agreement with the extreme views presented by one of their number.

Aran, too, was asked for a statement and a photograph but, though yearning for justification, wisely said that she had been seen and heard enough. It was small comfort that many of her accusers misquoted and distorted her statements, that the most vituperative had not even seen the program, but joined battle because of an oral account or another letter in the correspondence column; that all seemed to be working out an old grudge against a system under which they had failed, a subject which had defeated them, a teacher who had caused them humiliation.

Much more heartening were the public letters, fewer in

number but greatly superior in style, and the occasional editorial in her support. The excellence and accuracy of these favorable pronouncements, in several cases from prominent individuals, accounted, she supposed, for the lack of any official reprimand. There were earnest tributes to devoted and inspiring teachers of a former day, delightful pen-caricatures of the sufferings of parents assisting at homework "projects" progressivist-style, a discerning dissection of the content of the course in several "practical" subjects. A Professor of English, the Dean of a Faculty of Medicine, and several businessmen arraigned the system which allowed certain indolent illiterates with whom they had personal dealings to qualify as High School graduates. And in addition to the inevitable outbursts from slandered teenagers, several students at University and High School wrote thoughtful letters, deprecating the flabbiness of their present mental diet and wistfully contrasting their own culture and attitude towards learning with that of some students newly arrived from the British Isles and from the Continent. A few parents commented on what they called the "snide" remarks of the men towards Aran and, in answer to a particularly nasty attack, a former pupil, not "a brain" as he frankly admitted, wrote in glowing praise of the scope and liveliness of her remembered teaching.

This balm was by no means a successful antidote to the wound which each fresh cut opened, unhealed, in her spirit. Mentally she could weigh prosecution against defense and, discounting the prejudice, ignorance, and jargon of the great part of the former, find, naturally enough, the balance of logic, commonsense, and good taste heavily in her favor! Mentally she granted that a forthright proponent of any reform is a target for abuse and could even humbly consider herself blessed, since her persecution was for the sake of what she ardently believed to be truth and righteousness. In the inner being where emotion and physical feeling are imponderably interactive she suffered intensely. Sharply sensitive to criticism or hostility, she craved approval no less wistfully than many who sacrifice principle to win it. And in spite of the victory which dispassionate observers conceded to be hers, both in the actual encounter and in the subsequent discussion, the atmosphere of misunderstanding and opposition was exaggerated by physical weariness into a fog which weighed down her natural buoyancy.

If regular classes had continued, the very expenditure of energy might have dissipated it more quickly. As it was, teaching gave way to desultory presiding over June examinations; marking, averaging, totalling and balancing her register, the detested and procrastinated task of making out Personality Rating Charts, a dozen and one other sundries proper to the end of the school year left her mind insufficiently occupied and kept her more frequently in the company of colleagues whose silence on the subject she interpreted, unjustly enough, as tacit disapproval.

More than three weeks after TV had made her name a household word in education circles, Aran arrived at school earlier than usual. It was by no design of hers. A neighbor, to whom the idea was clearly preposterous that anyone would prefer to walk half a mile on a lovely June morning, had insisted on driving her to the very door. So it was without the healing of the walk, which she had needed more than usual, that she ascended the stairs to the second floor, realizing that she was taking them one at a time these days instead of two. An ugly letter had appeared in the *Globe and Mail* that morning, more devastating because well written, and exploding with the unexpected violence of a delayed-action bomb. She felt raw and exposed. Even Muriel's warm indignation and Boojum's attempt to lick her thoroughly — Boojum's maternal instincts were aroused by depression — had succeeded only in making her laugh without heartiness and leave the house joking for their sakes.

When she opened the staff-room door, she knew instantly

that the half dozen friends relaxed on the new comfortable chairs and lounges had been discussing her. The fractional silence had too obviously fallen on an interrupted remark, and Dorothy Simpson's effort to turn a sheet of newspaper under the cover of Joan's greeting drew her attention to the fact that it had been folded at the editorial page. Aran nodded at it.

"I see you've read the latest. I am now a cheap publicity seeker with the manners and mannerisms of the adolescents I ridicule. Wow — that hurt!"

Hilda Wright returned her diminutive clothesbrush to its petit-point case.   ,   ,

"Don't worry about it. The whole thing will be forgotten by fall."

"Anyhow," said Joan cheerfully, "you might have expected it. If you will get mixed up in public controversy, you have only yourself to thank for this sort of thing. People love to get their teeth in a teacher — particularly a woman. After all, we pay our Public Relations to do our fighting for us. This gets us nowhere."

Aran began to speak and found that she could not. Those confounded tears, as usual when she was angry enough to want to sound passionless, were behind her eyes. By breathing deeply and holding the eyes wide open she might keep them from falling until there was an excuse for turning away. But speech was impossible and her face was strained in its effort to appear unhurt. The pause that seemed endless lasted actually a few seconds before Terry broke it.

"Oh, drop dead, Joan!" Joan had come on the staff since Terry's student days and was accordingly treated with some familiarity, but this was not Terry's usual gentle approach. "You know perfectly well that Aran didn't ask for the job. All the points she made we've agreed on — most of us — in this very room over and over again. Only none of us would have had the nerve to make them in public — or could have done it so well. Can this smug onlooker attitude — "

Aran had recovered.

"Thanks, Champ," she called, taking letters from her mailbox and putting her gloves in it. "Joan is quite right, really. I'll live and — perhaps, though it's a lot to hope — learn."

That was the beastly part of it, she thought, escaping down the hall to her room, though no class awaited her there and she would normally have chatted till nine with any others who, like her, were not presiding at Upper School exams until afternoon. Somehow the larger the controversy grew, the more she was made to feel isolated, even by those whom she had tried to represent. Not by Terry — bless her and make her happy, in spite of George! — nor by Hilda. Hilda had become almost incurably pessimistic and in her eyes her friend had brought undesirable attention upon herself to no purpose. Nor were the rest estranged. The staff shower which she had given for Terry the previous Friday had been a gay and friendly affair and they had been loud in their appreciation of food and entertainment. Joan had probably some private annoyance which had sharpened her comment just now. But — she could mentally reproduce the remarks which had preceded her untimely entrance — there was a suggestion of skirt-drawing, of dissociation, of insinuation that if they had been in Aran's position (which they had wisely avoided) they would have conducted themselves irreproachably, achieved a happier relationship with the opposition, shunned "sweeping statements," a term Aran had come to loathe because it implied statements without foundation, and no one was willing to say which statements were sweeping or how, if every statement is qualified and ambiguous, progress in discussion can be made at all. The inference, too, was left to be drawn at will that since publicity inevitably attached to such performance, publicity must have been the aim and the reward of the performer. Though she would have been ridiculed or pitied if she had been wordless or worsted in controversy, her ability to uphold her convictions was construed as tendentiousness. Aran realized that she had become foolishly sensitive. But she was hurt that the tolerance and friendliness which she tried to evince in her private relationships had not sufficiently impressed to free her from the implied charge of interested motives. She was hurt secretly, too, though she admitted it to no one but herself, that strangers could watch her impassioned sincerity and be antagonized rather than won. Completely feminine in the matter of personal relations, she was uncomforted by praise for the barbed hurt inflicted by a few.

Ah, well — she shrugged, and fished from the bottom of a capacious desk drawer her three remaining sets of Personality Rating Charts — "Cease from idle dreaming, There is work to do, And rewards are waiting, For the good and true." A comforting little song that, another of her mother's, taught to the schoolboys of the nineties, who apparently had sung it without tongues in cheek. Well, why not? Was it any cornier than "Eliminate the negative, accentuate the positive" or the fatuous "Someone up there likes me"? Regardless of reward, the work to be done at the moment consisted of deciding whether Sandra Allin rated *A, B, C plus, C, C minus, D,* or *E* in appearance (Neatness, Cleanliness, Grooming), Character (Responsibility, Trustworthiness), Effort (Degree to which pupil tries), Co-operation (with students, with teacher).

That one always puzzles me, she meditated, wishing that her own Character (Responsibility, Trustworthiness) was sufficiently *E* to allow her to romp through the categories as she had often threatened to do, assigning *A, B, C, D, E; E, D, C, B, A,* an indiscriminate succession. Most often when they are co-operating with each other they are decidedly not co-operating with me — and vice versa. Voice, (Resonant, Clear, Monotonous, Enunciation). I suppose it's pedantic to wish that they wouldn't mix adjectives and nouns in a classification. Sandra has to be asked to repeat every answer so that she can be heard three feet away — in class that is; when she referees a basketball game she doesn't need a whistle! — but what she says is distinct enough; yet one letter has to cover both qualities. Well, C is the great leveller.

Arden Almhurst: *A* for appearance — actually most Grade Thirteen girls rate *A* these days unless one considers natural qualifications, and that isn't our business. The wardrobe of separates, of crinolines, of quite tasteful costume jewelry, the supply of hair ornaments, lipstick, nail polish, the constant warning, advice, blandishment re personal grooming in advertisements and Teen-Talk columns, all make for clean, attractively dressed adolescents without compare in my experience — above, that is, their anti-climactic bobby-sox and loafers. My entire college wardrobe — most of it made by Mother — would not satisfy our average High School youngster for a year.

Gerda Halstein: Emotional Control (Ability to take criticism), *D,* I'm afraid. Courtesy (Tact, Consideration), not too much for anybody except Gerda.

The boys, as a whole, rated a letter lower in appearance, a letter higher in audibility. Aran gave straight *A's* to one or two favorites, varied a line of *C's* with a *plus* or *minus* for several others, wondered what to do about Anton Potello, whom she vaguely remembered from a three-week, eventless session with her class before his silent withdrawal, first from her purview, then from the school ("A report is requested on every pupil taught even if in your class for only a few weeks!"), decided that it constituted average "effort" for Shaw to have his James Texts crib open at the right place when asked to translate — she did not otherwise allow cribs, but in view of the fact that Shaw had failed in his second and third year Latin ("Mr. Purvis will give him his Algebra; you can't hold him back for one subject when he has an average of 55") and with the help of a tutor achieved a pass of fifty in fourth year, Aran considered that any means justified an end so persistently pursued, and winked at the only thing which would keep him even in remote touch with the class. She knew that no wistful affection for the Classics kept her saddled with Shaw as year succeeded year but the unfortunate drop in his Grade Twelve French in which he had not taken extra lessons. Such jockeying between the languages, and the University Arts stipulation of Latin *or* two mathematics accounted for the presence of virtual conscripts in a class of presumed volunteers.

That set completed, she turned to the two Grade Eleven's, thankful that the later Charts had adopted a simple 1, 2, 3, 4, 5, marking system and cut down the categories to five. The innumerable silent debates which her conscience carried on with her enraged sense of proportion as to whether, in view of his capabilities, *C plus* was not a more truthful estimate of a pupil's Effort (Degree to which pupil tries) or whether *C minus* was not kinder than *D* for Ability (Resourcefulness, Initiative, Imagination), were here necessarily abrogated. And considering the probability that little Holt's adolescent acne would be cleared up by Grade Thirteen whereas Stelnick *could* clean his nails, wash his jeans, and tuck his sweatshirt in if he wanted to, she felt justified in giving them 2 and 5 respectively for Appearance.

Eleven-B done, she glanced at the clock. She might as well continue with Eleven-D to complete the job. The clock reminded her that she had not wound her watch, which lay, wristband broken, in her purse. Glad of a moment's change, she reached for the bag slung on the back of her chair, and noticed her morning mail. In the embarrassment and pain of her reaction to Joan's remark she had shoved the two letters into the open pocket and forgotten them.

Both were handwritten, one with an American stamp and a crest bearing the insignia of Queenstown College. So Lemuel Goodchild had not forgotten to thank her. It had crossed her mind once or twice in the thick of the recent polemics, that he had been rather remiss, although probably his verbal enthusiasm could be considered sufficient to discharge his obligation. In view of what the other letter — postmarked Peterborough, Ontario — might contain, she saved the President's as a potential antitoxin. In any case she had always reserved the choicest morsel, a piece of chop nearest the bone, a large mushroom, the maraschino cherry on her ice-cream sundae, for the last bite.

The Peterborough letter disappointed her apprehension. From a retired Toronto teacher, now doing occasional work from his family home, it expressed warm approval of her share in the panel program and gave a heartening account of the interest and agreement which had been voiced among his acquaintances. Aran thanked God audibly, picked up Goodchild's envelope, slit it open with one end of some pupil's abandoned compass, and prepared to purr.

Dr. Goodchild had not forgotten. A quick glance over the first paragraph discovered it to be so purr-producing that she settled down to savor it with slow and shameless enjoyment of every phrase. ("Aran is a dear little girl but she loves praise" — all right, Phil, and still does, even if she gives it less credence than she once did.) Her mood of the moment was pleasantly receptive towards American hyperbole and did not for once prefer English understatement.

The second paragraph at the bottom of the page began, teasingly enough:

"I don't know whether my ostensible reasons for the visit satisfied your curiosity" — Aran raised her brows and the sheet of paper simultaneously — "as completely as they seemed to. Naturally they were true if only partial. The whole truth is. . . ."

The whole truth was that Dr. Goodchild, convinced of the value of Classical studies and concerned that they had been deleted from the College curricula by his progressivist predecessor, wished to introduce a working compromise in the form of an intensive study of Greek and Latin literature in translation. Some attempt at such a course had been made, but it had been given as an English minor by a professor who was not himself versed in the original tongues; Dr. Goodchild believed, soundly enough, that a classicist, particularly with Aran's qualifications in Greek, would give depth to the translations, and awaken interest which might in time lead to a minor course involving a smattering of both languages. Mary VanLuven's enthusiasm on the subject of Aran's Greek travelogue had aroused his interest, and he had been more than delighted at the result of his investigations. He was, in short, empowered by the Governing Board of his College to offer her a position on their staff at a salary not, he regretted to say, as far exceeding her present one as he ultimately hoped it would become — Queenstown must be a substantially endowed College, thought Aran dazedly, to make such a generous initial offer to a woman in an "impractical" subject. The course would be in her hands to mould as she wished. He hoped that, in spite of his enforced delay in making the offer — several of the Board had been on a yachting cruise and he had been unable to hurry negotiations — she would be able to begin the fall semester. If she required more time to be released from her present contract, he would offer the course for the semester commencing in January. Other inducements — he was sending under separate cover the College bulletin and magazine — regarding domicile, grounds, access to New York, faculty life, and entertainment followed. And. . . .

"It will give me the greatest pleasure to receive a favorable reply from you in the very near future,
Believe me,
Yours most cordially,
LEMUEL G. GOODCHILD."

The familiar classroom, when Aran raised her eyes from the letter, seemed strange, as if seen from a new angle. Just so, itself yet unfamiliar, had the well-known north end of Queen's Park looked the first time she saw it from the Park Plaza roof, or the Waring island from a high hill across the bay. For twenty years this had been her room, her base of operations. Frequently, years ago, on the June day when her movables were put away and the cupboards had been given their annual and sorely needed tidying, she had glanced back from the door and tried to conjecture her feeling, if she knew that she was about to close it behind her for the last time. Sometimes amusedly she had wondered if perhaps this time *would* prove to be the last, if death or a grand unforeseen event during the summer might forestall the fulfillment of her matter-of-fact assumption that she would open it, cleaned and exuding its annual closed-in smell of furniture polish and floor wax, in September. Always on these now rarer occasions she had tried to view it, not as the empty, standardized room it was but as the memory-haunted permanent abode of an enriching part of her life. Now without effort she saw it so and remained, hardly breathing, suspended between the sure, accumulating past and the windfall, beckoning future.

The two walls with black slate boards placed too high for her to write on the top six inches: what uncapturable variety she had written on them of chalky effort to reach and inspire and communicate; what snatches of poetry in English and Latin and Greek, what proverbs and mottoes and fragments of magnificent prose — left for a day, then rubbed into oblivion, with the hope that they or their essence was indelibly written on someone's soul; and in the ordinary humdrum course which she never found humdrum, what hilarious mistakes — hers and theirs — what unexpected ramifications, what hare-brained illustrations, what burgeoning from a single word or reference or question of meaning and history and philosophy! The beaver-board squares facing her from the back of the room, now demurely bare except for the June exam time-table. Usually they were filled with a few annual constants and a revolving, unmethodically replenished selection of material: literary and classical maps, pictures to illustrate; cartoons on classical topics from *Punch*, the *New Yorker*, the daily Press; pertinent excerpts from surprising sources; Latin songs and mottoes; editorials and articles of general interest — remarkable how many she owed to the pupils themselves. Her busts of Jupiter and Juno gazed quietly into space from opposite vantage points on either side, even in atrocious plaster-of-paris reproduction suggesting a remote, divine tranquillity. As for the five rows of nine empty desks: there was not one but she could see behind it a particular face or link with a particular incident; and so interlaid were the strata of the years that her mind's eye shifted from a boy whom she had taught this year to another across the aisle who had gone from her room to the war.

'Hic Dolopum manus, hic saevus tendebat Achilles'

The seats near the front were most crowded and confusing, face melting into face, like the patterns in a kaleidoscope, for usually, though by no means invariably, these were occupied in school hours by the students who wanted to work, and always after school by the incalculable assortment of pupil, current or former, or student-teacher, who came to visit and to talk.

The telephone, too, was mute with suggestion of the steady increase in nuisance calls. Some days, as she complained, her room was like a railway station with youngsters called out: for dental inspection, for guidance interviews, for disciplinary action at the office re non-payment of school entertainment tickets or Christmas cards, for T.B. patch tests, and school magazine photographs — called out singly, as a class, in groups, but always returning singly — and once a month, with a precision that should have warned, but had never prepared her, so that it usually occurred at a most important moment of a most important class, the general unpostponable summons to buy Toronto Transportation Company student streetcar tickets. Of all that the telephone spoke, but of more: of unexpected personal calls to telephone familiar or unknown numbers — and once of the summons of impending death.

And the clock! with its unobserved speed to end a full and interesting period almost before it had begun, and its unreasonable, bewitched lagging if a class was restless and she was at the end of her tether: the clock, which, at least once a year, joined all the other room clocks in a general strike and then, moved by a Board of Education expert summoned to do esoteric things with the master clock in the office, proceeded to tick five hours loudly away to the unfailing and fascinated amusement of a class.

In this same room, "divine, dear, terrible, familiar," its surface changes unimportant, she had spent the working hours of almost half her life. Now, through no seeking or planning of her own, she could say the final good-bye which she had always anticipated. And her immediate feeling was of triumphant relief, such relief and such triumph that she was shocked by it. Never until a year or two ago had she considered the imaginary prospect with unmixed feelings. Always she had felt that, however attractive the cause — and she had never seriously considered seeking a cause — the parting would be a most painful wrench. She had experienced a similar shock some time earlier, to realize the change of attitude among the staff towards those of their number who were due for retirement. When she began to teach — and for years after — in spite of the "Thank God, it's Friday" with which her colleagues greeted each other on Friday afternoon, the general attitude towards their departing brethren had been one of unqualified commiseration: "She'll be completely lost," "What will he do with himself?" they had said, surrounding the victim in his last days among them with the concealed solicitude of visitors to a deathbed. Now, unexceptionally, the superannuate was the object of congratulation and not a little envy. Instead of counting oneself fortunate if one's birthday occurred after the contract-renewal date instead of just before, teacher after teacher, on Rivercrest's staff as on others, was retiring a year or more before the compulsory limit. The improved financial terms of superannuation were partly responsible for the action, Aran knew, but not for the eagerness of excellent teachers to take it. She recalled her own beloved Classics master, J. H. Mills, who had retired regretfully from a University-controlled school at seventy, thought of J. D. Morrow's exuberance when his teaching career was similarly lengthened by the war, and of the regret of many that the Toronto Board did not grant like extension. These days: "I may as well do it while I have strength to enjoy retirement," "Before I have a coronary, you know!" "I can hardly wait to do the things I've always wanted to do. Too tired when you're teaching," "No, I used to think I'd regret it; now I'm glad to leave before things get worse": she had heard all the remarks with variations, and the alarming aspect of it was the sincere or cynical acceptance of such an attitude by the younger teachers as sensible and inevitable. She had always regarded it, for herself, with horror. She would not stay in a job, so she thought, if that was her feeling about it. Hilda, she knew, was counting the years, as many as Aran's own, until her release. Even Thea Stone, that sweetest and gentlest of Rivercrest's staff, who had loved her job, her pupils, her colleagues, who had always been hurt when disparaging and critical remarks were made in the staff room — even Thea had found her work so unrewarding at the end that she had sadly admitted to Aran, in private, that she was glad to leave. It was not that age had sapped their energy either. Many of her acquaintance were working hard at other types of teaching, or at other jobs. Not for her such an attitude, she had thought arrogantly. And now— She looked down at Eleven-D's Personality Rating Charts with fine disdain. Confound P.R.C.! At last she would express her real convictions regarding all such pat, tabulated methods of estimating, and classifying human beings. She opened the envelope and began with a defiant pressure of her pen: 1,2,3,4,5, *E.A.W.*; the next 5,4,3,2,1, *E.A.W.* At this rate she would finish the thirty-five in three minutes and a half. Then she would go home and see how many Greek tragedies Gilbert Murray had translated!

Fourteen

"YOU MEAN you've turned it down?" asked Muriel, unbelieving.

Aran slipped her foot into the white mesh opera pump which she had just bought to wear to Terry's wedding and held it out for inspection.

"Yes. I'm so glad I could get these. My feet are too blunt for spectator pumps and they're all most stores have. It's a comfortable last too. Isn't it good that the rain has cleared up for Terry — poor kid!"

Muriel was impatient.

"You're the poor kid — and a poor chump too, if you ask me. I thought your mind was completely made up. In fact, I thought, when you came home after that last promotion meeting, you wouldn't go near the school again."

"I was annoyed, wasn't I?" Aran's smile was rueful.

"Annoyed! You were too furious to talk."

"And *that* for me is the ultimate in annoyance, huh? I know. It wasn't really personal either. I long ago got over feeling much resentment. And actually it is better than it used to be. 'Promoted — just failed in Latin and French' was the standard remark, and the science and math people used to look at us pityingly. By this time the desire — the conviction that they have a right — to side-step anything demanding concentration has spread to all the subjects. Whatever else can be said for Latin — and I can say plenty, as you know — the training in accuracy and logic and gradual accumulation of knowledge stood them in good stead in other subjects. So I find, rather smugly, that those who fail in Latin usually fail in two or three others —

notably one of the math subjects or sciences. And as for the classes which haven't elected Latin — you should see the results there!"

"It's a good time for you to get out of it," insisted Muriel stoutly. "I've always said you should be teaching English — and to more mature people."

"But it was for some of the younger ones," evaded Aran, "particularly Terry, of course. She's under enough strain just now and she was almost crying in the meeting. Frank Sansom is leaving, but young Wakeley isn't and all of them were asked again and again to raise their marks. 'Only down in your subject, Miss Maxfield.' 'We can't hold him back just for Geometry, Mr. Wakeley. Forty-nine, that's a dreadful average for a Grade Ten. You have some bright boys there. Look at these: Ross, Rankin, Tomasio — all good average ability.' It's all very kindly said, but the insinuation is that the teacher has failed."

"Well?" Muriel was being irritating on purpose.

"Well, he hasn't. Art Wakeley is a good teacher. Half that class were in Nine-C last year, played on the Bantam team, and were shoved through, in spite of being general nuisances and doing no work to speak of. They dropped Latin because one or two of them got the 'not practical; we don't need it' bug, although they had the ability to do it. So they all were put together again and have been making life cheery for Terry in English and for everybody else, including Wakeley, and Sansom. Oh, they're bright enough. They may fail in geometry but they can do simple arithmetic to figure out how many are kept back in any given year, and who passed with how little work, and how many, who failed in certain subjects, are promoted anyhow and taking the next year's work in those very things. And by some not too subtle reasoning they know that a teacher's results count against him or her and govern themselves accordingly."

"Aran — "

"That's the beastly temptation — and I strongly suspect

that George Madden and some others size up the situation and yield to it."

"In other words pad their marks?"

"According to George's philosophy, why not? If averages can be arbitrarily raised higher up, why shouldn't he raise his own and avoid opprobrium? But Terry didn't, and Wakeley and Sansom won't; so they receive it."

"But surely it comes out sooner or later?"

"How? Even if all an individual teacher's exam papers were inspected by the Head of his department, as they never are, there is an allowance for term work in almost every subject."

"Yes, but if he gives them marks for poor work, it will catch up with him when they come under another teacher."

"It will show, certainly, in the cumulative or carry-over subjects. But whom will it catch up with on a staff of forty-five? 'He did very well in geography — or math — or French until this year, Dr. Moorhouse,' 'I always got good with Mr. Madden last year,' 'Look at his record — what's the matter with you?' is the implication for the teacher in the higher grade."

"But the Heads — ?"

"Actually they — and whoever else teaches Upper School — are the ones who suffer. But remember, Heads can only suspect. And they aren't sacrosanct. If they complain that one of their subordinates always has better results than they have, it sounds like sour grapes, to say the least. 'Either the percentage passing in Middle School is too high or the percentage passing in Upper School is too low, Miss Waring,' as an inspector informed me during a run of large Thirteens and poor results I had a few years ago. I will say it was the only unpleasant comment I've had from an inspector and I did *not* take kindly to it. However, it was probably as well that 96 percent of that year's class in Latin got through and we acquired several scholarships."

"But surely the higher-ups aren't blind?"

"It's a vicious circle. Failure is bad for the pupil — so

as few as possible must fail; the percentage of failures is dictated from the Center, as is the desirable average, worked out by statistical graphs, omniscient and inerrant. Anything over that reflects unfavorably on a school and on its Principal. So he is enmeshed in the general struggle to appear successful. And if, by chance, an incompetent year — and don't let anyone ever tell you that some years aren't poorer than others, no matter what manipulated statistics prove — is properly slaughtered by one or more of the Upper School exams . . . either pressure is brought to bear on the examiners to boost the marks, at least the failure marks, from thirty-five up, or, if they refuse, there is a general outcry from the aggrieved public concerning the impossible University standards imposed on our able, conscientious young people. Yah!"

"Does yah mean that you are fed up with it?"

"To the teeth," answered Aran, walking deliberately into the trap.

"Then why on earth don't you take your opportunity to get out of it?"

Aran slipped off the white shoes and placed them in their box, lay down flat on the short, tapestried sofa (period piece, period unknown) with her feet over the end, and spoke to the ceiling.

"I don't know exactly. Perhaps *because* I'm fed up, *because* the situation is becoming worse. . . ."

"And you see how kindly they received your suggestions for improvement. What good did it do?"

"Don't fool yourself. The fight is on. I can't walk out just when it's beginning."

"I don't see why not. You've given the best of your life to it. You don't owe it anything. There are plenty of others who can't get a job teaching something they love to people who will appreciate it. Let them do the fighting."

"Muriel, you're a darling. But don't talk about my 'giving the best years of my life.' It sounds like the phrase neurotic women use to their hard-working husbands; only they add accusingly, 'bearing your children!' I've got plenty out of it. I never felt that I was teaching High School because I couldn't do anything else; that it was teaching on an inferior plane. It was that I was fitted to reach and interest more youngsters at that plastic age, at what I consider their most impressionable age, rather than to give more specialized instruction to those whose mental mould was already set. I've loved my work. That's why I'm so furious that it is being turned — needlessly — into something stale and unprofitable, though by no means flat! I grant you, at its best it's wearing. But it can be rich and rewarding and fun. What will happen to the next generation if all of us who feel that give it up?"

"I'm not concerned with the next generation. I'm concerned about you," said Muriel. And she was, Aran thought, wonderingly grateful at the unselfishness of her affection. Her departure would mean another revolution in Muriel's life, the stirring up of a pleasant and congenial nest, another period, perhaps indefinitely prolonged, of loneliness. Yet her joy at her friend's opportunity and initial excitement had been genuine, and she had urged acceptance, rather taken acceptance for granted, without the slightest reference to the adjustment entailed in her own affairs. "It's not good enough to keep yourself in a narrow groove for people who don't realize what you are trying to give them. You owe it to yourself to expand. Think of the good you can do at Queenstown among the University students. Teaching Euripides and Sophocles and, and — and Cicero, instead of pounding away at Latin declensions."

Aran winced. Muriel had unerringly touched her vulnerable spot: her sensibility of all that she had to give, which her classes were increasingly unable to draw out and too uninterested to take. Her tone became defensive.

"How do I know that Queenstown College students will respond to Euripides? Oh, I know it sounds 'inspirational' and 'challenging.' Actually it's the incidental reference, the off-beat, at which I do my best. That's why Latin . . . or

Greek or Ancient History provides so much in the way of parallel or analogy. I'm not nearly so good at dissecting a play or commenting on the structure of a chorus. And why are you so unflattering sure that my efforts are wasted here? I've always been amazed — sometimes years later — at the reactions of most unlikely ones. Tom McVittie — I haven't thought of him for years — was the first surprise of that sort."

"Who," asked Muriel dutifully, "was Tom McVittie and how did he get into this?"

"You asked for it, insinuating that my life-work has gone for nought! McVittie was in my Fifth Form Latin my first year at Rivercrest, a good-looking, assured boy, undemonstrative, with rather brusque manners — at least, I thought they were brusque then; they'd probably seem polished now. At any rate he sat in my classes, did his work, asked questions rather sharply as if he was trying to catch me up, and never indicated by word or sign that the lessons were more than routine duty. I nearly lost my teeth — to use your crude but vivid phrase — when he turned up after school in September to thank me for making Latin a completely new subject to him. He had never liked it, had to take it (in those days) to get into Meds. 'But,' he said, still brusquely, 'I got it, thanks to you, and I enjoyed it, which I wouldn't have thought possible. So I thought I'd come and thank you.' "

"That's fine," said Muriel. "That was twenty years ago — I know you've had plenty since. I meet them all over. But you yourself say that you have to drive and drive to get the basic facts home to them these days. You are in a rut. Why on earth don't you break loose and have a complete change?"

"Muriel I want to teach Latin and Greek, not English translations."

"Oh, don't be a fuddy-duddy. You know that English is the most important subject on the curriculum. You can reach hundreds that way who will never take Classics. What they *said* is what really matters and you can teach that in translation. How many of your pupils ever get to the stage where they can read — much less enjoy reading — two lines of Latin by themselves?"

"Touché. That hurt!" moaned Aran. She raised one nyloned leg and flexed her toes against the brick side of the fireplace. "But you're wrong, Muriel. Reading in translation is not the same. And apart from the meaning there is a value in studying even the rudiments of Latin or Greek. It's absolutely essential for real comprehension of English Literature. It sounds silly but I feel it essential to keep that study alive. Else I never should have taught in the — "

"All right. I should have known better than to start you off on that," said Muriel resignedly. She rose to look for her knitting — a sure sign of agitation — and paused in the doorway. "But Aran, come clean. That isn't the whole reason, or a good enough one. After all, Dr. Goodchild is all for re-introducing your precious Classics — a smattering of them at least. Why aren't you taking the position?"

"I wish I could explain," began Aran, sitting up in her effort and swinging her stockinged feet under her to the great detriment of the fragile sofa. How can I explain to her what I can scarcely explain to myself, she thought. No process of reasoning can account for the absolute conviction, after a brief heady period of recalcitrant anticipation, that I cannot accept. Perhaps I knew all the time that I should refuse, just as years ago I had occasional spasms of yearning to break loose from moral and conventional restrictions, spasms during which I indulged in the beginnings of glamorous imaginary adventures, at carnivals in Venice, or on the desert with highly civilized sheiks — knowing quite well, not only that I never could let myself go but that I really didn't want to. Only there morality and basic beliefs were at stake. How can I explain that this is as really wrong for me? It is such a purely personal thing. I could approve of anyone else's acceptance.

Muriel was waiting. She had seated herself in the large armchair and found the pattern of the jacket, which she had begun for her expected first grandchild, sufficiently intricate to keep her eyes away from Aran. The latter found it easier to formulate her apology.

"I suppose, basically, I don't want to go to the States."

"Aran, don't be provincial! You sound as if it's a foreign country. And what if it is?"

"Just that I'm Canadian. I owe my entire self — as far as my human life is concerned — to Canada and Britain. I know there are thousands of people who have had to become Americans — there might have been circumstances which compelled me. But I've always decried — and so have you — Canadians who took everything from Canada in the way of advantages and education and then flocked to the States just to earn a higher salary."

"This isn't a question of salary."

"What is it then? Prestige? Position?" Aran laughed. "I'm only reaping what I sowed! Remember when Paul went to New York and did so well? And his young sister prayed nightly for four years that he would come home to Canada. Which thing, amazingly enough, for he was no flag-waver like me, he did. How can I desert me country now?"

"I never heard of anything so absurd. It's jingoistic."

"You forget that I was brought up with the recitation going around — though my family always kept me from perpetrating it:

> *'And not a man dare lift a hand*
> *Against the men who brag*
> *That they were born in Canada*
> *Beneath the British flag.'* "

Muriel smiled at the piping, declamatory lisp and returned to the attack.

"This from a girl who hates racial discrimination and national pride! Who quotes with feeling: 'In Christ there is neither Jew nor Greek, barbarian, Scythian, bond or free.' "

"Ah, yes. In Christ that is true. But Scripture says noth-

211

ing about forsaking our own country just to satisfy personal ambition, or get an easier job."

"Rot. You owe something to yourself. As a University professor you can make a name for yourself. Here you're only a High School teacher — "

" 'Only a High-School Teacher' — by Horatio M. Alger," giggled Aran.

"Yes, and one who may have put herself in a pretty uncomfortable position. Aran, you infuriate me! I suppose you won't even tell Dr. Moorhouse."

Aran stared.

"You overestimate my nobility of character, friend. I shall certainly tell Dr. Moorhouse, probably tonight at the wedding, and anyone else I deem it politic to tell."

"I'm glad you're not quite mad. I wasn't sure what these weird sacrificial principles of yours involved."

"Muriel, you're a dear," said Aran, earnestly. "Believe me, I appreciate your concern for me. And I know that it's purely disinterested. Only come clean about it yourself. You know that the expansion, as you call it, of my personality doesn't depend on whether I teach Sophocles in translation or suddenly find something new in Virgil — or even Livy — which I have never noticed before, though I've taught it ten times over. In your conviction that I should take this position, isn't there an underlying thought that I shall be more likely to meet an eligible unattached intellectual, if I change my locale?"

"Perhaps. Is there any harm in that?"

Aran laughed.

"Not for you to want it for me. Only a certain degradation and childishness, more, a lack of faith in me if I should allow it to influence my decision. There is something pitiful about a 'nice' woman on the prowl."

"Oh, Aran. You wouldn't prowl."

"That's just why it would be pitiful. My prowling would have to be on such a high plane and so stealthy! But, failing that, don't you feel — confess now — that a spinster must find fulfillment in a spectacular career; that fullness of life depends on a change of environment, that there is glamour and satisfaction in pulling up stakes here, for instance, and venturing into an unknown American University town?"

"I suppose so," admitted Muriel. "Don't you feel it yourself?"

"A bit. At least I once did. Perhaps after travelling and watching people who have changed their habitat often I feel 'Caelum non animum mutant qui. . . .' Boojum! Do you have to do that?"

Boojum, finding the conversation over her head, had retired to the cool comfort of the rugless hardwood beneath the sofa. Now, with the terrifying unexpectedness of a rocketing pheasant, she bolted, squealing wildly, to the front door, leaped madly at the Evil Thing which was pushing things through the slot into her hall, caught one as it fell, and dashed back under the sofa to worry it. Aran retrieved it easily enough — a bone was the only thing about which Boojum was adamant in possession, and even then she managed a nice balance between the ominous growl of her front end and the ingratiating waggle of her rear. Muriel handed over three more missives and settled down to read her own letter from Yellowknife.

Aran was glad of the respite. Always willing to give a reason, she found it hard to explain even to herself her unassailable conviction that she should reject a course so obviously reasonable. She spent a much longer time than necessary studying her bill from the University Women's Club, her City Tax Bill, and the letter card from San Francisco, where Doris had gone for her holidays.

That's that really, she said to herself, while her eyes under veiling lashes re-read the message without seeing it. Everything I have told Muriel is true and it adds up. Perhaps I should accept the position if it were in Canada. I'm certainly not indispensable. I could leave the school — even gladly — if I had a strong sense of duty calling elsewhere. But it goes deeper than that. I'm refusing as a sort of protest against the — the rootlessness of modern living: perpetually seeking the bluebird by change; acquiring lovely homes to tear away from at the week-end; regarding a change of employment as necessarily an improvement; forming no ties or friends or associations which cannot be sacrificed for self-interest or to avoid difficulty. Perhaps — I don't know — this is a needed discipline because I am naturally ambitious for great things, things, that is, which people in general consider great and exciting. For a short time I felt that this offer was my destiny — but only for a short time. Perhaps my earthly destiny is to live fully and excitingly in a fairly circumscribed area, to show that ordinary things are not ordinary but may be forever new and interesting, that mediocrity lightly borne is victory. Perhaps my Christian witness before those who find life humdrum is to demonstrate that I have found the Secret "in whatsoever state I am therein to be content." And Dr. Goodchild's offer is not irrelevant. Without it my position would not have the dignity of decision and choice. It has restored meaning to the moment when I unlock my door again next September, a day that has always been stirring to me, fraught with unknown possibilities. Paradoxical, that every new year of teaching at the same school should give me the sense of adventure which is usually associated with rounding a curve in an uncharted river — or appearing in a new play — or going in a rocket to the moon. "Behold, I make all things new." I've always known that verse as true. Then, too, Dr. Goodchild has completely removed the unhealthy bitterness and self-pity I was nursing over the TV panel and the general school frustration. Now I feel like rising to fight another round. And to accept his offer would be running away. Crazy it sounds, but it's true

Having satisfied herself, she became aware of Boojum's slightly crumpled contribution unopened in her lap. The rounded, firm handwriting looked familiar, as most handwriting looked familiar to her teacher's eye, but it told her nothing, nor did the Toronto address, punctiliously written at the upper left-hand corner of the envelope.

A minute later Muriel, glancing across, saw Aran staring at the letter in her hand, her teeth catching her lower lip, her eyes wide with tears. She put her knitting aside and crossed the room.

"Aran, tell me. Has something happened?"

Aran shrugged, swallowed, and turned her expression into a deprecating smile.

"Sorry to make a fool of myself. I'm just tired. This — well this is part of your answer."

She hesitated, then put the letter into Muriel's hand and went over to the piano.

"Who is Rhoda Lake?"

"A lovely kid — naturally I'd think so now, but I always have, and I've taught her for three years — in Grade Thirteen."

To the hesitant, but determined, opening bars of "The Fountain," one of Aran's prized recollections from her almost barren years of piano lessons, Muriel read the letter. Beautifully, if youthfully written, gracefully and sincerely expressed, the warm tribute of gratitude for Aran's teaching filled two closely written pages.

> "Speaking on behalf of all your upper school pupils," she concluded, "may I say that we are leaving High School with a more valuable background than that demanded by the course of study alone. You have given us some laughs, some common sense, some appreciation, and many many thoughts.
>
> "Thank you very much for your interest, a portion of your learning, and the part of your personality which you leave in every student.
>
> Yours most sincerely
RHODA LAKE"

"I feel like crying too," said Muriel soberly. "Of course, she's only one but — I'll be glad to get you up North for a rest, though. You look all in."

"I'll be all right after a week of swimming and lying in the sun. Who knows? I may even write another chapter of my secret autobiography."

"Well," said Muriel practically. "I must press my dress for the wedding. And you ought to get your car washed. It's a disgrace." She glanced at Aran sitting limply on the piano stool. "The occasion calls for something. How about 'O Canada'?"

"I will not!" Aran flared. "Besides, I can't play it. 'God save the Queen,' yes. Or if you insist on a good Canadian song, I think I can remember this."

Singing to drown out the accompaniment, she began:

    " *'In days of yore the hero Wolfe.'* "

Muriel stood beside her and joined in to uphold the faltering piano, which rose in crashing triumph at the end.

    " *'God save our Queen and Heaven bless*
      The Maple Leaf forever.' "

Boojum, nose straining at the ceiling, echoed the sentiment.